VOICES IN A MASK

෴

VOICES IN

A MASK

STORIES

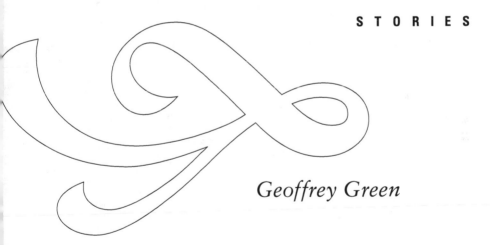

Geoffrey Green

TRIQUARTERLY BOOKS
NORTHWESTERN UNIVERSITY PRESS
EVANSTON, ILLINOIS

TriQuarterly Books
Northwestern University Press
www.nupress.northwestern.edu

Printed in the United States of America

10   9   8   7   6   5   4   3   2   1

This is a work of fiction. Characters, places, and events are the product of the author's imagination or are used fictitiously and do not represent actual people, places, or events.

Library of Congress Cataloging-in-Publication Data

Green, Geoffrey, 1951–
    Voices in a mask : stories / Geoffrey Green.
        p. cm.
    ISBN 978-0-8101-5209-0 (pbk. : alk. paper)
    1. Opera—Fiction. I. Title.
    PS3607.R4328V65   2008
    813.6—dc22

                        2008009853

♾ The paper used in this publication meets the minimum requirements of the American National Standard for Information Sciences—Permanence of Paper for Printed Library Materials, ANSI Z39.48-1992.

To Marcia

"Da quel che ti mirai
palpitai per te d'amore,
da quel giorno, al 'ultimore
Sì, questo cor, sì, per te palpiterà.
La mia vita io ti sacrai
nella gioia e nel dolore,
fin la morte in questo amore
dolce e cara a me sarà."

"From that day when I first saw you
I have been on fire with love for you,
from that day to my last hour,
Yes, my heart will always beat for you.
I have dedicated my life to you
in joy and in sorrow,
and, loving you,
even death will be dear and sweet to me."

—ARTURO TO ELVIRA,
I PURITANI, ACT 3

CONTENTS

VOICES IN A MASK

OVERTURE

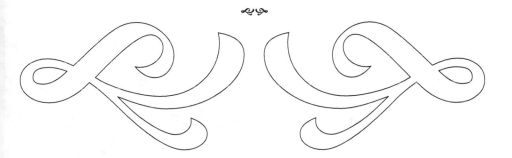

Ladies and gentlemen. May I have your attention, please?

I have your undivided attention now, I trust. You are all on the edge of your seats, so to speak, waiting intently for my announcement. And why is that? Why not go on with your activities—talking, laughing, reading the program, clearing your throat, coughing, doing the necessary fidgeting that will prepare you for your subsequent interval of uninterrupted sitting?

Let us be frank. On normal occasions, you pay your money, take your program, find your seat, occupy yourself with the aforementioned functions until the music begins and the curtain goes up—and then you're *safe!* Home free, under cover, in the nick of time: the commencement of the music and the visual action indicate that you are *in* the work, it has already begun. Regardless of your ultimate opinion of the finished product, you are now already in the midst of it.

My appearance changes all that. The possibility that I might be here just to say hello you rule out as far too quirky and unusual. Therefore, I am here to interrupt the normal passage into the work of art. I am here to tell you something that you need to know before you may begin properly. My presence suggests that something is amiss. What could it be? Is it possible that *one of the principals has canceled*?

Anything but that!

But which one? Under extreme circumstances (not preferring or even desiring this outcome in the slightest, of course) you might be willing to accept the absence (with good reason) of *that* principal, or that *other* one, as long as *this* one remains. Best of all in this arduous situation would be the announcement of the cancellation of one or more of the minor characters. After all, who cares about them, right? But not the principal!

It is possible to conceive of several related dilemmas: what if the principal is indisposed but has agreed to appear anyway? You initially breathe a sigh of relief, but then comes the realization: Do I want this, in truth? Do I want to experience said principal in circumstances that might produce an uncharacteristically weak performance? Still, this is to be preferred to an outright cancellation. The problem with cancellation is your response to it: the principal had better have a good excuse! Look here, I've paid good money for this and now you've dropped out. You didn't quit last night, or last week in Geneva, so why tonight for me? Am I not suitable enough?

And what if the nonappearance results from a mere excuse, a frivolous rejoinder that masks a conflicting commitment that is judged to be more pressing, more important? Pneumonia, say, or leprosy, or even death (none of these things are desired, of course, naturally) might be conceived of as appropriate excuses, but an attack of hives that nevertheless allows one to perform the next evening in Madrid—this is not to be endured!

Relax, please, I beg of you.

All of the principals are in good health and will appear presently. I know them all quite well and feel privileged to have close working relations with them. I can't explain what impelled me to appear here before you simply in order to welcome you, but somehow, that's what I wanted to do. Highly unusual, I grant, but is this what I deserve? Your distaste, your suspicion, your lowest insinuations? Under the circumstances, I find it suitable to conjecture that you want to preserve the illusion of the artwork emerging whole—full grown and armed, like Pallas Athena emanating from the head of Zeus—onto the stage before you. You wish the curtain to remain inviolable until it is opened; you do not wish to see me address you in front of it.

If you conceive of me as your general director, it is altogether appropriate for me to remain backstage until the work is completed. Keep off the stage! My presence is perceived as an intrusion that reminds you of the process by which art is made, reminds you of the unpredictability of performance: things change, catastrophes occur, people may be boorish as well as kind, some nights are better than others. My absence, on the other hand, is oddly comforting: each night is regularized by routine, everything is as it should be, nothing irregular will occur, all is under control, soon it (the work itself) will begin before you.

I would rather that you think of me as your facilitator, as one who makes easier the transition from your perspective into the otherness of an alternative perspective and then back again. But you ought not to deny that such a transition is involved. A great deal has taken place so that you might be sitting there with me here before you. All of that might be said to color the performance that you are about to experience. Without denying that there are some things of a private nature about which you are better off not knowing, I nevertheless have insinuated myself here, on the one hand, out of good fellowship, to say hello and extend my best wishes, and, on the other hand, to remind you that even though my function is ordinarily implied and not experienced directly as a presence, it does not follow that such a function does not exist. Here I am. I will continue to exist throughout our proceedings even though my station may change or be modified.

As I retire, then, may I repeat that I welcome you here and hope that your enjoyment will be intensified as a result of this brief interruption designed to familiarize you with our performance customs. Thank you.

VOICES IN A MASK

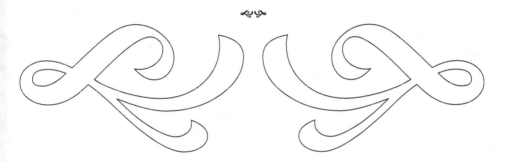

Krista Vitek, arts and leisure reporter for the *New York Times,* shot bolt upright in her bed: it was three in the morning of January 5, 1996, and her telephone was ringing. My God! Was there no peace to be had? She staggered to the phone and hastily, awkwardly, lighted a cigarette as she cradled the receiver. It was the chief of her news desk, Warren. Of all the nights to have quested for the perfect martini! Damn!

"Warren, you swine, do you know what time it is? Have you no decency?" It was apparent that Warren *did* know the time and the etiquette, but he had been forced to call out of urgent necessity. Krista lurched to the shower to regain some sense of sobriety. It really *was* incredible: Sir Flanders Floyd Lubber, the greatest luminary in the American and English musical theater, the composer of *Jesus of Nazareth: Dude; Moses and the Remarkable Marble Tablets; Checkers; Indira!; Candlelight Special;* and *Specter of the Balcony,* was in town for the premiere of his latest musical extravaganza: a musical life of the nineteenth-century diva Maria Malibran, the world's most admired opera singer—it was called: *Maria!* Sir Flanders was at the opening with his fourth wife, polo specialist Honey Divine Johnson, when a disturbance erupted in the theater. Retired opera singer, former director of the New York City Opera, and now best-selling author Emilia Marty leapt onto the stage, sprayed Sir Flanders and his wife with red paint, and uttered derogatory oaths through a portable microphone (*Maria!* was a hoax, a sham, a travesty! Floyd Lubber was a whore, a fifth-rate hack who stole his best tunes from Puccini!) until she was apprehended by New York City's finest.

Emilia Marty was a remarkable publishing phenomenon: readers purchased her books, several of them a year, with a devotion that was heartwarming to her publisher. These loyal readers seemed to believe she had invented romance. Each current release set dramatic new publishing records and then was optioned to Hollywood or the networks or cable for a blockbuster film. Emilia's attorney, William Kunstler, had already called a press conference to announce his defense plea of "women's rage": the idea that Emilia's disruption and vandalism at the theater were the delayed response to years of sexist oppression. The situation was particularly thorny: Sir Flanders, it seems, had actually swallowed some of the red paint and was "in hospital," as they would say in his country; his wife was by his side with a dislocated pelvis. Emilia was refusing to meet with her lawyer; instead, she phoned the entertainment desk and insisted that a reporter and crew pick her up in a car as soon as her bond was posted: she wanted to give an exclusive statement to the *Times*! Krista marveled at how media savvy Emilia was: the name of the game was public relations; for Emilia to get her story out to the world first, simultaneously with the breaking news of her arrest, would "spin" the news in her favor. Krista had been privy to many disasters that had been mollified by the damage control of a timely interview: in some cases, a major scandal had been averted and even transformed into a media triumph!

Nevertheless, as she labored to appear presentable at three thirty in the morning, Krista was puzzled by the whole situation: she was familiar with Emilia Marty (she had seen her on public television introducing highbrow music specials of the sort Krista would avoid watching), but she was positively *enamored* of Sir Flanders! He was an entertainment phenomenon: every musical he had ever written was running simultaneously to capacity crowds in both New York and London! In addition, touring companies traveled around the world with repertory versions of his productions—usually starring one of his three ex-wives or one of his publicly designated mistresses. Single-handedly, he accounted for one-half of all the theater productions on Broadway and three-fifths of all the titles in the West End. He was a one-person music industry! His songs had been colossal hits for decades, turning gold and platinum consistently—and, of course, winning award after award. The music critic for *Time* magazine had devoted a year of his life to writing a coffee-table book on Sir Flanders, hailing him as *the* musical genius of the century. Still, there were those persistent, troublesome rumors—none that Krista could make any sense of, but mostly accusations that Sir Flanders had appropriated most of his compositions from opera composers whose work was in the public domain. "Music of the Evening," for instance, from *Specter,* was said to have been taken from some Puccini opera or other.

Krista knew from the media blitz that *Maria!* was a musical set in New York City, Paris, London, and Venice in the early 1800s. It told the story of the career of Maria Malibran, the most famous opera singer of all time and the first "superstar" of the modern era. Although the show had premiered earlier that evening, it had been previewing for several weeks, and Krista's colleagues had hailed it as a major sensation. Several of the songs from the new show were rising hits: Krista could even hum the words to a few of them. She was especially fond of Barbra Streisand's version of:

> Stand back, Old New York City!
> Because you've gotta learn what you're gonna have from me
> Just the merest bit of
> Just the merest bit of
> Just the merest bit of Diva-bility!

There was also the heartbreaking ballad that Maria sang just before her tragic death in northern England:

> Don't cry f'me, Manchester, England
> To tell the truth, I never abandoned you
> Despite my craziness
> My operatic frenzy
> I kept the faith with you
> Don't walk away from me.

Krista loved the recording of that song by Helen Reddy: it was big enough to launch her latest comeback!

Krista phoned for a cab and flipped through the pages of the recent magazines to refresh her memory: yes! there had been some sort of minor furor about a song from this opening musical, the title song—there were charges that Sir Flanders had stolen the song from some old-timer, Leonard Bernstein. Krista had no way of knowing one way or the other: these CDs should really come with warning labels or something! But she adored the Michael Bolton version of the title song, "Maria":

> The loveliest name I've ever called:
> Mar-i-a! Mar-i-a!

I've just heard a girl sing named Mar-i-a!
And suddenly that word
Will never sound absurd
To me.

Mar-i-a! Mar-i-a!
I've just heard an aria by Mar-i-a!
And all at once that song
Can nevermore be wrong
For me.

Mar-i-a:
Pronounce it noisily and seventy-six trombones are blaring
Pronounce it quietly and it's the same as caring
Mar-i-a!
I'll never stop reiterating:
Mar-i-a!

If she had to admit it, Krista really loved the way Michael Bolton winced as he sang out that plaintive, yearning appeal to true love: it was a sign of his sincerity as a performer. Why did her friends on the *Village Voice* have such a low opinion of Michael Bolton—and Sir Flanders Floyd Lubber as well? Krista attributed their criticism to envy and resentment.

In the cab, Krista picked up Bobby, her cameraman, and Julie, her video operator, at the *Times* office; then they headed downtown to the city jail to meet Emilia. Her associates were both wired with excitement! Bobby, especially: "Can you believe it, man? After all those years of lobbying for this part? I mean, really, for this to happen to Madonna? Bummer, man!" Apparently, Madonna had staged a one-woman stakeout at the entrance to Sir Flanders's estate in Kent (this had become the subject for her third successful documentary about herself) until he had agreed to cast her as the lead in *Maria!* Sir Flanders was called a "cutthroat" by his critics, and his friends described him as "pragmatic"—whatever the term, he had doled out several million-pound settlements to actresses (such as Glenn Close, Faye Dunaway, and Patti LuPone) whom he had fired at the last minute without any cause. Thus, Madonna had sweated every second of the previews until opening night. And now this had to happen: this was, without question, a media emergency!

Krista and her crew arrived just as Emilia Marty had been released. Krista was dismayed to see that a press brigade was already in attendance, primarily composed of scandalmongers and reporters from gossip sheets. As she maneuvered her way into the crowd scene, Krista was taken with how striking Emilia Marty was: after the episode, the arrest, the hours spent in prison—this was a woman whose face revealed extraordinary character, grace, and serene dignity. She controlled the press corps with dexterity and quiet strength. "So you see, I was compelled to make my objections known—I really had no choice. I meant no harm to Floyd Lubber himself (not that he was harmed in any way! Is he saying that he was?) and regret the inconvenience to the theatergoers. But the truth must be told: someone must stand up to Floyd Lubber and his musical vampirism! Maria Malibran was a great, a resplendent artist, and I shall not allow her memory to be desecrated by this viper who masquerades as a composer." She turned to the left to accommodate the needs of a photographer. "Do you realize that Maria Malibran sang the first Italian opera heard in America not far from here—at the Park Theatre—in 1825? There would be no Metropolitan Opera without her, no American musical tradition! But Floyd Lubber has her singing *his* wretched song travesties throughout the show! And what's the business with Karl Marx as a commentator on Malibran's career? Marx was seven years old when Maria first sang in New York; he was eighteen years old at her death: but Floyd Lubber has him as the mature author of *Das Kapital* discoursing about her fame and career!"

"Miss Marty, are you aware that Sir Flanders has announced his intention of filing charges against you in court?" Emilia turned to face the video camera.

"I welcome my day in court. I informed Floyd Lubber of the gross errors in his show after he invited me to preview it. He told me the audience would love it regardless of how silly and insipid it was. When I disagreed and suggested that he change the play, he dared me to do something about it: well, I daresay I have risen to his challenge!"

Emilia spotted Krista as she approached the center. "Thank you, one and all, for your interest—especially at this ungodly hour. But now you must excuse me as I have a commitment to give an interview to Miss Vitek at the *Times*. Please feel free to contact me later for a statement—after we've all slept, that is!" Emilia took Krista's arm and steered her toward the exit door. Bobby and Julie followed. She whispered in Krista's ear in what must have appeared to be an intimate and friendly manner, but the fact was, they had never met. "Do you have a car waiting? Splendid!"

"Where would you like to talk, Miss Marty? At the *Times* offices? It really is quite early," Krista carefully inquired as Emilia waved ta-ta to the reporters.

"No, don't be silly! I keep a suite at the St. Regis: we'll be more comfortable there. I desperately need to unwind after all this excitement. By the way, thanks so much for coming on such short notice." And they were off!

Emilia Marty's suite at the St. Regis was beyond anything Krista had ever seen: even the photographic spreads in *Architectural Digest* did not do justice to what met her eyes—room after enormous room of ornate and tastefully elegant paneling, paintings, and antique furnishings. From the moment they had arrived in the hotel lobby, Emilia Marty had been accompanied by a supporting procession of hotel functionaries. Inside her expansive suite, one person rushed off to run Miss Marty's bath, another adjusted the lighting to her specifications, and yet a third was dispatched to fetch refreshments: tea with honey, cola, and crumpets for Krista and her associates; for Miss Marty, an unusual Greek coffee concoction into which Emilia Marty poured a dark, aromatic liquorlike elixir from an antique flask.

"Thank you, thank you, leave us!" At the instant Emilia Marty pronounced these words in a soft, almost whispered voice, all the hotel functionaries departed. "Now, Krista, I am beginning to tire, so what I should like is for your crew to take the pictures you need and then leave so that the two of us may talk." Krista could discern no trace of exhaustion on Emilia Marty's face, with the exception of a weary edge to her voice. As Julie ran her video camera and Bobby shot stills, Krista noticed that Emilia Marty switched "on," as if she had been wired to the circuit of a light. It was not that she had been at all tired previously—she had eons more energy than the very tired Krista—but she seemed to tap into some secret reservoir of dynamic vitality. In the camera's lighting, Emilia Marty posed, smiled, preened, luxuriated, threw back her head, took on postures and expressions of charm and seductive appeal: Krista had to admire how seasoned Emilia was in front of a camera. After fifteen minutes of fast-paced shooting, Emilia abruptly slumped into a chair, flicked her index finger in the air, and announced, "Yes, wonderful. Through those double doors you will find Carl, the butler of my suite, who will show you out. Nighty-night!" Julie and Bobby looked at Krista with slightly bemused expressions as they exited. It was exactly half past five in the morning.

"If you don't mind indulging me for just a moment, Krista, I would like to make myself comfortable." Krista nodded, poured herself more tea, and reached for another crumpet. Emilia Marty left the outer living room for her private quarters within her suite. When she returned at six, Krista was astonished: Emilia had bathed, restyled her hair, modified her makeup, and changed into a formal evening lounging outfit of black silk. Whereas Krista felt a pervasive tiredness looming in the recesses of her brain, Emilia appeared as if she were beginning the day after a most refreshing evening's rest. This was a woman, for God's sake, who had created a public incident, been arrested, held a press conference, spent the bulk of the night in jail, conducted a photo shoot, and now was emitting an aura of radiance! Krista, for all her news experience, was literally speechless: she had never seen anything like Emilia Marty!

"Miss Marty?" Krista began, haltingly.

"Please, child, call me 'Emilia.'" The voice was soft, intimate, confiding.

"Emilia, then. Thank you for requesting that I interview you. I wonder, however: You're a successful, best-selling author, a former opera singer, former director of a major opera company, and from your quarters here it's obvious you lack for nothing, so why would you wish to take such drastic action over a Broadway musical? What do you have against Sir Flanders Floyd Lubber? I confess that I don't know much about him, but, after all, isn't he a knight of the realm?" As she spoke, Krista realized, with pleasure, that she was gaining confidence and strength. She leaned toward Emilia and the cadences of her voice moved with animation.

Emilia Marty sipped her drink. "Do you know the story by Hans Christian Andersen of 'The Emperor's New Clothes'? The king is persuaded to parade down the street naked and all his toadies and hangers-on won't tell him the scandalous truth—that he's disgracing himself. Finally, a child looks with naïveté on the scene and exposes the king's folly. No one else would—or could. Well, I think in this matter I may be playing the role of the child. To my way of thinking, art makes a difference: it's important. I know that may not be chic or in vogue, dear, but that's how I feel. Listen: Puccini worked long and hard on his opera, *La Fanciulla del West*. It premiered here in New York at the Metropolitan Opera in 1910. The great Caruso sang the aria that Sir Flanders stole, retitled it 'Music of the Evening,' and claimed for his own in his *Specter:* why should Floyd Lubber receive royalties for work that he did not compose?" Emilia grew more excited. "Puccini's style was uniquely his own; Caruso sang with elegance and pure emotion: why should this tenth-rate hack receive acclaim for the pilfering of a true artist's accomplishment?"

Krista responded that Emilia was citing an old controversy. Why not protest years earlier, at the premiere of *Specter,* rather than now at the opening of *Maria!*? "Many years ago," Emilia began, "I sang the role of Tosca in Puccini's opera. Tosca sings: '*Vissi d'arte, vissi d'amore.*' I guess I feel the same way. I live for art and love. I trained to be a singer. During her short career, from 1825 to 1836, Maria Malibran produced the most haunting singing anyone has ever heard. She inspired me, she truly did. She literally mesmerized Europe and the United States. She, and her father, Manuel del Pópolo Vicente Rodríguez García, brought Italian opera to the United States. Their family—the Garcías—presented the first version of *Don Giovanni* ever heard in this country. Her father was a great tenor: he created the role of Count Almaviva in Rossini's *Il Barbiere di Siviglia.* Through her brother (who lived for a hundred and one years) and her sister (who lived for eighty-eight years) the tradition of 'beautiful song' (what we call *bel canto*) in opera has been sustained and preserved. Her life matters to the tradition of art: we need to remember such things or they're lost!"

There was a fragile hush in the room as Emilia Marty spoke. Krista knew very little about opera itself, but when Miss Marty spoke, Krista felt herself deeply affected. There was an extraordinary presence, an intense sincerity to Emilia Marty, and Krista took note of it precisely because it was sound journalistic practice to resist such appeals of the heart. At that moment, the double doors burst open and Carl, the St. Regis butler, bounded into the suite: "Miss Marty, I beg your pardon, I truly do! But this . . . man! . . . just insisted on gallivanting in here! Some of us know better and tried to tell him to be decent, but no! this self-important moron simply could not be stopped!"

Krista heard steps and then was face-to-face with a tall, thin man dressed in evening clothes early in the morning. His face was pale and anemic, and he had a distinctive curl to his upper lip when he spoke. "Miss Marty?" He rolled the *r* as he pronounced the name. "Miss Emeeeelia Marty?" He took note for an instant of Emilia's brief nod of distaste. "I am Unctuous Jones, Esquire, attorney-at-law. I do so regret disturbing you at this early hour of the morning (and may I, despite the awkwardness, take this opportunity to wish you a very good morning indeed!), but, you see, my law firm—Jones, Fahey, Mamounian, and Phelps—represents Sir Flanders Floyd Lubber. It is my unique pleasure to act as the surrogate for Sir Flanders in the matter of serving these court papers upon you, madam (though may I say that it is a sad moment for all of us when a luminary of your status must be tainted with the likes of legal papers of any sort: this brings me no joy, none at all, I assure you!), on account of the lawsuit that Sir Flanders and Lady Honey Divine Johnson Flanders are bringing down upon your most distinguished head. At another moment, Miss Marty, I should so enjoy the opportunity of meeting you and even nurturing the rare thought of representing you (on matters other than this, of course!), but, for now, it is my burden to notify you officially that you must appear in court to answer these charges. However—"

"Cease and desist!" Emilia Marty had risen from her couch. "Sir, I have known fleas and bedbugs less ignoble than your wretched presence. You are a scoundrel and a miscreant! My one consolation is that you are precisely the appropriate individual to represent Floyd Lubber. Good day!"

Unctuous Jones was fuming: "Miss Marty, I will not be addressed by you in this insulting tone of voice! May I inform you that my law firm is proud of its distinguished and honorable reputation. Why, we are defending Sir Flanders in a new and highly complex litigation that was filed against him only yesterday—by the heirs and estate of the late maestro Leonard Bernstein, the well-known composer Stephen Sondheim, and the distant relatives by marriage of the late Maria Callas—all over his new show, *Maria!,* and the alleged similarity of one of its songs, "Maria," to one of the same name by Bernstein and Sondheim and to the name of Miss Callas. Sir Flanders called upon us, madam, to defend him!"

"And by his choice shall he be judged!" thundered Emilia Marty. She quaffed in one gulp the remainder of her coffee concoction. "Mr. Jones, I am unimpressed by your tired repertoire. Neither am I intimidated by you or your client. It seems to me that your client ought not to be *initiating* litigation at a time when he is hard-pressed to defend himself against existent litigation. It is so deliciously ironic that three other parties are suing Sir Flanders for artistic theft and chicanery while he is suing me for charging him with those exact offenses! I shall have you know, sir, that I, the subject of a play and an opera, am sufficiently ensconced as an historical personage to know a passing fraud when I see one!" The index finger twitched again in midair. "Carl, Mr. Jones will be slithering out now; if he does not care to follow your lead, do not hesitate to phone security, the police, or the local animal shelter."

Mr. Jones left in a huff and a shambles. Krista could not resist a chuckle at how furious he seemed. She wondered why Sir Flanders (who seemed such an agreeable sort) should hire such counsel. Emilia Marty asked her patience while she made a telephone call. There was no way for Krista to avoid eavesdropping on the conversation. "Emilia Marty for Mr. Kunstler. Thank you. Bill? No, I haven't been avoiding you! Who told you that? I need you to neutralize immediately a creature called Unctuous Jones. Yes, he was just here, and Bill, he left some papers, right, from Floyd Lubber. You'll take care of it? I knew I could count on you. Bye!"

"Miss Marty? Uh, I mean, Emilia? What did you mean when you said that an opera and a play had been written about you?" Krista wanted to get this interview back on track.

"Why, yes, Krista, of course: I thought everyone knew about that by now. I am the subject of the well-known play by the Czech author Karel

Čapek and the renowned opera by the Czech composer Leoš Janáček—both are entitled *Vec Makropulos,* variously translated as *The Makropulos Thing, The Makropulos Case, The Makropulos Secret,* or *The Makropulos Document*—in any case, if it's 'Makropulos,' then it's me! In fact, I was attracted to you as a suitable interviewer because your name coincidentally is the same as one of the characters of the play—Krista Vitek, called Kristina in the opera—who dotes on my character and ends up being the recipient of my character's secret inheritance."

"Are these recent productions, Emilia?" Krista was both delighted that an artistic character shared her name and embarrassed that she knew so little about this realm of the arts.

"If you mean this century, then: yes! The Čapek play opened in 1922. Janáček's opera debuted in 1926. In fact, I am absolutely delighted that the Metropolitan Opera is performing my piece this evening for the very first time. Would you like to see it? I have several complimentary tickets. Right, there you are. Why don't we talk again tomorrow morning? Ta! Oh, Carl!" And with that, Krista was escorted to the elevator.

That evening, Krista stood out in a huge crowd of people outside the Metropolitan Opera. She had always had a conception of the Met as being the epitome of "high culture" (whatever *that* was), but here she was, dressed to the nines, surrounded by other stylish individuals, all pushing and shoving and insinuating themselves for the best possible position when the doors opened. It was like a herd of cattle on the verge of a stampede. What was this about? Didn't everyone have a ticket? What was the point of this absurd jockeying for position? She replayed the day in her mind: She had taxied home and taken an emergency nap. She had phoned Warren and then typed in a brief feature story of the "Marty Case" (as it was being called) to date. In the afternoon, freshly showered, fed, and changed, she rushed to the New York Public Library to read the Čapek play and the libretto for the Janáček opera.

Both works related the story of a woman, Elina Makropulos, born in Crete in 1585, who was the daughter of Hieronymous Makropulos, the court physician to Hapsburg emperor Rudolf II. The emperor refused to be the first recipient of Hieronymous's eternal-life potion, so the physician tested it on a guinea pig, his sixteen-year-old daughter, Elina. This was in

1601. She experienced terrible pains and became deathly ill. When she recovered, however, she had been granted three hundred years of life. She became an opera singer and, with world enough and time, was able to master the technique of flawless musical vocal expression. Every seventy years or so, she would change her name to avoid detection. But each name preserved the identifying initials—"E.M.": she was, after Elina Makropulos, Ekaterina Myshkina, Elsa Muller, Eugenia Montez, and Ellian MacGregor.

As the play opens, in 1922, she is "Emilia Marty"! Marty becomes involved in a hundred-year-old lawsuit because a document she is searching for is secreted within the papers of the disputed estate. As the elements of the case are revealed, documents that Emilia produces indicate that she has an unexplained memory for historical events before her lifetime and a signature that matches exactly that of the significant participants—all of whom, Elina and Ellian, were alive in previous centuries. It becomes clear to the other characters that Emilia Marty *is* Elina Makropulos and that she is 337 years old! This is amazing to them, not least because she is so youthful and charismatic in appearance. She obtains the "Makropulos thing"—the document with her father's secret for three hundred years of life—and, pressed by the litigants to account for her coldness, her steely, dispassionate detachment to all things human, she admits that perennial life is dreadful: only a delimited human existence allows people to care and become involved in the evanescent details and circumstances of life and love. Cynically nihilistic, she offers the "thing"—the secret—to the woman who most admired her vocal artistry: Krista Vitek! At the end of each work, Krista burns the Makropulos secret of eternal life.

As the crowd of people was herded into the opera house, Krista reviewed the burning questions she had established. Could it actually be possible for a human to live for hundreds of years? (Krista dismissed this as the stuff of myth or legend.) If not, how could it even be possible for the stylishly midfiftyish Emilia Marty to have inspired a play back in 1922? Wouldn't that make her something like ninety-five or a hundred years old? Krista would not believe Emilia to be that old—no way! She actually appeared, at most, to be in her late forties. Why should Janáček and Čapek be inspired by her in the first place? Was she even Czech? True, she spoke with a slight accent, but Krista (who was of Czech ancestry) did not associate it with the accent of her grandparents. Worst of all, Janáček died in 1928 and Čapek in 1938: if Emilia were born in the year Janáček died, she would have to be much older than she appeared, and even so, how could an infant have inspired this play and opera?

The lights in the hall dimmed and the opera began. Initially, Krista was shocked that the music sounded as it did—was all opera like this? To tell the truth, she preferred the tunes she had heard from Sir Flanders Floyd Lubber's *Maria!* to the music of Janáček. With the play fresh in her mind, the dramatic action seemed to proceed in slow motion, each sentence being sung ponderously as opposed to the rapid verbal repartee of the play. But as the opera unfolded, an odd phenomenon occurred: she became drawn into the spell of the musical drama. The interaction of theater, music, costumes, sets, lyrics, sound, and voice created a total impression that captivated her. At the end of the opera, as Elina Makropulos, near death, renounces the "thing" of eternal life, and Krista's own double—Kristina—burns it, Krista felt herself deeply moved. There was a poignant emotion in the hall, a feeling that the commonplace assumptions of life had been turned about. Rather than bemoan the brevity of human existence, it was precisely life's brief duration that created all the human elements about which we cared: life, love, freedom, art, human dignity, human rights! The Metropolitan Opera audience, so nervous and agitated at the onset, filed out of the hall as if in a trance. As she stepped out into the night, Krista could still hear traces of the music in her mind. The sensation was remarkably appealing. Mind you, she could not hum a note of what she had heard, but the traces of the concluding waltz and the spell it had cast on the members of the audience were pervasive in her senses. The city seemed *different* as she returned to it, as did the Krista who stood in front of the opera house. For no discernible reason, she wanted to linger, wanted the moment to endure. What would it *really* be like to have experienced all human history since 1585? At that instant, two things happened simultaneously: Unctuous Jones bumped her from behind as he rushed for a taxi, and Emilia Marty waved to her from across the courtyard, calling, "Wasn't it marvelous? I'm going backstage to kiss Jessye Norman! See you tomorrow, Krista, darling!"

❧❧

Emilia Marty's face froze for an instant in response to Krista's question. It was the following morning and Krista and Emilia were in the living room of the suite at the St. Regis. Krista had learned early in her career to tolerate silences, so now she gazed out the window and waited for Emilia to answer. With a willful effort, Emilia Marty prodded herself back into character and initiated a tight smile: "Well, you certainly don't beat around the bush, I'll give you that, my dear! I am delighted that you so enjoyed the opera, but isn't the important issue that it stands as a tribute to me, rather than the purely inquisitive (some might call it nosey, dear!) pinning down of my exact age? Here, have another scone!"

Emilia thrust the serving basket under Krista's chin, virtually forcing it against Krista's neck. Krista leaned back in her chair so that she could face Emilia directly by staring at an angle around the basket. "If I take this scone, will you answer my question?" She could see Emilia nod eagerly. Krista helped herself to a scone and the basket was withdrawn. She took a dainty bite and chewed, waiting.

"I do not appreciate these negotiation tactics, my dear! No upstanding woman of any respectability cares to reveal her exact age—you'll understand that as you get older." All of a sudden, Krista noticed an abrupt, almost racy, flash of a grin dart across Emilia's expression—as if she were recalling some vision from the past that brought her pleasure. "I was born, Krista, on the island of Crete in 1585. (Isn't this splendid, my dear? It's a moment precisely from the opera!) My father was Hieronymous Makropulos, the court physician to the Hapsburg emperor Rudolf II. When my father, in response to the emperor's command, invented an elixir for perpetual youth, Rudolf refused to try it. Unbeknownst to me, my father fed me, a sixteen-year-old girl, experimental doses. I became deathly ill and—"

Krista stood up and walked stridently to the window: she was furious. "Now look here, Miss Marty, uh, Emilia—or should I now say Elina Makropulos?—I saw the opera, I read the play! I *am* curious as to how you might have inspired Čapek and Janáček to write about you in the 1920s, but now you have the audacity to claim that—that—"

Emilia spoke very softly. Krista could barely hear her voice. "That I am Elina Makropulos. I do, indeed. Now, please, take your seat: there is nothing to be gained by cheap theatrics. That is the territory of Sir Flanders Floyd Lubber. I am four hundred and eleven years old. But I prefer to count my age from the year in which I received the potion, in 1601: thus, I am three hundred ninety-five years old. Please, calm down! I never claimed this is my unadulterated face. I employ the finest cosmetics consultants in the world. I confess to you (off the record, mind you!) that I have had several sessions with the plastic surgeon. But here I am, in the flesh. I date myself from 1601 not merely because it was then that I received the potion but also because in 1601 were published the first operas."

"You ask me to believe," Krista spoke slowly and clearly, "that you have lived for centuries despite the fact that all scientific evidence contradicts your little ghost story? You must take me for a fool, Miss Marty, and, let me assure you, I am no fool!" Krista's frustration expressed itself in frenzied movements: she waved her hands in the air and opened her mouth to speak, but no words came out. For no particular reason, she pulled aside a curtain, allowing the sun to flood the room with bright morning light.

Emilia Marty shielded her eyes with the palm of her hand but did not otherwise move. "The first opera I remember was *Euridice* by Peri and Rinuccini in 1601. I remember it appeared close in time to the first novel I recall, *Don Quixote,* by Cervantes. My dear Krista, pretend for a moment that you are in the position of Orpheus, the great mythic musician whose music was so beautiful that he was able to descend to Hades to bring back to life his beloved, departed wife, Euridice. Do not, Krista, make his mistake and look too earnestly at my face before it is time. You will force me back whence I came. When Orpheus looked at his wife before they were both completely returned to the world, she was compelled to return to the realm of death: even his song of eternal loveliness could not save her, and eventually he was torn to pieces by an angry mob."

Emilia pressed a button and the curtains shut electronically. She removed her hand from her brow and made a gesture with her upturned palm. "I often compare myself to Orpheus. My life—my eternal life—began with opera. I was fascinated by this unity of music, theater, and the soulful depiction of our innermost spiritual states. One of my earliest and most persistent memories is the mournful song of Orpheus as he bemoans the loss of his beloved to that other world, most especially in the version by Gluck of 1762: 'What will I do without my Eurydice? Where will I go without my beloved? What will I do, where will I go? . . . Ah, no help is left me, nor hope, from earth or from heaven!' This is how I felt, Krista, when I realized that I would live for centuries. I did not understand at first. But gradually, I came to see that I would not die: Where would I go? What would I do? Who would help me? Opera was invented and I found it or it found me. Suddenly, I was not alone: I could sing out my feelings! I could sing and transform myself into other beings, other people, other characters. I could reinvent myself through song. People in the galleries— the audience—could marvel at my transformation and shower me with praise and adoration. Ah, Krista, first through opera, then through the novel, through the evocation of human feeling, I was able to mask myself and appear in altered form: through that disguise, I could touch and move my fellow humans as I would never be moved—I could make them appreciate the sublimity of the precious human life. What is a human life? A few absurd moments of pain and ecstasy: what does it matter? But pretend for a moment that I am speaking the truth to you—imagine that I am not lying: what a wondrous story I am bestowing upon you, to reveal to the world!"

Krista returned to her seat on the couch. "What do you want from me, Emilia?" Her voice conveyed her frustration and impatience. "You must know that I can't write a story in the *New York Times* about a four-hundred-year-old diva and her impressions on life. You realize, naturally, that I would be laughed out of the business. Level with me, please: what is all this truly about?" She could resist no longer: she reached in her bag and asked hastily of Miss Marty, "Do you mind if I smoke?"

Emilia Marty removed an impressive mahogany humidor from beneath the coffee table that separated them. It appeared to be an antique of extraordinary value. "Krista, my dear," she began, "I thought you'd never ask." Within the humidor was a variety of aged cheroots. Emilia Marty selected one, and, with a small, guillotine-like device, clipped off the tip, and lighted it. "Would you care to join me?" This was not what Krista had in mind, but she opted for the sociable gesture to defuse the tension. Miss Marty reached over and offered her a light. Emilia leaned back in her chair and exhaled. "I first met Maria Malibran's father, Manuel García, in Naples, sometime around the second decade of the nineteenth century.

VOICES IN A MASK

We were both students of the great Ansani. Now I had been singing for at least two hundred years, but I confess to you frankly that I did not entirely have control of my instrument. I had my splendid nights—nights where I would be toasted and saluted and serenaded outside my balcony—but I also had evenings where I was ignored, barely acknowledged. Why, I shall never forget that disgraceful debacle when that insidious Anna Strada received an ovation grander than mine! She sang like a goat, I tell you; why Handel should feature her in his 1735 opera *Alcina* I'll never understand, but where was I? Oh, yes: I needed a sense of technique. García was a stunning specimen with real stage presence, but he, too, desired some ability to master his voice. Ansani had the secret: the art of the bel canto, beautiful song. We both yearned to master that art."

A timer beeped in the suite. Carl, the butler, rushed into the living room to shut it off. "Miss Marty, your program is starting."

"Thank you, Carl. I'll flip it on immediately." Emilia pressed a remote control on the coffee table, and the television switched on: Regis Philbin and Kathie Lee Gifford were interviewing Sir Flanders Floyd Lubber. Regis was speaking: "So then she *shvitzes* you with the red paint right there from the stage? I don't believe it! I don't believe it! I mean, what if it was me? You know, Joy and me, sitting where you were, and the paint lands all over us? I'd be outta control! I'm outta control right now, just thinking about it!" The audience applauded wildly.

Kathie Lee contributed her distinctive laugh: "Oh, Reege! You're just saying that! But if it was me and Frank was there, he would have taken care of that harpy! She would not be sitting down at the moment, I don't mind telling ya!"

Emilia Marty switched off the television set. She tossed the remote control onto the coffee table, forcibly shutting the lid of the mahogany humidor in the process. "There! That's why I need you, Krista! I don't care a snippet for the details of *my* story being made public, but I am desperate that you reveal the truth about opera, about the art of bel canto, about the real Maria Malibran. You see that fraud, that human toad, gallivanting about the public airways with his preposterous claims to talent when the most extraordinary voice I have ever heard is being nightly maligned in his musical revue!"

Abruptly, Emilia Marty stood up and began to sing scales of ascending and descending notes on the same vocalized syllable. Krista was astonished at how distinctively youthful and lovely was the voice to which she listened. Emilia Marty paused. "Ansani taught this to me and to García: this is his method—to direct one's voice into 'the mask,' the hollow regions of the face beyond the eyes and nose. When your voice is properly placed—in the mask—you become the character you represent: you are no longer yourself. The most natural syllable to sing is the vowel *i*, but the human 'I' disappears when you sing naturally! Great singing, I learned, is the art of self-effacement in the service of beauty. Floyd Lubber is the opposite of bel canto, Krista, darling: he is the epitome of self-promotion in the service of the fatuous!"

Emilia Marty closed her eyes and sang softly:

> "Ah! non credea mirarti
> Si presto estinto, o fiore,
> Passasti al par d'amore,
> Che un giorno solo duro . . ."

Krista was stunned; she had never heard such exquisite tones of haunting loveliness. The voice faded gradually and haltingly into silence, yet Krista could hear it still, within her memory. A new voice, a theatrical speaking voice which she had never before heard, filled the room with a stage whisper:

> "I hadn't thought I'd see you,
> Dear flower, perished so soon.
> You died as did our love,
> That only lived for a day."

Emilia opened her eyes. "That was Bellini, my child, from *La Sonnambula*. But no one could sing Bellini like Maria Malibran. In every role she sang, she set the standard and created the character. I had learned the bel canto technique with her father, but I did not appreciate it until I heard her sing."

Miss Marty sat down and ignited her cheroot. "Let me tell you this,

Krista, and you may transmit it to your readers. It doesn't matter what I've done; tell them this. Maria Malibran spent only a few weeks in Venice, from late March to early April of 1835. And in that time, she sang so bounteously and so angelically that she changed the geography! The Teatro Emeronittio was nearly bankrupt when she arrived in Venice for her engagement at the Fenice opera house. Giovanni Gallo, the desperate manager of the Emeronittio, begged La Malibran for help in saving his hall. Maria, as always, was generous: I am proud to have counted her as my friend. She donated all of her proceeds to save the theater. At her last performance in Venice, she performed a benefit at the Teatro Emeronittio: Franz Liszt was there and so was I, and I remember distinctly that I attempted to keep my distance from him as a result of a sordid past experience. But we both heard (from our separate seats) the half hour of concerted applause, witnessed the thirty-six curtain calls after her depiction of Amina in the Bellini opera from which I just sang. The evening concluded with Signore Gallo's revealing the new name of his theater: Teatro Malibran! Maria Malibran's artistry was able to make a difference! A theater was saved as a result of her voice. Do you think it would matter to Maria that the name—Teatro Malibran—would remind her of the man whom she wished to divorce from the moment of their marriage? I think not. What matters is what Maria Malibran gave to that audience and what she received in return: something magical transpired, and I know that Liszt called out to me that he would transcribe it in his diary and in his correspondence. At the time, I had little interest: the man was a lecher! But now, in the light of posterity and his enduring piano music, I call it to your attention."

Emilia pointed to a book on the couch, *A Dying Fall*. "When I was on a book tour to publicize that novel, Krista, sometime last year, I found myself in Venice and traced my footsteps carefully to the spot where I recalled that Maria's theater was located . . . and there it was: it was boarded up, shut down, faced with hard times once again. At first, I was devastated; but then I realized what I was seeing. One hundred sixty-one years ago, when I was merely two hundred thirty-four, this theater received the name of my friend, Maria. La Malibran sang, and the theater was named in honor of her artistry, and her gift, and the joy she bestowed. *That name was still there, still on the marquee.* Although the theater was not in use, the name was a part of Venice: people would say (in Italian, of course!) 'meet me by the Malibran,' for instance. All around me, in that eternal, timeless city, were the spirits of those with whom La Malibran had shared her voice: I could *feel* her presence, I could sense her infectious smile, I could hear her cascading peals of song."

A sad, momentary remembrance passed over Emilia Marty's countenance. "I am at least three hundred ninety-five years old, Krista. Of course a play and an opera were conceived in my honor! What difference should that make: at some point the numbers play out in your favor—eventually, the odds prevail! But my friend Maria walked on this earth for a brief twenty-eight years. And she altered the history of opera and left her impression on a city! Last year in Venice, I peered between the cracks of the boarded-up windows: I fancied I could discern a performance of *La Sonnambula* in the version Bellini composed for Maria's voice. My eyes are not what they were, but I swear to you I could hear Bellini's notes: swirling ecstasies of the most intense sensation and empathy. La Malibran was alive in song, and her voice—proudly and divinely alive in her mask of bel canto—provides me even now with a sense of ethereal bliss."

Carl, the butler, entered the suite determinedly. "Your midmorning appointment is here, Miss Marty."

Emilia Marty responded with a barely perceptible movement in her butler's direction. "Thank you, Carl. Please tell Mr. Larry that I'll be with him shortly. Now listen, Krista: this is important. García taught Ansani's method to his son, Manuel Jr., and to his daughters, Maria Malibran and Pauline Viardot. Unlike their sister, Manuel Jr. and Pauline lived long lives. From Pauline's great singing and teaching and from Manuel's teaching all of the preeminent contemporary singers are descended: that sense of bliss about which I spoke is the reality of time being transcended on wings of song. When you hear bel canto, you, Krista, are like me—hundreds of years old—privy to bygone eras and artists who are no longer with us. Art is eternally alive, my dear, and the mask—the art of bel canto—allows us all to share in the unbroken line of great singers and writers and artists."

Krista was startled by a shocking change in Miss Marty's voice. It sounded as if it originated in the center of the earth and traveled thousands of miles, gaining volume and intensity. "BUT FLOYD LUBBER WOULD BREAK THAT LINE! Floyd Lubber has no concern for history, time, or traditions. The hell with that, he says! Who needs to compose new music? He merely plunders the compositions of composers who are no longer alive. Who needs great singers who are trained to place their voices in the mask? The hell with that! He merely outfits them with microphones. Their voices will then be irrelevant: the entire production may be cast in terms of physical appearance. Or, better still: he has them lip-synch the entire production to a recording while on roller skates! Who will be able to tell? Well, I can tell! And I can testify! As long as someone—anyone—listens and is moved by the passion of art, the Floyd Lubbers of the world will not prevail."

Krista felt all of her journalistic instincts warn her that she was becoming emotionally involved. On the one hand, she rejected utterly the malarkey that Emilia Marty was really the multicentenarian Elina Makropulos. On the other hand, Miss Marty spoke with genuine emotion and fervor, and Krista sensed herself being affected. She attempted to reason with herself that Miss Marty was a consummate performer, capable of staging dramatic effects, a singer and actress of resourcefulness, a writer, a spinner of words whose agenda was concealed temporarily but nevertheless ought to be recognized. "No one will believe your story, Emilia. It's as simple as that. No one. It doesn't matter whether I believe you or want to tell your story. No one will accept how long you claim to have lived. They'll say you're nuts!"

"My dear Krista, leave me out of it, completely out of it. If you merely expose Floyd Lubber's travesty of history and art, my story will be told. Present the real Maria Malibran. Tell them what bel canto is all about. But here: I have a better idea. Carl? Carl? You may show in Mr. Larry now."

At precisely the moment that Emilia Marty reached for and tasted yet another scone, into the room hurtled a tall, muscle-bound man, outfitted in a salmon skintight T-shirt with a rust-colored Hugo Boss suit. He wore unlaced high-top athletic shoes and sported a flowing pocket handkerchief. "Hullo, hullo, hullo!" he called out. "Emilia! Darling, put that down! Uh, uh, uh, no! What did we say about our fat intake? Are we really going to eat that silly scone? I don't think so, uh, uh, no, ma'am!"

Miss Marty laughed stylishly and polished off the rest of her scone. "Krista, darling, this is Mr. Larry. Mr. Larry is my dietary adviser. Mr. Larry, this is Miss Krista Vitek of the *New York Times*." With her finger, she gestured delicately but unmistakably for Krista to take her seat. "Now I forgot to mention, Krista, dear, that Mr. Larry is also my hypnotist. Mr. Larry, I *know* we were supposed to review my calcium supplement dosage, but I would *much* rather utilize your talents as a channeler to stage a séance right here for Miss Vitek!"

Mr. Larry took a seat on an antique settee and reached for a grape. "We have certainly had our fun with our little séances, haven't we, Emilia? But, dearest, I didn't bring the table, or the candles, or the cassette of the special channeling sounds. Really, can't we do this next time?"

Emilia spoke to Krista: "Mr. Larry often appears to forget who it is that puts those thousand-dollar suits on his back. Perhaps Mr. Larry would prefer to return to the YMCA in Astoria?"

Now Mr. Larry spoke to Krista: "Isn't she fantastic? What a sense of humor! I just love it when she's decisive. I love her to death! Mmm-wah!" He mimed a kiss and blew it in Emilia's direction.

While Emilia summoned Carl to fetch the accoutrements for a séance, Krista lighted a cigarette and considered the situation. This was very wacky. How did she get into this? It was clearly time to leave. Once again, she rose. "Miss Marty, I really must be going. I need to transcribe my notes and—"

"Not now, Krista." Emilia was emphatic. "I neglected to mention *who* we would conjure at this séance—my good friend, Maria Felicia García Malibran! With Mr. Larry's special talents, you will hear her speak in just a few moments!"

"Yes, indeedy!" agreed Mr. Larry. "Maria Felicia García—who? I love it! Wasn't she the Gloria Estefan backup singer who died in that bus crash? To think that could have been Gloria herself! I could just cringe!"

"*Mr.* Larry! A word with you, sir!" boomed Emilia. Then, in a soft tone: "Krista, would you be a dear and fetch me the elixir in the small pink dram from the desktop in the inner room? Thank you." While Krista retrieved the bottle, she could hear decisive murmurings behind her back: Emilia was doing all the reprimanding and Mr. Larry was on the verge of tears. In the nick of time, Carl the butler arrived.

On the desk where she found the elixir, Krista noticed a leatherbound weekly calendar, opened to the current week. She could not resist a rapid scan of the listed appointments: one name recurred on a daily basis—Aeros Mortati, M.D., Ph.D., D.C. Krista made a mental note of the Park Avenue address and returned to the outer room of the suite. There, Carl the butler was spreading a cloth over a round table. He then proceeded to light a series of candles. She handed the bottle to Emilia, who uncapped it and downed the liquid contents in one draft.

"Thank you, Krista, my dear. Now please join us at the table. You know, it really was time for my formula—I could feel it! After all these hundreds of years of being obsessed with this so-called magic elixir, imagine my surprise when I had my chemists analyze the contents and found it to be a solution of what you would today call melatonin! Available at any pharmacy. Isn't that remarkable? I had hidden a copy of the formula in the Park Theatre where Maria Malibran sang shortly after her performances there in 1825. It was on Park Row near Ann Street. Lorenzo Da Ponte (Mozart's librettist who was then a professor of Italian at Columbia College) showed me a suitable hiding place. When I returned to New York recently, I could not find the Park Theatre: I must have somehow missed the news that it had burned down in 1848! At any rate, there, in its location, were the brownstone shops that John Jacob Astor's family had constructed in its place. I spotted a huge conglomerate—J & R Music—and went inside. Within a few hours, I had located the desolate corner of the theater where I had concealed the parchment: it now contained a feature display of Julio Iglesias compact discs! I choked back my resentment and retrieved the document and it was from this that I concocted the draft that my chemists analyzed. But all of that is old news. Here, sit by me and take my hand."

Krista's right hand was held by Emilia, and her left hand was grasped by Mr. Larry. Except for the candles, there was no light in the room. Mr. Larry giggled. "Isn't this delicious? We could all be around the campfire, singing, 'Kum-ba-ya, my Lord, Kum-ba-ya' . . . ouch!" Krista realized that Mr. Larry had just been kicked beneath the table by Emilia! "Now what we do here, Krista (yes, Emilia, I'll be good!) is focus on Emilia's concentration. In this way, my parapsychological and paranormal abilities are directed onto Emilia. She will then be a channel to summon forth the spirit from the world beyond. All righty? Now we need to recite something mellifluous and soothing. Look at me, Emilia: look into my eyes! 'There once was a man named Michael Finnigan / He had whiskers on his chin-nigan / The wind came along and blew them in again / Poor old Michael Finnigan! Begin again!'"

"Mr. Larry!" Emilia's grip on Krista's hand was so tight that she could only imagine how brutally Miss Marty clutched Mr. Larry's hand in dis-pleasure. "Mr. Larry, *you* will lull me with your hypnotic powers while *I* recite some verse!" The voice that continued impressed Krista for its reso-nance and lyric sonority. "From Longfellow . . . I used to know him . . . years ago.

> Tell me not, in mournful numbers,
> Life is but an empty dream!—
> For the soul is dead that slumbers,
> And things are not what they seem.
>
> Life is real! Life is earnest!
> And the grave is not its goal;
> Dust thou art, to dust returnest,
> Was not spoken of the soul.
> . . . .
>
> Art is long, and Time is fleeting,
> And our hearts, though stout and brave,
> Still, like muffled drams, are beating
> Funeral marches to the grave.
> . . . .
>
> Trust no Future, howe'er pleasant!
> Let the dead Past bury its dead!
> Act,—act in the living Present!
> Heart within, and God o'erhead!
>
> Lives of great men all remind us
> We can make our lives sublime,

And, departing, leave behind us
Footprints on the sands of time. . . ."

Krista could tell by Emilia's heavier breathing that she was either now in a trance or else wanted Krista to believe she was—it was becoming increasingly difficult to distinguish between these two possibilities. Mr. Larry called out, "Who's there? Who is with us? Enter our séance and identify yourself!"

A voice that Krista had never heard before answered. She saw Emilia's lips move but the voice was higher, lighter, and spoke with a very different (and more pronounced) accent than did Emilia. "My name is Maria Felicia García Malibran."

Mr. Larry asked the voice, "Where are you speaking from, Maria?"

"I am behind the curtains of the Park Theatre. Holding my fingers in a deliberate fashion, I obtain a glimpse of the gold columns of the auditorium. I stare at the figures of Tragedy and Comedy for I believe that my young life to date contains elements of both these realms."

Krista did not know whether to burst out laughing or listen in rapt attention: the scene was simultaneously bogus *and* genuine. Mr. Larry whistled. "Tell us, Maria, why your life is both tragic and comic." Was Mr. Larry reading from a script?

"I have just completed the vocal exercises that Papa taught me to put my voice forward in the mask. When my voice is so placed, I will be able to assume the character I am representing tonight. I will walk out onstage and the audience will applaud me, just like the divine Giuditta Pasta who is the goddess of all singers. I am not yet called 'Malibran.' I shall be playing Desdemona tonight, in Rossini's *Otello*. It is the eighth of February in the year 1826 and Papa is forcing me to play Desdemona to *his* Otello."

Mr. Larry interrupted to comment, "Notice, Krista, that Maria's voice is being channeled through Emilia's body. In phony séances, the voice would come through my body—"

"Hush!" Emilia's lips were still moving.

"Sorry, Maria! Please, continue."

"I do not want to play Desdemona and be held and kissed by Papa like that. I am frightened when Papa embraces me and then when he comes to kill me on the stage. He has berated me and castigated me for not depicting my character in a sufficiently convincing manner. In our rehearsals, Papa has threatened me: 'You will do it, my daughter, and if you fail in any way I will really strike you with my dagger!' This terrifies me, for when we assume our roles there is an intensity that is so real as to be haunting. I walk out onstage for the last act of the opera. The audience is overwhelmed by my singing of 'The Willow Song.' Now Papa enters as the deranged Moor. (Oh, excuse me . . . the spirits here inform me that there will be a subsequent *Otello* by a composer named Verdi that is more faithful to the Shakespeare play, but for me, *this* is *Otello,* so I am not bothered by the discrepancy that Otello carries a dagger.) To continue: I notice that Papa is not carrying the stage prop dagger with which we had rehearsed. He is carrying a real dagger! I sing out my line in Italian: '*Ah padre! ah che mai feci! / E sol colpa la mi di averti amato*' (Ah father! ah, whatever have I done! / To have loved you is my only crime). I am overwhelmed with fear! Is he angry at me for not infusing my performance with enough passion? Does he want to murder me? Or is he so overcome with dramatic artifice that he believes himself to *be* Otello and believes me to be Desdemona, his supposedly unfaithful spouse? Am I to die tonight? Does Papa mean to enact his threat? Will I perish on the stage of the Park Theatre?"

Mr. Larry gasped. "This is so exciting! Tell us, Maria: what happens next?"

The masked voice continued: "I move on the stage to a position where we are separated by a table. Papa/Otello circles the table in an effort to grab hold of me. He lunges at me with the authentic dagger. I scream out: 'Papa, papa, *por dios no me mates*!' Those in the audience fluent in my Spanish mother tongue know I cry out: 'Papa, papa, for God's sake don't kill me!' In that instant, he grasps me! Desperate to escape, I bite the hand of Him that created me! Papa screams out in pain, but appears to come back to a sense of himself: he is Papa, merely playing Otello (or so I believe!), and thus we continue the scene to its conclusion. I mime my death and Papa completes the opera. Afterward, we are called before the curtain again and again for tumultuous applause. I feel like the great Pasta, but I am shaken profoundly to my very core of being. What happened to Papa on that stage? I am not sure whether he was Papa or Otello or some infernal combination of the two. On that evening, I became La Malibran (although I would not marry Malibran for another six weeks or so)."

Krista leaned over to Mr. Larry. "May I ask her a question?"

Mr. Larry grimaced. "Absolutely not! Only I may communicate with the spirit."

Krista was unperturbed. "Then ask Maria whether she is Elina Makropulos."

Before Mr. Larry could relay the question, Emilia's lips conveyed the masked voice's answer: "Before I was Maria Malibran, I was Elina Makropulos. In 1826, when I played Desdemona onstage, I was thought to be seventeen years old, but Papa misrepresented my age to the proprietor by one year: I was actually sixteen years old! I see myself now, at age sixteen, in 1601, at the court of Hapsburg emperor Rudolf II. My father, Hieronymous Makropulos, is chasing me round a table with an elixir in his hand! I do not want to imbibe it; he screams out that he'll force me! I bite his hand: he pours the dastardly fluid down my throat and chokes me until I gasp out and swallow! I *am* Elina *and* Maria: we share the same event, the same moment, we leave the same footprints on the sands of time!"

Krista released her clasp of both hands and stood up from the table. "Well, then, thank you! Thank you, Emilia/Maria/Elina—or whatever the hell your real name is! I believe I've had quite enough of this performance. But I don't mean to sound unappreciative: it was better than the theater, or rather, it *was* theater, arranged—all of it—for my viewing pleasure! Don't bother to summon Carl: I'll let myself out!"

Mr. Larry grabbed hold of Krista's arm. "Ssshhh! Can't you see Emilia's still in a trance?"

Krista nodded, cynically, "Yeah, right!"

"No, really," Mr. Larry asserted. "She hasn't heard a thing you said. Here, I'll bring her out of it: I just need to recite some lines she likes. 'John Jacob Jingleheimer Schmidt! / Your name is my name, too! / And whenever we go out, / You can hear the people shout: / There goes John Jacob Jingleheimer Schmidt—'"

"Ahhhh!" Emilia Marty's lips were moving. Her voice was again her own, the deep, resonant, stage whisper. "Poe, Edgar A. He lived near here . . . in the Bronx."

"Or *she* can recite some lines to break the trance: it's all the same thing in the end," commented Mr. Larry.

Emilia continued, quoting,

> "Take this kiss upon the brow!
> And, in parting from you now,
> Thus much let me avow—
> You are not wrong, who deem
> That my days have been a dream;
> Yet if hope has flown away
> In a night, or in a day,
> In a vision, or in none,
> Is it therefore the less *gone*?
> *All* that we see or seem
> Is but a dream within a dream.
>
> I stand amid the roar
> Of a surf-tormented shore,
> And I hold within my hand
> Grains of the golden sand—
> How few! yet how they creep
> Through my fingers to the deep,
> While I weep—while I weep!
> O God! can I not grasp
> Them with a tighter clasp?
> O God! can I not save
> *One* from the pitiless wave?
> Is *all* that we see or seem
> But a dream within a dream?"

But by the time Emilia had completed her recitation, Krista Vitek was gone. "Mr. Larry! Turn on the lights! Krista! Darling, please don't leave!" But the *Times* reporter was on her way to the hotel lobby. "Mr. Larry, take a letter: 'My dear Krista, According to Hugh Holman, "all fiction is in some sense a story told by someone; all self-consciously artistic fiction is told by someone created by the author and who serves, therefore, as a mask." . . .'"

Dr. Aeros Mortati frowned pensively. Seated behind his massive desk, surrounded by his framed diplomas, artifacts of distinction, and testimonial certificates, he appeared at first to Krista as a figure in a diorama: elaborately arranged, configured, and posed but not, ultimately, real. She had gone for a long and bracing lunch, phoned in to the office, and then taken a cab over to the office of Dr. Mortati. Her inquiry concerned the enigma of Emilia Marty. Dr. Mortati stroked his beard and ruminated on his options. "Ordinarily, Miss Vitek, if you had come here inquiring about a psychiatric patient of mine, then there would be a clear and simple response to your entreaty: no. Absolutely, positively, no, without equivocation. But—and here's the rub—although I am decidedly and unreservedly a psychiatrist (and therefore owe my psychiatric patients a vow of professional confidentiality), and although the frequency and regularity of Miss Emilia Marty's visits would suggest that she was seeing me for psychotherapy or some such treatment, in reality I am also a doctor of chiropractic, and it was for this variety of care that Miss Marty would frequent my offices. I gave her daily chiropractic adjustments and see no reason why I ought not confide that to you. No professional vow is lapsed and nothing improper has been revealed." Dr. Mortati stared out the window at the dimming light of the early evening. "Now (how shall I say this?) I am sufficiently concerned about Miss Marty's recent notoriety to perhaps speculate—hypothetically, of course!—from a psychiatric capacity on the particular features of the personality of the individual whom I treated on a chiropractic basis. I do this for the *New York Times* and for no one else. Please note the distinctive spelling of my name and also that I have additionally a doctorate in existential philosophy."

Krista learned from Dr. Mortati that a woman named Maria Estella Monterone was born in 1900 in Vienna of Italian parentage. Early on, she had decided upon a career in music, and she studied with a Marianne Brandt, a Viennese singer of considerable fame who had herself learned to sing from Pauline Viardot, the youngest daughter of Manuel García and the sister of Maria Malibran. Marianne Brandt provided vocal instruction in Vienna from 1890 until her death in 1921. Maria Estella Monterone had been one of her last pupils, from 1919 to 1921. Not much is known of Monterone's early performance experience, but it is certain that she was a member of the cast of the 1929 Frankfurt production of the Janáček opera *The Makropulos Case,* conducted by Josef Krips. This was the third production of the opera but the first production to attract international attention. Maria Estella Monterone, Dr. Mortati believed, played the role of Krista Vitek in that Frankfurt version of the opera. But as a result of that experience, two certainties were established in her life: she dedicated herself without hesitation to the art of the voice, and she viewed the story of Emilia Marty as representing the secret of life through the masked voice.

At some indeterminate point after the Krips Frankfurt production, Dr. Mortati speculated, Maria Estella Monterone convinced herself that the fictional character who was the subject of first Čapek's play and then Janáček's opera was, in fact, real and that she, Maria Estella Monterone, was none other than Elina Makropulos herself! Dropping the "Maria" in her name provided her with the requisite "E.M." initials. She then continued her operatic career following the script of the Makropulos story: every decade or so she would change her name to another "E.M." variant and, like the phoenix, create herself anew in a fresh manifestation.

"It is decidedly worthy of note that Estella Monterone's operatic career began (as Krista Vitek) with that 1929 Frankfurt *Makropulos Case* and ended (playing the part of Emilia Marty under her current name of Emilia Marty) with a San Francisco production of the opera in November of 1966. I was there!" attested Dr. Mortati. "It was thoroughly stupendous! She looked every bit as ravishing as she looks today. No one would ever have suspected that Emilia was then sixty-six years old—the same age I am now. I often traveled with her in those days, in the latter stages of her career, because she required from me complex chiropractic maneuvers to keep her voice and body limber. Shall I confess to you that I fell in love with her almost immediately? I saw her honestly as a remarkable woman in every respect. (I am relying on your discretion in this regard, Miss Vitek.) Despite the fact that she sang stunningly, the San Francisco performances unnerved

Emilia in some deep and disturbing manner. It is my opinion that playing Emilia Marty while being Emilia Marty induced in her an excessive identification with the character. She suffered a devastating breakdown which, as an existential psychiatric chiropractor, I treated with chiropractic. (And why not chiropractic, since where does the mind exist except in the skull? And what is the skull but that which is connected to the spine? Thus, by adjusting the spine I am treating the inner psyche.) During her breakdown, she became convinced that she was a 'shadow,' a projected image created by some author or composer. In effect, she lost confidence that she was an authentic being. Her sense of herself was that her life was a fiction, a dream, a representational state of existence imagined by some other creature whom she referred to as a 'persona' or 'mask.' To resume her life, she had to dispose of one Emilia Marty. Thereafter, she recovered and wrote romance novels: writing, I believe, was an alternative reality for her."

Dr. Mortati leaned back in his imposing leather chair and gestured toward a set of photographs on the wall across from him. "All of these are of—us." Krista walked over for a closer examination. "I wanted her all to myself. I wanted her to live with me exclusively. To my way of thinking, what did she need opera for—or writing or directing? Our love would be sufficient. But whenever I would reprise this theme, she would recite to me from opera: most frequently the aria 'E sogno? o realtà' ('Is this a dream? or reality?'), from Verdi's *Falstaff*, I believe. 'Mortati,' she would say to me, 'how do you know that time spent with you is real?' Or else, she would render Prospero's final speech from *The Tempest*, ending with: 'As you from crimes would pardoned be, / Let your indulgence set me free.' She would follow this by saying, 'Mortati, if you keep this up, I won't be spending any time with you at all!' Reluctantly, I realized she needed a realm of her life that was not Mortati, that was outside the scope of Aeros Mortati! I came to understand that I would have to share her with everyone else—certainly, with her other lovers! But, sharing her—a woman devoted to art, a work of art herself, an artist—allowed me to become closer to her than others ever would, and, for this, I am thankful." Dr. Mortati shrugged.

Krista paced back and forth before the framed photographs on the opposite wall: Emilia in Nuremberg, Paris, Venice, Munich, Seville, New York, Rome, Milan, Los Angeles, Salzburg, Vienna, Bakersfield, Catania,

San Francisco, Prague—what sort of enigmatic individual could inspire this visual itinerary? Only when she squinted her eyes could Krista detect a glimpse of the faint image of Dr. Mortati in the photos. On the adjacent wall were framed the jackets of Emilia Marty's many books and the posters of the operas she had performed. "Why do you have this shrine to Emilia on your wall, Doctor?" Krista asked, without fully understanding her question—for, indeed, Krista was becoming aware that she was at least as obsessed with Emilia as was Dr. Mortati.

"I used to reserve that wall for graphic scientific charts of the spine and skull," he responded, "but somehow, for some reason, they made her uncomfortable. These personal images are what she wanted here . . . when we would meet. And I . . . it was as if I were one of *her* creations: loving her, I existed to please her, to carry out her will, her creative design. I removed my specialized charts, erasing a part of myself, to make room for her . . ."

Krista felt dizzy from all she had absorbed; she was so frustrated she wanted to scream. She struggled with intense vertigo. She labored to regain her composure. "Doctor! I have heard a description of past events and I have observed your office decor. Now answer me this: is she Emilia Marty or Elina Makropulos or what?"

Dr. Mortati stood up. "She is, for me, Maria Estella Monterone. She saw her life as a vast opera and cast herself as its leading character. When her interpretation was revealed to be only a characterization, she seized on another role and yet another, finding solace in the process of creation rather than its outcome or result. Life, in its unfolding possibilities, was an unending schedule of impending performances. And by this means . . . she lived! She confused life with art, dream with reality, to her personal and perpetual detriment; but this same determination provided a vast and ceaseless enrichment for her audiences and readers—past, present, and future. Art was the mask she wore to face the world—or perhaps it was the other way around."

"That lummox said *what*?" Emilia Marty nearly fell forward out of her lounge chair. It was the following day and Krista had returned to the

St. Regis for tea, at Miss Marty's invitation, and recounted the narrative she had been told by Dr. Mortati. "Really, my dear, that is too much. Did Mortati disclose to you that I no longer avail myself of his chiropractic psychotherapy or any other services? Did he confide to you that he is currently writing some sort of confessional book—What do they call it? A 'kiss-and-tell book!' Yes, that's it!—and that my purpose for seeing him this week was to prevail upon him not to publish his particular brand of tommyrot? No? I thought as much!" Miss Marty leaned toward Krista and refilled her teacup. "How much credence should you place in a man whose determined purpose is to concoct fantastic lies in exchange for a colossal advance against royalties from his sleazy publisher?"

"But, Miss Marty!" Krista now allowed herself to convey some measure of her own frustration and irritation. "His story is more reasonable! According to Dr. Mortati, you're a ninety-six-year-old woman who, as a result of unbelievably skillful plastic surgery, appears to be half that age. In your version of the fable, you are either three hundred ninety-five or four hundred and eleven years old and you've confounded medical science by means of cosmetic surgery, chiropractic, and melatonin! His version, though far-fetched, at least has some degree of plausibility; your account is utterly preposterous!"

"Look around you, my child." Miss Marty's voice was soft and soothing. "The curtains are closed so as to blot out the light. In this soft light, does it matter so much whether I am ninety-six years old or four times that age? When you suspend your disbelief to accept Mortati's tale, how much more effort is needed to embrace the details of my story? Opera and fiction are both like that, Krista. They occur in their own special realms, apart from life, but—in their own unique manner—connected to life. Once you enter the opera house and the lights dim and the curtains part, once you open the pages of your novel and the actual world recedes, your attention is focused on a projected, masked stage—a theater of imaginary beings and voices conveying elusive and evanescent glimpses of eternity. I live for those flashes of uncanny insight, Krista. It is my calling to evoke that sudden shudder of empathy and ecstasy that we associate with what is beautiful and human both."

The telephone rang. Emilia spoke into the receiver. "What? Floyd Lubber and Jones are in the lobby? And Mortati, too? Well, send them up—but, Carl, do not admit them to my room in here: I will come out to them when I am ready!"

Emilia stood and reached for a book from the armoire. She pressed a switch and the room was flooded with music. Krista was not entirely sure, but she believed she was listening to the haunting and eerie concluding melody from Janáček's *Makropulos Case*. Emilia spiraled in waltz-like movements around the room while reciting lyrics from the libretto in Czech. After a few moments, she called out: "According to Čapek's play, Krista, I should bequeath to you the parchment that contains the secret to my immortality. But, as I already told you, melatonin is available everywhere: in fact, there's a health food store down the street that offers a type that dissolves readily under your tongue or in a warm beverage. But I need to give you something. I want to give you something." The music came to an end, and Emilia returned to her seat.

Emilia took Krista's hand in both of hers. "Please, my dear. Allow me to tell you about my next novel, the novel I am in the process of writing. Remember, Krista, that there is the so-called real world and then there is the imaginary world of fiction. If the fictional world is artistically rendered, it becomes more real than reality itself. In my novel, many characters are depicted, many events are described—and all of them are fictional. There is an imaginary character named Maria Estella Monterone, an old and tired woman who is born in 1900 and who studied with Marianne Brandt (a student of Maria Malibran's sister, Pauline Viardot); in 1929, this Maria Estella Monterone plays the part of Krista or Kristina in the Frankfurt production of Janáček's opera, and she becomes convinced that she is actually Elina Makropulos, the woman who has been alive for hundreds of years. There is another imaginary character in my novel, a woman of German-Italian ancestry. Born in 1930, she sings under the name of Maria Tod. She is aware, of course, that her name means 'death' in German, and this fact has disturbed her in the past. She is cast for the part of Kristina/Krista in the San Francisco Opera production of *The Makropulos Case* in 1966. She identifies with her role as the heir to Elina Makropulos and becomes convinced that if *she* really is Elina Makropulos, the woman who has lived for hundreds of years—or, at least, Elina's current manifestation, Emilia

Marty—then she will overcome her destiny of death and become eternal through art."

The telephone rang and Emilia Marty ignored it. She retained her hold on Krista's hand. "Many imaginary events take place in my novel, Krista. For instance, do you remember the other night, when we both went to the Metropolitan Opera premiere of *The Makropulos Case*? In my novel, a tenor named Richard Versalle plays the role of Vitek, Kristina's father. And in the premiere of the opera, he sings out the English equivalent of the Czech, 'You only live so long,' and then he sustains a heart attack and falls ten feet from a ladder to the stage where he dies! Isn't that incredible? The character in my novel actually dies at the logical moment in the opera where the text preordains his death! The audience, ironically, would be confused as to whether Versalle or Vitek was actually dying (in life) or depicting death on the stage. In my novel, Jessye Norman would never get to sing the role of Emilia Marty on the night of the premiere because the performance will be canceled! You see, in my fiction there is a strange tradition of dream and reality being confused at the opera, Krista, just as it is in all fiction. The great baritone Leonard Warren died on the stage of the Met in 1960 during a scene from *La Forza del Destino*. The 'force of destiny,' indeed! And the historic baritone Lawrence Tibbett killed a man onstage at the Met during a rehearsal of an opera based on a Browning text in which he was creating the role of a murderous villain!"

Emilia Marty released Krista's hand and pressed a switch to play yet another recording: the music was conspicuously different than the Janáček a few moments before—it was lively, pulsating, spirited, and energetic. "This is the climax of Rossini's *Otello,* Krista, the music Maria Malibran sang at the Park Theatre in New York in 1826 and which she sang in Venice at the Fenice in 1835 when they named the Teatro Malibran after her. In my novel, the grand Fenice opera house—the house that was named after the phoenix for its ability to be reborn from the ashes after being destroyed by fire, a creation that (like Elina Makropulos!) stood for hundreds of years—burns to the ground: it dies, just as Elina does at the end of the Janáček opera! There is an end to everyone and everything, Krista. Even my attorney, William Kunstler, dies in the fictional realm of my novel! What I mean to emphasize in my novel is that life would not be precious if it existed forever; it is invaluable precisely because it is finite! Unlike life, only art is eternal: the forms and traditions of art, while never being actually alive, transcend death by remaining vital and moving people passionately again and again for hundreds and hundreds of years. Art is the mask of life, Krista, and through its projected voices life is perennially born and reborn!"

As Emilia Marty spoke vibrantly, Rossini's music reached its climactic conclusion. Emilia reached over, grabbed a bottle, and tossed it into the trash. "Krista, that's it for me! I'm through with melatonin! *No mas!* No more! Please understand, my next novel will be a colossal success: now that I have my own Emilia Marty Web site and fan club and my public awaits my book tours and autograph signings, there is no question but that this novel will be a best seller like the rest of them. But, Krista, I leave to you this reality: that a woman who *really has* lived for hundreds of years is now declaring that her life must end—not in suicide, perish the thought! But I will not artificially prolong my existence any further. What lies in store for me I will face, without elixir, or potion, or parchment, or melatonin! Here am I—Emilia Marty, Elina Makropulos, Ellian MacGregor, Eugenia Montez, Maria Malibran—a woman and her art! Through the opera and its text, through the words and their music, I will enact my operatic destiny on the stage of life—now and forever, eternally! Krista, I am talking to you! This is all there is, and all there ever was!"

But Krista was paying only slight attention. She realized that her quest for the true Emilia Marty had no closure or, at least, was ongoing. What seemed to matter more than anything else was traversing the distance between the fiction and the reality: comparing the imaginary with the actual in order to obtain a sense of the possible.

Krista rushed over to the trash bin, retrieved the overturned bottle of melatonin, and secured the bottle cap; then, carefully, deliberately, she placed the container in her purse along with the other bottles on Emilia Marty's table. What if Emilia Marty were correct? What harm could result from taking melatonin, what wrong could ensue from living on and on to witness the incredible wonder of the human predicament? At the very least, her search for the perfect martini would continue for a good deal longer than she had ever expected.

The telephone rang. Emilia picked up the receiver. "Carl? Yes, I see. Sir Flanders Floyd Lubber is waiting in the outer room? Listen: there is a recording I should like for you to play for him while he waits for me. It's on the bureau and I've marked the track for you to play. Yes, the Puccini, *La Fanciulla del West*: do you know? I not only think he'll enjoy it, I think he'll recognize it! And present Mr. Unctuous Jones with the facial mirror I placed on the counter for him: that will keep him occupied for unlimited hours of momentous pleasure! And for Dr. Mortati, reward him with the book I left on the shelf, Leslie Fiedler's *Love and Death in the American Novel*; inside it, I've inscribed a quotation, from Hugh Holman: 'The persona can be not a character in the story but an "implied author"; that is, a voice not directly the author's but created by the author and through which the author speaks'—I think he'll appreciate the sentiment. Thank you, Carl. I'll be in momentarily."

Emilia Marty opened a drawer and withdrew a long, flowing scarf: she tossed its ends around her neck with a flourish and observed its decorative tassels as she moved. "Do you know, Kristina? In my novels, I am famous for my characteristic irony, for a detached quality that allows me to emphasize certain dark or unfathomable impressions. If this scene right now were to be included in my novel, I would strike a morbid bargain with Sir Flanders Floyd Lubber: I would, in exchange for credit as the coauthor of the book for *Maria!* and an actual revision of the text to correct the facts about the life of Maria Malibran, apologize for my unseemly behavior and pay over a small, token financial settlement. I would even, in the novel, endorse the rewritten *Maria!* and encourage my readers to see it. I would expect, in return, that Floyd Lubber would drop his lawsuit against me and invite me to star in his next production. We would be thick as thieves, I assure you!"

Emilia paused and listened to the music from the outer room. She heard the familiar strains of Puccini that Floyd Lubber had illicitly appropriated. "But life is not fiction, Kristina. In life, there are no 'mock executions.' All of us are the authors of our own lives!" In fascination, Krista watched as Emilia Marty threw open the door to the outer room and walked determinedly and intently to face the music.

THE KEEPER OF THE LIST

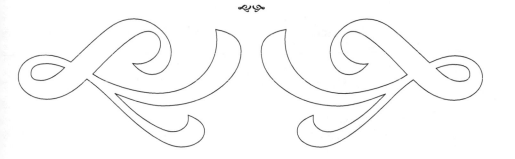

There he stands in the distance: a tall, stalwart young man, elegant, with haughty demeanor and an air of condescension. What do we know about him? As we approach, we notice, first of all, his stately presence, his characteristic combination of detachment and charm. But his detachment is imperfect, breaking at times to reveal hasty glances at his surroundings: eyes darting in the midst of a steely countenance. The charm, as well, veils a coldness, a heart of stone, as a particular servant of his was once known to remark.

So secure is he in his privileged hauteur that he is able to give his word—grandly, with great swagger—and then withdraw it instantly as if nothing whatever had transpired. Promises, for him, are only tactics, strategic moves that enable him to reach a particular goal. When a certain Z., with whom he was striving to be intimate, urged him to remember that she was engaged to another ("But, my lord, I have promised to marry him"), his response was that "such a promise is worth nothing."

He likes to make things up. In the midst of wooing Z., he was confronted by a previous amour, a certain Donna E.; not wishing to make a scene, he whispered to Z., "The unfortunate woman is in love with me and out of pity I must feign love." This, however, was not true—that is, while it was true that the woman was in love with him, it was not out of pity that he felt obliged to feign love.

He likes women; specifically, he likes to have sexual intercourse with women. While he is most fastidious about his toilette and his personal appearance, he is enthusiastically undiscriminating about the selection of those women with whom he likes to have sexual intercourse. On the account of his manservant, a certain L. (who, incidentally, is not to be relied upon absolutely since he nurtures a deep-rooted envy of his employer; he once commented, in a public place before witnesses, on the nature of the employer-employee relationship that he "want[s] to be the gentleman, [he] no longer want[s] to serve"), he has had sexual intercourse with 2,065 women.

The number 2,065 describes a quantity that is difficult to bring forth to the memory in a simultaneous fashion. If, for instance, one consumed 2,065 bottles of, say, Bordeaux, over a period of time, one would possess a certain overall sense of the experience; but one would have difficulty recalling in a specific sense the individual qualities of one particular wine or another. If one wished to recall or compare or savor one or more of these bottles after the fact, it would be necessary to devise some system of categorization.

It is not surprising, then, to discover that he keeps an elaborate catalog. He likes to write things down. Or, rather, due to his elevated station, L., his manservant, is assigned the actual task of transcribing, but at his direction and conception. The catalog establishes categories of reference so that he might better maintain control of the concept underlying the number, 2,065.

The women with whom he has had sexual intercourse are indexed according to their nationality. Specifically, he has had 640 sexual partners in Italy of Italian ancestry. (Note: it might be possible to maintain that while in Italy he slept with women who were not Italian; nevertheless, it is my contention that the intention behind the list is to indicate nationality.) Another 231 women were of the German nationality; 100 of his sexual partners were French; there were 91 women of Turkish background; and finally, there is evidence for a marked predilection—a predisposition, if you will—for Spanish sexual partners since the number of Spanish women with whom he has had sexual intercourse totals 1,003. Needless to say, he enjoys traveling.

The women are cross-referenced by means of their class affiliation: peasant, servant, town girl, countess, baroness, marchesa, princess, et cetera. There is an additional cross-index for physical type and yet another for chronological age. Hair color is established as a category of reference: fair hair, dark hair, white hair, et cetera. Remarkably, this latter category is subfiled in terms of the particular flattering remarks he prefers to make to that subgroup! Another highly unusual correlation is the one he draws between body type and season. Although he is obviously an extremely thorough individual, this does not eliminate a certain creativity for organization.

A closer look at the catalog, however, reveals a fundamental quandary: despite the existence of the classification subgroups, they do not seem to have a significant purpose. For instance, although it is clearly indicated that he shows a marked preference—a predominating passion—for sexual partners who are young beginners, he will also have sexual intercourse with old, highly experienced sexual partners simply for the purpose of adding them to his list despite his specified preference! Let me be clear about this: He has established categories, for instance, of wealth, physical beauty, and physical repugnance. These exist as descriptive subgroups to organize the listing but not as standards or criteria by which he chooses the women with whom he will have sexual intercourse. In other words, physical repugnance and beauty have nothing in themselves to do with selecting the particular sexual partner; rather, they exist as means to structure the experience after the fact and to keep a permanent record.

The single criterion by which sexual partners are selected is that they be women; as L. has expressed it (in his inimitable way), "If she wears skirts, you know what he does!" Here, however, a problem reveals itself: If the categories exist as an aid to memory, as a means of structuring experiences whose number is excessive, why does he occupy himself with activities devoted to increasing the size of the catalog? Is the catalog a record of his life experiences (of a specialized sort) or is his life lived in order to catalog?

Something must be said concerning his olfactory keenness: L. has observed that he is able to detect the presence of a woman by means of the sense of smell exclusively. By way of clarification, it ought to be mentioned that this sensory gift applies not to the accoutrements of scent with which it is customary for women to adorn themselves—perfume, cologne, powder, and the like—but rather for the actual, *essential,* if you will, aroma of womanness. Thus, his discriminating organ, his perfect nose, would not be fooled by a man wearing a woman's powder, perfume, and scented garments.

On the other hand, his uncanny ability to sense an *odor di femmina* does not seem to be connected to his cataloging disposition. In one notable instance, he announced to L. the presence of a beautiful woman by means of scent alone. On closer, *visual* inspection, the woman was identified as Donna E., a previous sexual partner, cataloged as number 994 under the subgroup Women of Spain, category Well-born. It is thus quite evident that his olfactory identification of Donna E. as a woman did not provide him with any precise information that she had already been included in the catalog. To the contrary, he was attracted to the woman as a future sexual partner (by means of scent) *until* the visual appraisal confirmed that the woman had already been listed; at this point, sexual attraction was contraindicated. It would appear, therefore, that the catalog has primary significance in and of itself as a separate and distinct entity from its function of ordering and preserving moments from life. In this one suggestive example, a scent derived from life provided the impetus for his feeling a desire to achieve coitus. Circumstances were such that this goal was entirely reasonable (although he had behaved badly toward Donna E., he had slept with her previously and she retained a tender inclination for him despite her very appropriate anger at his behavior): life had brought these two individuals together, so to speak, in order for them to resume a state of affairs that had existed earlier. But the preexistence of Donna E. as an item in the catalog took precedence over the affinities suggested by life. Evidently, repetition is forsworn from the catalog. His responses in life were modified by the reality of the catalog: Donna E., whose scent had so enticed him, was transformed instead into an enemy from which he felt the necessity to flee.

Another means of escape which he enjoys thoroughly is the masquerade—dressing up in the garb of others so as to suggest another identity. On one notable occasion, he wrapped himself in a cloak as a preface to attempting sexual intercourse with a certain highborn Spanish woman, Donna A. The cloak had the effect of concealing—temporarily, at least—his identity so that Donna A. at first mistook him for her fiancé. (But the circumstances of this event are so shrouded in controversy that they threaten to overwhelm the concept at hand. It will be necessary to return to this important incident presently.) It is more suitable to cite, at this point, his exchange of clothing with his manservant, L. This was a recreational transposition, it must be emphasized. Nothing in the condition of his own garments at that moment made them dysfunctional or impossible to wear. Rather, the donning of his manservant's clothing served at least two purposes. First, since he could not continue to relate to Donna E. as a possible future sexual partner (as a prior sexual partner, she had already been *listed,* if you will, she was already a character in his text), he found it amusing for L. to seek her out while wearing his clothing. The gratifications of this arrangement are apparent: if L. does not manage to sleep with

Donna E., it is of no consequence since he, L.'s employer, has already slept with her and cataloged her and L. is a mere employee. If L. does sleep with Donna E., this may be attributed to his appearing before her in the guise of his employer, her previous lover. Since he will not or cannot sleep with Donna E., it is only fitting that L., his representative, should do so in his stead. Second, by outfitting himself in his manservant's costume, he is now able to attempt sexual intercourse with Donna E.'s maidservant, a woman who has not previously been listed in the catalog. In this case, even if the maidservant has sexual intercourse with him because she mistakes him for L., it is he who has prevailed by arranging this tactical maneuver: it is he, L.'s master, who would achieve the catalog listing (although a delicious irony would be that L., whom he has cuckolded in a decidedly unusual manner, would actually write the entry).

Nothing in this recreational attire swap should be taken as eliminating a more serious aspect to the exchange. Those who would describe it as exclusively a frivolity are in error. Masquerading as another presents him with insights of a decidedly self-revelatory nature. Many of those who have encountered him have commented upon his characteristic reticence at talking about himself, revealing his inner feelings, and the like. But this, in itself, is not a flaw or even a problem. Who of us has not been oppressed, on one occasion or another, by some individual whose incessant chatter about self fills the air with noxious fumes, so to speak? We must be wary so as to avoid an excessive characterization based on insufficient evidence. There is, however, a simple observation—a condition, really, that, taken together with his reluctance or inability to disclose himself as a personality through discourse, reveals a significant amount: *he has no friends*. The closest thing to a friend he has among males is his manservant, L., and he abuses the kind feelings that might exist by treating him in a crass and inconsiderate manner. His female associates are sexual partners and not friends, at least in his eyes: this point must be insisted upon. An example of this exceedingly provocative manner toward L. may be seen when he was describing to his manservant how he had very nearly succeeded in having sexual intercourse with yet another woman who believed him to be L. L. asked him, "And you tell me this so casually?" His reply: "Why not?" L.'s query: "Suppose it was my wife?" His response: "Better still!" Thus it may be seen that his extreme reticence and lack of self-description are part and parcel of his isolation, his aloofness, his remoteness.

Dressed in L.'s clothing, on the contrary, he is a veritable fountain of information about himself. Phrases that would have struck him as being unseemly and profoundly inappropriate fairly leap from his tongue while in the guise of L. It is instructive to explore in some substance an exchange that took place between him (disguised as L.) and M., the fiancé of Z. (the peasant woman mentioned earlier whose favors he had sought to win), as well as a large group of M.'s associates. M. and his associates were in a surly temper and were not inclined to be kindly disposed toward him, or L. either, for that matter. Their intentions were hostile, in other words. Who would not forgive, under these circumstances, a degree of reticence? Who would be moved to reprove an element of discursive discretion? Nevertheless, in this situation, seeming to be L., he spoke at great length about himself, achieving a degree of lyricism that is most noteworthy: "If a man and a girl," he noted, "walk through the piazza, and if beneath a window, lovemaking you hear: wound him! It will be my master. On his head he wears a hat with white plumes, a great cloak around him, and a sword at his side."

Really, this is extraordinary! What is disclosed by this passage is his willingness to see himself from another's viewpoint—indeed, the necessity of assuming the other's position in order for him to be able to see himself at all. He is describing himself almost as a mythical character: wherever you might roam, should you encounter a man romancing a woman in the piazza, that's him (me). He might be here, he might be there, wherever you least expect him—all of us are familiar with the routine. Under any circumstances, should you happen to hear a couple making love under a window, *that's him* (in other words, me, he's saying). But once you find him, wound him, strike out at him, it will be my master. The ability to see oneself as a legendary or mythical character is most unusual. If we combine this with the talent and resourcefulness of so becoming the other that one shares the other's perspective—in this case, homicidal rage—about oneself, then we have a remarkable ability to be no one and someone simultaneously. And all of this is achieved by means of the masquerade.

The disguise, moreover, does not deprive him of his central purposefulness: in the midst of the self-revelatory paean to himself and his empathy for the contemptful reproach of the individuals he has encountered, he does not fail to send M.'s associates off on a futile excursion in order that he might isolate M., disarm him, and then inflict on him a beating of the most excruciating variety. He shares with other people a contempt for himself; yet he has contempt for those—including himself, it would seem—who have contempt for him.

That self who so persistently elicits contempt is, nevertheless, a contrary one; despite his propensity for cataloging and his inclination to disguise, he possesses marked counteraffinities—he appears to detest all categories and classifications in life that apply to him. It has been noted that his desire for women with whom he might have sexual intercourse is not harnessed to class distinctions, hierarchies, or social customs; he has no use for these implements of power except as the means to obtain new names for his list. If the list is placed for the moment to the side, he may be seen as detesting the social order, for indeed, of what use is it to him? Being already at the top, as it were, and engaged as he is in the spirited endeavor of itemizing (in a grandiose sense) the infinite varieties of womanhood, he refuses to be enslaved by those categories that are not of his own making. At a party that he hosted for the express purpose of soliciting new material for his catalog, he provided these directions to his musicians: "Without any order let the dance proceed, for some the minuet, for some the follia, for some the allemande."

All of us have undoubtedly had the experience of attending a dance and observing the precise and ritualized manner in which the routine unfolds: the principals inaugurate the event, so to speak, by dancing alone at the onset; then, others join in, and a careful and highly ordered series of dances is then initiated. The overall effect is elaborately designed, constructed from a series of slight variations of tempo, mood, pace, and effect. But he would seem to reject such distinctions! "Without any order let the dance proceed": What sort of spirit is this? What kind of event can proceed without any order? Indeed, how might one distinguish a single event if there is no order, no meaningful progression? The entire concept of subjugating one's life to one's environment, one's circumstances, is called into question: when one dances, one performs a series of formalized steps that are synchronized to a particular type of music. Even the "freer" dances depend on an associational relationship between bodily movement and originating music. But what does it mean for the minuet, follia, and allemande to be danced simultaneously? Does that mean *against* the music? Or regardless of the music? What are the larger consequences if such an aesthetic principle were to be applied in a broader swath, so to speak?

There is no question that his behavior provides an answer to this last inquiry. Perhaps inflamed by this dancing-without-order, he proclaimed as he opened his doors for his party, "Anyone is welcome: *viva la libertà!*" Now, it has been noted for many years by commentators too numerous to mention that the idea of a party is based upon the concept of exclusivity: you may attend, but you, alas, are not welcome—only by inviting some and restricting others is a party invented, so to speak. Otherwise, there would be no difference between a party at one's home and the uncorking of a bottle of champagne on a city street for the consumption of a disparate group of traffickers. How is one to arrive at a satisfying solution of this enigma? Is he a champion of liberty, one who epitomizes the universal pursuit of happiness, the ability of every human being to develop and arrive at an individualized conception of pleasure? Is he nothing more than an anarchist, a negating spirit whose inclinations are against structure and order, an opponent of systems building, a foe of any sort of category or mode? Is he an enemy of the ancien régime, a principled resister of the archaic and oppressive codifications of power? Or might it be suggested that these enigmatic positions against order and in favor of liberty are, in fact, *postures* that carry him toward a surreptitious goal: the adding of names to his catalog!

Back to the catalog and again to the masquerade! For it might readily be suggested that the party itself was a peculiar sort of theater designed to contrive a disarray so substantive as to allow him to seduce the object of his desire, Z. If the creation of chaos has, as its end, the satisfaction of an elaborate design, then it is reasonable, at least, to suppose that the chaos represents a *concealed order*—a single-minded order disguised as disorder. Were the dances to proceed without any order, it would be that much more difficult to keep track of the dancers. Could that be the intent behind the extravagant gesture? (Might the fact that he did lure Z. away from all the other revelers and nearly succeeded in seducing her be taken as reinforcement of this concept?)

But no, the notion that a solution to this conundrum might be found is, in itself, outrageous: Why must it be that he had one intention for all this cacophony? Isn't the impulse to costume, to disguise, to don the masquerade, a reflection of a nonunified nature? Could it not be that he had more than one affinity, or even contradictory affinities? Will you allow that it is at least possible that he was genuinely confused? For instance, while declaring "*viva la libertà*," he nevertheless fully took advantage of the pronounced rank and social advantages he enjoyed over M., Z.'s fiancé, so as to isolate M. from Z. and allow himself the opportunity to attempt a seduction of Z. on her wedding day. M. was reduced to the sarcastic mutterings appropriate to his rank: yes, sir, I understand, sir. In fact, when apprehended in the act of forcing his attentions on Z., he had the temerity to foist the entire responsibility onto his beleaguered manservant, L., an accusation so preposterous that no one in the company believed it for an instant and yet all were prevented, by means of his rank, from even questioning the veracity of his bold assertion.

Later that evening, he was overheard declaring: "I don't know what I'm doing, and a horrible tempest, O God, is threatening me." Surely this would serve to support the possibility that he was experiencing some sort of volatile state. On the basis of his public comments, it would appear that he resolved this confusion, albeit temporarily and fragilely, by resorting to a new brand of unifying spirit: "But my courage doesn't fail me. I'm not lost, I'm not confused. Even if the world should fall, nothing will ever make me fear." Somehow, the declaration of courage is the mediation between "I don't know what I'm doing" and "I'm not confused." Which emotion is worn as a cloak over the essential body? Which is the disguise and which the more nearly essential feeling? Is it at all possible to discern? Before answering, it is at long last time to consider more thoroughly the controversial circumstances involved in the affair of Donna A.

It was a wretched night, fierce with wind and rain (we have this on the authority of his manservant, L., who was, on the evening in question, overheard complaining about the weather conditions while he stood watch in the vicinity of Donna A.'s window). It was late at night and Donna A.

was alone in her room. All at once, a man wrapped in a cloak entered her quarters. Was the cloak draped around him in such a fashion as to conceal his identity? This is unclear. But really, how thoroughly is a plain cloak able to conceal anything? Let us consider an example: If God and Satan were each wrapped in cloaks, would we be able to tell them apart? Does there exist a cloak vast enough to obfuscate the eternal light that would emanate from the one visage? You grasp my point, I trust. In the first instant, Donna A. mistook him, L.'s master, the man in the cloak, the man in question, for her fiancé, Don O. (We have this as a result of her delayed account of the events, a rendering made tardy, presumably, by the extent of her distress.) But, in truth, how similar are they? How reasonable are the grounds for this confusion? On the one hand, we have Don O., a cautious, reticent, restrained aristocrat of sensitive mien and bearing, engaged (in the most oppressive, restrictive manner) to Donna A. for the purpose of securing matrimony—an individual content to remain exclusively bound to one woman in the most banal and dreary contractual arrangement, a veritable cream puff who exclaimed in public, seconds after the murder of Donna A.'s father, "You have husband and father in me." On the other hand, we have the gentleman in question, a brave, stalwart, flamboyant cavalier of courageous stance and demeanor, irresistible to some 2,065 women—a restless, fearless quester for erotic sensation and sensual fulfillment, a man who likewise pronounced in public, "Here's to women and good wine, the sustenance and glory of humanity!" The one subjugates himself to the sole object of his desire (one of his most revealing pronouncements supports this analysis: "On her peace my peace depends, what pleases her gives me life, what displeases her brings me death"); the other orders the world in the service of his desires. The one is content to be listed, the other is the Keeper of the List! Donna A. mistook the one for the other: what does that solemn fact reveal about her?

But is that fact (that is, that she was confused between the two men) itself so incontrovertible? Donna A.'s sworn statement attests that the intruder attempted to force himself upon her: he held her tightly, she cried out, resisted, saying the rogue had "tried to steal my honor!" But surely it is evident that had Donna A. begun crying out at the *first instant* that she sensed another presence in her room, the intruder would never have been able to arrive at such an intimate posture so as to be able to clasp her to his breast and attempt an indecent kiss! Why is it that she did not begin screaming immediately? Her answer: she mistook the intruder for her fiancé. But what respectable female would not begin shrieking immediately at the unannounced and unexpected presence of her intended in her room in the middle of the night? Let us allow for a moment that she did misperceive the intruder as Don O.: Was he any *less* of an intruder? Would his presence in her room in the black of night be a typical event, a welcome occurrence, one that would *not* provoke shock and outrage? What purpose would there be to such an indiscreet and inappropriate visit? Could they not converse the following morning? Or, if a matter of some urgency (my invention temporarily fails me), could a servant not be dispatched who would return with a communication in writing? It is clear that Don O. lives in the immediate vicinity: Donna A. is able to fetch him and return with him to the scene of her father's murder with great rapidity. No, I am afraid that the temporary assumption that the misperception was valid leads only to the most troubling insinuations about the nature of Donna A.'s propriety, her very decency and honor! Was she accustomed to entertaining Don O. in her chambers? Perish the thought! Therefore, why did she not cry out sooner?

Now it is necessary to contrive for an instant that Donna A. did not misperceive the intruder for Don O. (This, considering the vastly different natures of the two gentlemen, is really such a logical inference that it exhausts me to belabor this point so agonizingly; nevertheless, in the interests of fairness, I proceed.) Since she did not cry out instantly at the sensed presence of her intruder in her room, it is essential to wonder why. Undoubtedly, she was frightened, but if so, why did she not scream? Could it be that she was not frightened? Is it possible to presume that—for the merest fraction of a second—a semblance of a smile crossed her beauteous countenance? That would explain things, would it not? It is impossible to smile and scream simultaneously; try it yourself if you have remaining doubts. And at what might she be smiling (for the briefest of moments)? A smile at the thought of some welcome adventure in the most maudlin and constrained of existences, a bit of brio in the midst of monotony? A smile, perhaps, at the possibility of unanticipated pleasure? A smile in recognition of the glimpse obtained, despite the cloak, of a comely and gallant visage presenting himself unto her with valor and love? Again: why did she not cry out? It is feeble indeed to continue to deny the obvious conclusion: she did not cry out because she did not wish to—*she wanted to be silent.*

Silence is many things: intimacy, empathy, understanding, complicity— but, above all, it is one thing . . . consent! I sense, by your silence, that you have taken my point.

Now we may proceed to consider the question of why she abandoned that silence for shouts and resistance. But why? Whatever difference does it make that she ended the silence eventually in comparison to the fact—the fact, mind you!—that she must have been silent in the first place? There are countless possibilities here, none of them particularly interesting or absorbing: she had second thoughts, as the saying goes, she became frightened at the great leap she was about to take, she was overcome by self-recrimination . . . things of that sort. Far more enticing is the realization that once her account is found to be distorted, even in the slightest detail, other distortions are possible, even likely! For instance, it is ungallant but, in the interests of truth, crucial to propose that the timing of her account may have been distorted. Perhaps the screams, the resisting, did not come until *after* the event that would logically follow the silent visit to a room late at night and the silent, smiling response. Would guilt and delay make the screams louder? Would the resistance be that much more spirited for not occurring at the time it would have prevented *the act*? These thoughts are inescapable to entertain. Indeed, even the unfortunate Don O., after attending to Donna A.'s account, spoke of his need to "undeceive her"—that is, she was deceived, even to him.

But look, you, at how our portrait of the figure in question is modified by the realization of Donna A.'s unreliability! His effrontery becomes a woeful misunderstanding; his perfidy may be construed as a well-intentioned miscue. Even Don O. is inclined to ambivalence: he wondered "how to believe that such a terrible crime could be committed by a cavalier": how, indeed! Up until now, the crime of indecency has been considered. What of the crime of murder, the deadly and demented assault on the person of Donna A.'s father, the commander?

Pause for a moment and dwell upon the posture and stance of he who is mighty and he who is meek: "Fight with me," insists one individual; "I do not deign to fight with you," replies the other. If the two of them are drawn into battle, who may be said to have instigated the conflict? The exchange is repeated, more or less: How many times must this occur? How often must one repeat one's desired inoffensive goal before it is reasonable to retreat to self-defense? Was the commander defending a nonexistent honor? If so, was he not the true aggressor? Were not the words "miserable man, stay, if you want to die" (attributed to the supposed intruder) uttered out of a sense of tragic, despairing inevitability, a profound dignity in the midst of outrageous provocation?

Of course, it is possible to cling to the notion of the vile treachery of the stealthy intruder. This is without question. Each of us, as individuals—we do what we can, and we believe what we must. But does that belief not reflect the face of the believer? Do some beliefs serve as the garb of deception by which we disguise from ourselves our true and essential natures? What I mean to convey is that as long as there is a degree of ambiguity in this matter, as long as the matter resists being "merely this" or "precisely that"—then, at least, the issue retains its life and its vitality. And on that note, allow me to continue.

Late one evening, the gentleman in question and his manservant, L., sought refuge inside the walls of a church graveyard. They were seeking a haven from the scores of pursuers who were motivated to harm them as a result of the recreational masquerade we discussed previously. It is appropriate to wonder: what sort of sensibility would find a graveyard a source of comfort and security? I confess that I am not sure. Are there not many reasons that one might visit a graveyard? Paying one's respects to the deceased, admiring the design of the gravestones, checking on the date for a birth or death? All right, yes, I will admit that these activities would most appropriately take place during the daylight hours. But nevertheless, I resist the characterization that mere presence in a graveyard implies a funereal nature or a grotesque sensibility. Why not be content with the allowance that our cavalier was possessed of a radically skeptical disposition? His was a nature that allowed him to relax comfortably in a cemetery. Often skeptics are made, not born. Who would not share precisely such a radically skeptical disposition and enjoy the restful atmosphere of a graveyard after having been thought ill of for an entire lifetime? But still, there are many sorts of skeptics and many possible interpretive nuances involved in achieving a meaningful understanding of his character.

At any rate, while amusing himself in a diverting fashion in the cemetery, our cavalier's discourse was interrupted by a stern voice that informed him he would cease his laughter before dawn. Since he and his manservant, L., were the only apparent living sojourners in the graveyard at this particular moment, it seemed appropriate for him to wonder about the origin of the voice. L.'s theory—that the words emanated from an otherworldly ghost whose intention was that they should apply to the chevalier—was rejected by the figure in question. For, after all, as a radical skeptic, what basis was there for him to believe in supernatural tampering? It was readily apparent that he and L. were alone. Thus, when he inquired as to the source of the voice and received the answer—"Audacious rascal! Leave the dead in peace!"—it was thoroughly appropriate for him to assume that "it must be someone outside who's making fun of us." How many of you, upon hearing yourself addressed by a voice whose source you could not immediately ascertain, would assume with confidence that you had been addressed by our Lord? Or, let us say, by the archangel Gabriel? Would it not be more responsible, more rationalistic, to assume that the voice proceeded from a human source that was, in some way, concealed, say, behind a tree, for instance? Of course.

What I wish to emphasize in this matter is that our aristocrat's skeptical approach was thoroughly in keeping with the circumstances that were presented to him. We are, none of us, in the habit of being addressed by creatures from the spirit world. Thus, when he found that he and his man, L., were at the feet of a statue of the commander, Donna A.'s father, whom he had (perhaps) slain inadvertently, who had (arguably) provoked him into a fatal sword fight, he directed his attention to it as a relief from the tension that is inherent to all instances of supernatural illusions until they can be explained in a reasonable manner. Imagine his frustration, his extreme distaste, when his servant refused his simple request: that he read the inscription on the statue! Really, we live in a bustling modern world; such behavior is tantamount to an inferior refusing to carry out a trivial errand on the grounds that a black cat had crossed his path, or some other such nonsense! Subservients often must be handled roughly when their implicit superstitiousness impairs their ability to carry out directions. So it was that L.—in the midst of some exotic distress—was ordered to read the inscription, and he prattled on about the commander awaiting vengeance against the man who put him in his grave . . . something like that.

A vulgar prank is evidently in progress: crude liberties would seem to be taken with your dignity in that jokers from outside the cemetery walls are pretending to be the voice of a ghost or spirit. Meanwhile, your deranged servant, thoroughly taken in by this idiocy, has lapsed into a state of comatose delusion, haunted by what you are certain is an inept contrivance: Who would not lapse into a mode of response that reflected a degree of distaste and irony? What to do with this dangerous (ha! ha!) Man of Stone? Why, tell him that he is invited to dinner: "I'll expect him to dine with me this evening."

Now, when your servant has been compelled to transmit that invitation and both of you perceive what appears to be the statue of the commander nodding his head in assent to the invitation and an accompanying voice affirming, "Yes," who, then, would not feel as if an elaborate jest were being perpetrated upon oneself? Unusual to the supreme degree, truly a "bizarre scene"; nevertheless, what is one to do? There would seem to be nothing for our figure to do but withdraw and, with dry amusement, enter into the preparations for his late evening meal.

And what a feast it was! "Since I'm spending my money, I want to be entertained!" Such was the aesthetic philosophy of our cavalier. To the live accompaniment of a group of musicians playing familiar operatic excerpts, he ate and drank lustily, consuming from a wide variety of delicacies, while monitoring the audacious greed of his manservant, L., who sought to sample some food on the sly. In the midst of these festivities, his previously listed paramour, Donna E., appeared and, interrupting his enjoyment, harangued him to "change his life."

His manner, I must say, in responding to her utterances, was impeccable. When she knelt before him, he urged her to rise or else he would not remain standing. When she accused him of deriding her, he responded gently, "I, deride you?" When she urged him to change his ways, his response was "Brava!"—wry, witty, concise, but without the slightest trace of rudeness. Then he asked her permission to continue with his feast and invited her, an uninvited guest, to join him if she wished. Why, he even toasted her! Nevertheless, she fled the hall and his graceful company and, in the alcove, uttered a diabolical cry.

Sent to investigate, our chevalier's manservant, L., returned with hysterical babblings about a man of stone, a man in white, and an ominous pounding noise. It was then that *he* appeared: the commander, Donna A.'s father—not, that is, the actual person (for, you may remember, he had been killed in the inadvertent exchange with our cavalier) but rather the walking personage of the statue from the cemetery (who, it must be said, was at least an invited guest—unlike Donna E., who had burst in unannounced). What had seemed, after dutiful reflection, to be a prank—the contrived throwing of a voice over a wall to appear to be a talking statue—is revealed as reality: the supernatural come to life!

With stern ferocity, the stone guest explained that he had been invited and has now arrived. The response of our figure in question speaks volumes about his character, about his essence. Faced with a truly uncanny event, a turn in life that defied all his ability to anticipate or predict, he answered with poise and control: "I would never have believed it, but I'll do what I can!" His manservant, L., was then directed to have another dinner brought in immediately.

What is there in our cavalier to admire? Why has there been, throughout history, all this—so to speak—beautiful music about him? It is here that I must take exception to Donna E., who condemned his consistent odious nature and called for a redemptive change. In my view, what is most admirable about our figure is precisely his volatile presence, his willingness to improvise. Who is there among us who has not been chastened by life, presented with its chilling rebuke? And yet, how many of us, when all of our anticipated hopes and plans have been dashed, have the dignity to carry on, to shrug philosophically—stoically—and say, "I would never have believed it, but I'll do what I can"?

So: on this count, I find him worthy of admiration. But there is more: The stone guest, as a celestial being, did not "partake of mortal food." The cavalier's ironic invitation to dine was then turned back on him in earnest. Having issued the invitation, would he agree to dine with the commander's statue—that is, in the other world? L., quivering beneath a table, urged a strategy of deceit: he should reply that he had no time, sorry. But our figure announced: "I shall never be accused of cowardice." To the stone commander, a man who (it might be argued) had arrived to seek his rightful vengeance, our figure was steadfast: "My heart is steady in my breast: I'm not afraid, I'll come!"

And why not? Is this not a supreme new adventure? What is there in life to hold one back? Life in its essence has no essence: it must be embraced wholeheartedly, with a certain brio, an accommodating spirit that enables one to bear, if not wholeheartedly welcome, the perverse changes and reversals that are hurled at us. But there is a distinction to be made between doing what one can—with no fear or hesitation—and repentance. Our figure offered his hand as a symbol of his valorous honor—only to be again tormented with the relentless refrain of "*pentiti, cangia vita*" (repent, change your life)! But our cavalier will not. Would you? I put it to you: Are we ultimately at fault for the bizarre permutations of life? If all is predetermined by the fateful hand of our Creator, how may we repent for deeds over which we had no control? Is not repentance the final indignity? Our chevalier will tolerate everything life offers him, he will never complain, but he will not repent.

And so, our aristocrat is dragged down to hell by the icy grip of the stone guest: a most unsatisfactory and undeserved fate . . . but what is that pounding?

DON GIOVANNI! YOU INVITED MY OPINION AND I HAVE ARRIVED!

What are you doing here? This is not the performance!

IT IS ALWAYS THE PERFORMANCE WHEN ONE IS ONSTAGE.

I never would have believed it, but I'll do what I can. Leporello, have another dinner brought in immediately.

CEASE YOUR CHARADE: YOU HAVE MASQUERADED AS YOUR OWN SERVANT AND NOW AS THE NARRATOR.

Speak, then! What do you ask? What do you want?

I SPEAK: LISTEN! I HAVE LITTLE TIME!

Speak, speak, I am listening to you.

YOU INVITED MY OPINION AND I HAVE ARRIVED! YOU KNOW YOUR OBLIGATION. NOW ANSWER ME: WILL YOU CONSUME WITH ME THE MEANING OF THIS NARRATIVE?

Have you been reading me—eavesdropping—all along?

YOU INVITED ME TO SHARE THIS FEAST.

Are you my audience, then?

I AM YOUR INVITED GUEST. WHAT IS YOUR MEANING?

I shall never be accused of cowardice.

HAVE YOU NOT BEEN ENGAGED IN A MASQUERADE? CONTEMPLATING YOURSELF IN THE GUISE OF ANOTHER? RESOLVE!

I have already resolved.

I CHALLENGE YOU: WHAT IS YOUR MEANING? YOUR INTENTION? YOUR SUBSTANCE?

My heart is steady in my breast: I'm not afraid, I'll come and chew with you the meat of this discourse.

HAVE YOU NOT OBFUSCATED MEANING? INCLUDED SOME DETAILS AND EXCLUDED OTHERS?

Bravo!

YOU OMITTED YOUR DISDAIN FOR THE COMMENDATORE: "HE ASKED FOR IT. TOO BAD" IS WHAT YOU SAID AFTER KILLING HIM. IS THIS NOT CONTEMPT FOR YOUR AUDIENCE?

Bravo!

YOU HAVE TWISTED AND CONFUSED THE TRUTH.

There is no truth.

FOOL! ADMIT THAT EVERYTHING OCCURS FOR A REASON.

No! Some things merely happen—for no reason.

WILL YOU NOT SAY THAT ALL IN LIFE HAS MEANING?

No! Some things have no meaning. Meaning, at any rate, is never clear or evident.

GIVE ME YOUR HAND AS A PLEDGE.

Here it is. Alas!

WHAT IS THE MATTER?

VOICES IN A MASK

What is this icy coldness?

PENTITI! REPENT YOUR INDETERMINATE WAYS. CHANGE YOUR DECEITFUL, FICTIVE LIFE. IT IS YOUR LAST MOMENT.

No, I do not repent.

REPENT, VILLAIN FICTIONEER!

No, obsessed fool!

REPENT YOUR CRIMES TO MEANING.

No!

LOOK ON HOW THIS HAS DETERIORATED. REPENT!

No!

YES! YES!

No! No!

AH, THERE IS NO MORE TIME.

With a desperate effort, I wrenched my hand away from the fiend. All right, then! I stand accused, but not convicted. Perhaps I have concealed myself in the guise of the narrator (as I have disguised myself as Leporello), but did I not admit that masquerading as another is what he—Don Giovanni—I—like to do? Have I not the right to feast on multiple courses of meaning for their own sakes? I maintain that this is not *the* performance. I am not afraid of you. I acknowledge a degree of knavery, certainly. I will allow for a touch of chicanery. But I will never repent. But what is this? What is this unfamiliar trembling that overcomes me? I feel the spirits assail me . . . I am surrounded by vortices of fire and horror!

No doom is too great for your sins! Worse torments await you below!

Whose voice was that? When I engaged in this disguise, this masquerade, why couldn't I be doing it for my own amusement? Why couldn't I be talking to myself, speaking rhetorically? Why must I always be addressing someone other than me? What is this that lacerates my soul? What is it that so agitates my innermost recesses? What torture! What frenzy! I may be condemned in your eyes, but you will not dispose of me so easily: hypocrite reader!

No doom is too great for your sins! Worse torments await you below!

Zitto! Silence! Why can't I be alone? What is such a crime about solitary dissembling—fabulating? What torture! What frenzy! What hell! What terror!

Ahhhhhhhhhh!

This is the end of those who do evil: their death will be equal to their life.

❧

Oh, hello.

Yes, hello, Donna Elvira, Zerlina, Don Ottavio, Masetto.

Greetings to you, Donna Anna—and to all the rest of You. Where is my master? Where is Don Giovanni? Where is the liar? I am afraid that he is not here. He is certainly not here, absolutely not here! (*Zitto! Mi pare sentir odor di femmina!*)

He was carried away, amid smoke and fire, the stone man, right down there, the devil swallowed him up.

It really happened.

Don't ever hope to see him again, don't look for him anymore—he went far away, he went far away . . .

A FLOOD OF MEMORIES

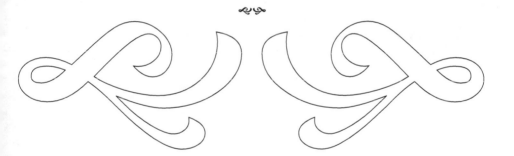

Here are the first few pages of a story which I am only now completing:

The stars were shining on that November evening as Enrico Cavaradossi crossed Fifth Avenue at the corner of East Sixty-fifth Street; strange for them to appear so early in the evening—it was barely dusk: an unexpected pleasure, he thought, and made his way onto the cobbled path which led into Central Park. Ordinarily, he would never have considered walking through the park: he took pride in his rational sensibility, which insisted that a guy could get killed in there (Hadn't he read only the week before about the elderly man who, after willingly offering his wallet to the mugger, had been blinded by the freaking lunatic so he would never identify him in the lineup?), but today he especially needed to save time. The shortcut would save him nearly twenty minutes: he would arrive at his apartment on West Seventy-ninth with plenty of time for the shave, shower, and ample primping he required before leaving for work at the Metropolitan Lounge. Enrico was the featured vocalist at "the Met" (as the frequenting crowd affectionately termed the cocktail parlor and restaurant); he had been singing there for over eleven years—he was just a kid of twenty-two when he began—but in recent years his residency attracted crowds and critical attention. People came to the club expressly to listen to his voice, to marvel at his artistry and sensual moves. Already the out-of-state offers were mounting: he had played to packed houses in Newark; Jersey City; Fall River, Massachusetts; and Providence, Rhode Island. And a syndicated columnist for the Pittsburgh *Journal* had dubbed him "Mr. Sophistication"—yet that bum Tony still gave him grief about coming late! (Hey, Tony, I'm a professional: we don't punch clocks—you understand what I'm saying? But that animal would never listen—probably only responds to grunted four-letter words—and besides, who cares?) Tony was lucky to have him in the first place for the freaking peanuts he received as salary.

Wait a minute: peanuts, animals—he was near the zoo, the Central Park Zoo! Papa used to take him there as a boy. He had never enjoyed the balloons that other youngsters carried; instead, he would beg his father for an unlighted stogie cigar—to match the one constantly between old Giacomo's teeth. The zoo: what fond memories he had of the elephants, the tigers, the giraffes, and, best of all, the Monkey House, where gorillas, gibbons, chimpanzees, orangutans, and baboons frolicked in perfect abandon. With an intense nostalgia, Cavaradossi realized that he wanted to visit the zoo. Would it still be open? Of course; the sky was scarcely dark. The shortcut would enable him to manage a brief visit—Tony could take a flying leap if he so much as said anything—and not only that: he deserved it, for Enrico Cavaradossi had endured an exceedingly enervating day. This morning (this afternoon, really, but morning for him) he had been awakened a little after two by a frantic pounding at his door. When he released the bolt, Angel had burst in, or rather Cesare Angelotti, freshly escaped from jail and looking like a crazy man—eyes crossed, perspiring heavily, spittle running down his chin—forcibly entered his living room and crouched behind the piano bench. (Hey, Angel, you crazy or something or what? You know you woke me up? You think that's funny?) But then he recalled that Angelotti had been in jail: he had stared at the shivering, disheveled figure pathetically trying to camouflage himself against the beige piano: the guy was scared, frightened. So what the hell.

Well, how do you like it so far? Does it live up to your expectations? Is its effortless flow beguiling to your sensibility? I must admit that I marvel at my own ability to evoke the New York milieu of a certain ethnic group and socioeconomic level. But this is all superficial: Isn't it wondrously witty? Don't you find that its intellectual conceit is dazzling?

What? Oh, I see . . . yes, you're right, I am being a touch presumptuous by asking you to evaluate the remarkable breadth and sweep of my conceptual creation on the basis of only a few glistening pages. After all, it has been frequently postulated that we do not truly comprehend any work of art at one sitting, as it were; rather, it has been said that we "read" it once and absorb that response, then read it again, testing our initial reaction, synthesizing this information into an interpretation, and only then do we conventionally read it and produce what amounts to a subjective interpretation of that text. If this is true, then it would seem to be well-nigh impossible to expect you to grasp my intentions at such a premature juncture. With sadness, I withdraw my question.

But can it be that Joseph Conrad was right when he wrote that "it is impossible to convey the life-sensation of any given epoch of one's existence—that which makes its truth, its meaning—its subtle and penetrating essence. It is impossible. We live, as we dream—alone"? I confess that I have always regarded this idea with skepticism. After all, I have never been the sort who adheres to the "teacher-disciple" mode of the author-reader relationship—that one writes *for* an audience and that the audience members are veritable peons who slavishly adore that author, and so forth. Instead, I hold to the "self-other" mode, whereby I conceive of my reader as an alternative form of myself. Thus one does not write *for* an audience (an attitude which is intrinsically patronizing) but *with* a reader who is another version of the author (an attitude built on mutual respect and admiration).

Do you see, then, that my oversolicitousness toward you was motivated by a form of love . . . by an encompassing affection which dared to believe that you might, in fact, be my other, that you might intuit my sense of this story even as I was conceiving it for you now for the first time . . . that you might be so sympathetic as to return that love even before all the supporting evidence for your judgment had been produced?

It may be that to ask this of you is to ask too much. But look here: Is not at least some of the framework of my story apparent to you? Is it not evident, for instance, by the use of the names Cavaradossi, Giacomo, Cesare Angelotti, that I was contemplating a contemporary version of Giacomo Puccini's *Tosca,* which was itself an operatic version of *La Tosca* by Victorien Sardou, a nineteenth-century play designed for Sarah Bernhardt? No? Well, what if I reveal that the fiction opens with the line "the stars were shining," which mimics the opening line of the opera's most famous tenor aria, "E lucevan le stelle"? And surely, from the use of the names Enrico and the Met, it was clear to you that I had in mind Caruso, the majestic tenor and supreme interpreter of Puccini's works? And if you had realized this—not so much to recognize, actually, if you are my kind of reader, that is, my alternative—then you would have caught the idea that Enrico (as opposed to Mario, the character's name) Cavaradossi, the singer, was, in some sense, a combination of Caruso, the singer, and Cavaradossi, the artist in the opera. But perhaps all this was not apparent to you. (After all, you only read it once and not the stipulated three times.) Do not worry, I do not blame you: I blame myself. If you, my other, are not cognizant of my purpose, then I have not adequately projected it for you. Allow me, then, to interrupt the unfolding of my story in order to share with you the story of how I came to want to write this story:

First, the opera: in *Tosca,* Mario Cavaradossi, a painter, runs afoul of Baron Scarpia, the chief of police for the city of Rome, when he helps conceal an escaped political prisoner, Cesare Angelotti. Scarpia exploits the jealous temperament of Cavaradossi's lover, Floria Tosca, a famous singer, in order to disclose the prisoner's whereabouts. Mario is arrested and tortured. When the news arrives that Napoleon has been victorious and will soon liberate the city (oh, yes, all of this takes place in June 1800), Cavaradossi denigrates Scarpia and is condemned to death.

Unbeknownst to Cavaradossi, Tosca has cemented a deal: Scarpia will spare the painter in exchange for her favors. But Mario must go through a mock execution. Then he and Tosca will have safe conduct out of the city. At the last moment, Tosca cannot live up to her side of the arrangement and instead stabs the chief of police. It is at this point that we encounter Mario, at the opening of act 3, alone in his jail cell, awaiting his execution at dawn. He has one hour left; he asks for pen and paper in order to write a last letter to Tosca.

When the writing materials arrive, the libretto reveals that "Cavaradossi sits on the bench. He thinks awhile, then begins to write. After a few lines, he is overcome by a flood of memories and stops." He then proceeds to sing the aria, "E lucevan le stelle," which is introduced by a plaintive clarinet solo. I can already hear it in my mind; perhaps this will enable you to hear it in yours:

> *E lucevan le stelle*
> (And the stars were shining)
> *e olezzava la terra,*
> (and the earth was perfumed,)
> *stridea l'uscio dell'orto,*
> (the garden gate creaked,)

e un passo sfiorava le rena.
(and footsteps grazed the path.)
Entrava ella, fragrante,
(She entered, all fragrance,)
mi cadea fra le braccia.
(she fell into my arms.)
O dolci baci, o languide carezze,
(O sweet kisses, languid caresses,)
mentr'io fremente,
(while I, trembling,)
le belle forme disciogliea dai veli!
(unloosed the veils, revealing her beauty!)
Svanì per sempre il sogno mio d'amore—
(Gone forever that dream of love—)
l'ora è fuggita,
(the hour has fled,)
e muoio disperato!
(and I die despairing!)
E non ho amato mai tanto la vita!
(Yet never before have I loved life so much!)

Imagine, the enthralling poignance of the scene: he wants to write; he cannot write; he is overcome with memories of his life; these memories convince him that now, as he is about to die, he has never loved life more! And all this emotion is only upon a first encounter with the opera. The aria becomes infinitely richer in profundity upon the second or third encounter because one knows beforehand what will happen to Mario subsequently.

He never is able to write down his thoughts, for immediately upon completing the aria, Tosca enters, shows him their letter of passage, and reveals that she has killed Scarpia. Thus, Cavaradossi faces the mock execution with giddy anticipation: he is certain that he will imminently reclaim his freedom and his love. Imagine how shocked and disheartened he must feel when he realizes—if only for a mere instant—that there's nothing mock about his execution! And who could forget Tosca's words to

Cavaradossi as he falls—"*Com' è bello il mio Mario! Ecco un artista!*"
(How splendid my Mario is! What an actor!)—only to discover he has not
been acting. And of course, when Scarpia's body is found, the jig is up for
Tosca: she hurls herself from the highest parapet.

In my story, the setting is changed from 1800 Rome to contemporary
Manhattan. Not wishing to be banal, I scrupulously inserted the plot into
an indigenous environment: thus, Floria Tosca, the Italian singer, becomes
Flora Costa, a Puerto Rican singer-dancer (note, as well, how Costa is an
anagram of Tosca); Scarpia is transformed into Nunzio Caprisa (another
skillful anagram, don't you think?), the godfather of the Upper West Side;
Cesare Angelotti retains his name but is given the nickname Angel and
becomes a Mafia hoodlum. The political motif—so dramatic and exciting
in 1900 when the opera premiered—becomes cumbersome in a topical setting, so I discard it and substitute a more suitable theme of big-time crime.
Through this device, the opera which so moved me over three or more lis-
tenings is brought closer to me and to my own experience; rather than attempting to empathize through time with Mario Cavaradossi, I whisk him
to me, as it were, on wings of story, if you will excuse my exuberance.

But now, in the darker regions of your mind, which I affect to know so
thoroughly, I sense an impediment: you've got your nerve, Geoffrey Green!
Merely by updating *Tosca* to New York City and setting it in the world of
Italians and Puerto Ricans, of mobsters and cocktail entertainers, how do
you bring it closer to you and your own experience? Who do you think you
are, Giuseppe Verdi or something? Where do you get off with this swill?
The next thing, you'll be telling us that your family came from Sorrento
or Naples . . .

This is not a matter to be taken lightly. The fact that I have anticipated your objection (that I have, in a sense, invented it) does not vitiate
the pain such thoughts instill in me. To a certain extent, this is a natural
occurrence. There is nothing more reasonable to suppose than that human
beings reading fiction will occasionally obfuscate the barriers between fiction and reality—especially so, in this case, when a bond exists between an
author and his reader and said reader asks himself: How does my authorial
double fit into this fictitious world? When do I encounter his actual self
(and thus myself) amid this fiction? Once again, I hold myself responsible

for this difficulty. Were it not for the infernal linearity of my endeavor, I might have cleared the matter up pages before, but as it is, I shall deal with it forthrightly and without hesitation.

I do not think it is any secret that I am not an Italian or of Italian descent. Once, at a resort, when my mother had been asked if she were Italian and answered no, her questioner continued, "Are you *sure*?" But aside from Dino's Pizzeria, which was located near Tony's Candy Store, against the wall of which we used to play handball, my familiarity with things Italian was derived from my peculiar affinity (judged to be bizarre in my family) for the music of Mario Lanza and Louis Prima. All of this, however, was secondary to the copious sagas I was told, by my parents and relatives, about the awe-inspiring gifts of Enrico Caruso. The greatest singer in the world bar none, my father told me, and I believed him completely for he had, as a small boy, seen Caruso in the flesh—witnessed him and heard him sing at the New York Hippodrome. Listening to an old scratchy recording of Caruso singing the aria "Vesti la giubba" from Leoncavallo's *Pagliacci,* I mentioned to my father that Caruso sounded as if he were weeping. That's because he really was crying, my father said: every time he sang, he cried.

Everything about Caruso was amazing: a voice like his comes only once in a thousand years, they told me. Impressed by Mario Lanza in the movie *The Great Caruso,* I was informed: that's nothing compared to Caruso. Even his death was spectacular: it was my impression that, on the stage of the Metropolitan Opera, Caruso, while singing, had burst a blood vessel in his throat; spouting blood extravagantly, the impresario had begged him to leave the stage, but Caruso refused, continuing the aria and expiring in the process.

Growing up as I did with the notion of Caruso as a demigod, my response to the discovery, many years later, that he was tantalizingly mortal was pure and absolute astonishment. But after my surprise had faded, I found that my profound admiration for Caruso the man had intensified.

According to Stanley Jackson's biography, Caruso had been arrested on November 16, 1906—for allegedly squeezing a woman's buttocks—in the Monkey House of the Central Park Zoo. The tenor insisted on his innocence all the way to the Park Station; once in police custody, however, he was overtaken by emotion: scuffling with two patrolmen, he was pleading on his knees when thrust behind bars.

Release on five hundred dollars' bail did nothing to assuage Caruso's nerves; during his hearing at the Yorkville Police Court, James J. Kane, the arresting officer, testified that Caruso had not been particularly interested in the monkeys. Rather, he had approached several women, culminating in the pinching of the posterior of Mrs. Hannah K. Graham. Mrs. Graham then socked him, shouting, "You loafer! You beast!"

Caruso, under attack, denied any wrongdoing: eye contact had been established, smiles had been exchanged—*fine*. When pressed, Mrs. Graham refused to take the stand, claiming that Caruso's supposedly ruffian friends would manhandle her—a fishy excuse! But then, a veiled woman in white, out of some Wilkie Collins novel, testified that Caruso had reached out and touched her one night while both were in audience at the Met. This accusation was thrown out of court, but it seemed to offset the discovery that Officer Kane had been the best man at Mrs. Graham's wedding.

The deputy police commissioner, undoubtedly confusing Caruso with his role as the profligate Duke in Verdi's *Rigoletto,* lashed out at the tenor as a "moral pervert," an alien who threatened the virtuousness of American females. He tossed in the assertion that Caruso had earlier assaulted still another woman to whom he had given a ride in his auto—but she (if she existed) had not pressed charges.

A monkey trial, you say? And I could not agree more. It ought to have been held in the Central Park Zoo. Nonetheless, Caruso was found guilty and fined ten dollars. On appeal, the judge held that the tenor had assaulted not only Mrs. Graham but "public order and decency" as well.

And all of this notoriety no doubt served to inflame the earlier accusation, by a New York newspaper, that while acting in the role of Cavaradossi, Caruso had hurled propriety to the winds and kissed his Tosca, Emma Eames, with a brio that transcended the requirements of the role. What an ordeal! Who could say for certain that, in subsequent *Tosca*s, Caruso's mind did not dwell upon that monkey house and his own personal agony as his artistic reputation was placed before the firing squad of public criticism. I must say that I find this interpretation compelling. And if he did cry out during "E lucevan le stelle," was it as Mario Cavaradossi or as Enrico Caruso? We may never know.

Needless to say, my discovery of the Monkey House Scandal, as it was termed, thrilled me: it seemed as if some mysterious and sublime duplication had occurred involving life and art in a portentous design. And when I discovered that my own father (who had first acquainted me with Caruso) had been born on the anniversary of that monkey house incident, I was convinced that it was up to me to fashion something enduring from out of this accumulation of astonishing details and impressions.

Now, I trust, my intention has been clarified. Since it was I who had realized that the opera and the event had overlapped, it was my responsibility to create a story in which this correspondence was given actuality. So, you see, in my story, Enrico Cavaradossi is about to enter the Central Park Zoo Monkey House where he will be arrested by Officer Kane and accused of accosting Mrs. Graham. When Enrico offers to plea-bargain to lessen his charges, Caprisa, the godfather, will mistakenly assume that Enrico is planning on fingering racketeers in the entertainment industry. The chieftain then has him kidnapped from his cell and taken to a tenement where he will be shot at sunrise. He has one hour left; he asks for pen and paper to write to Flora Costa, his lover, who, at that moment, is murdering Caprisa for his vile advances. Enrico wants to write; he cannot write; he sings "E lucevan le stelle"—thus enveloping the opera and the historical event within the timely contemporary perspective from which I first perceived the unlikely symbiosis of life and art.

But my instinct for divining these fateful correspondences did not cease here. The events described in the Monkey House Scandal did not seem to have originated within historical life (and such staid figures as the president of the United States at that time, Theodore Roosevelt) but, in my view, seemed a pastiche which had emanated, perhaps, from that dark and comic fiction by Kafka, *Amerika,* in which the protagonist is "packed off" to the United States because a girl "had seduced him." To be sure, this assertion appeared to me, as well, like a wild and unfounded association. But then, with dizzying clarity, I realized that Kafka had penned a story entitled, "A Report to the Academy," in which an ape describes his transformation into a man and his subsequent success as an entertainer: what if the Monkey House were filled with such beings?

Bedazzled by such cosmic reciprocity, I dutifully set out to chart my own fictional vision. I wanted to write; my conceptualization was in order; I had been selected, as it were, to write this tale. I sat down at my desk. Naturally, I thought awhile; then I began to write. After a few pages, I found that I was overcome by a flood of memories: memories of the opera, memories of Caruso, memories of my family acquainting me with Caruso, memories of my responses to Caruso playing Cavaradossi remembering Tosca as he breaks off his narrative, memories of my idea to juxtapose these fictional and actual lives. Unlike Kafka's ape, who found that his "memory of the past has closed the door against me more and more," I found that, for me, the door was open and memories were rushing past me with astonishing speed: memories of my childhood, memories of music, memories of my life among memories, memories of love, memories of memories!

Overcome by a flood of memories, I stopped, paused, and reflected upon my recollection of what I had set about to do. Deeply moved by the power of art, by its passion, I noticed that the stars were shining; it seemed as if I could smell the fragrance of life. You appeared to me then, you for whom I was striving to write all along. I considered that when you would read the charged words of him who adores you, of my prose, that your innate beauty would be revealed from beneath its veil: on the page, where your eyes caress my words, and in the languid air where the vaporous ideas signified by the words kiss and embrace your ideas concerning them. And I trembled in an ecstasy of voluminous love!

But that dream of love has gone forever. Its hour has fled. Now do you see why I asked you earlier for your reaction, for your approval? Is it not obvious that had you answered then, we might have avoided the sheer torture of this inescapable moment? Although it was never my intention, it is now entirely evident that I was never able to complete my story of how the plot of *Tosca* intersected the life of Caruso. Indeed, like Mario Cavaradossi, a character of Puccini, and I had hoped, a character of mine, who ought—confound him!—to have remained a flimsy figure subject to my authorial control: I say, like Cavaradossi, I have been coerced by a flood of memories to break off my narrative and stand before you here. All this was minutes ago; might it have been an hour ago? Like Caruso, I appear before you.

I am now beholden to your judgment. It might be argued that, since I have failed to complete what I originally intended, I am deserving of your critical condemnation—to be struck down, as it were, before your disapproving eyes. On the other hand, it might be suggested that since I have continued to narrate the story of my story, my failure is contrived, that the possibility of my artistic execution before you might be a fake, a mock execution arranged as a prelude to my ultimate freedom—in which case, you might (I implore!) allow blessed mercy to enter your heart. Still a third view contends that whether or not I continued the story or the story of the story, it was all designed to conceal the Cavaradossi/Caruso-like doom which my creative undertaking was destined to achieve: if this is so (and I hope not!) then perhaps your mercy itself will be an illusion, disguising a real execution of your own conception. I do not know.

I do know that I nurture deeply within me the memory of that idea that you, my flower, and I might be free to express our love for each other together. (The memories are flooding my consciousness.) Everything I have attempted here was wagered in order to obtain that sunny vision: Will I attain that paradise? Will I hear the creaking of the garden gate, your footsteps grazing the path? I had hoped as much, and yet it is conceivable that now I shall die despairing. (What? How can this be?) Yet never before have I loved life so much!

FINE

"THIS VERY VIVID MORN"

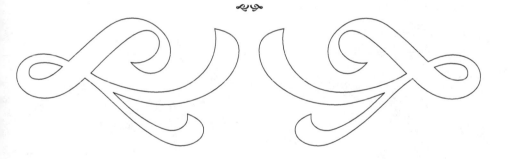

Here is a deluxe remastered digital recording of your favorite opera singer.

He murdered a man in cold blood! Does it matter?

He used a dagger! Does that matter?

What if I told you that a man was killed but it was only an accident? Does *that* matter?

Listen:

I.

Mr. Lawrence Tibbett, featured baritone of the Metropolitan Opera, had not planned on attending the dress rehearsal of the opera *Caponsacchi* on the morning of January 26, 1937. After all, the particular scene in question had been rehearsed forty times previously; there would seem to be no doubt whatsoever that he had mastered it thoroughly. As one of the principals at the Met and the dominant villain of the opera, his professionalism was beyond dispute. Nevertheless, Met stage manager Desire Defrere had reminded him, this was to be the world premiere of the opera. The composer, Richard Hageman, would be present at the rehearsal and desired his attendance: would he not reconsider? Naturally, he agreed.

Throughout his illustrious career, he had championed the idea of English-language opera for English-speaking audiences, and here was an opera that could illustrate many of his contentions on the heightened drama of vocalized English. Tibbett was a consummate musician, but he had no use for the custom of endless rehearsing for its own sake. In singing, he had written, "it is far more important to concentrate on the spirit of the thing, even with a mistake here and there, than to sing a score letter-perfect without reaching for its inner life." On the other hand, hadn't he always been cooperative with the directors at the Met? Had he not, twelve years earlier, assumed the role of Ford in Verdi's *Falstaff* on very little notice? His singing of the aria "E sogno? o realtà" ("Is this a dream? or reality") had electrified the audience at the opera house, and they had demonstrated thunderously for him—a complete nonentity!—to take curtain call after curtain call, eclipsing the master, Scotti, as Falstaff. From that ethereal moment—thirty-five hundred persons cheering him alone: a dream come to life!—his ascendant career had proceeded: as Metropolitan Opera *divo,*

Hollywood film star, recording luminary, and radio sensation. So why not be accommodating?

Although Hageman titled his opera *Caponsacchi* (after the play of the same name), both opera and play were based on Robert Browning's long poem *The Ring and the Book*. That poem was itself derived from an "old yellow book" that Browning found in Florence in 1860 that related the details of an actual Roman murder trial of 1698. The central character, the one who stands accused of the murder of his wife, Pompilia, and her father, Pietro, is Count Guido Franceschini of Arezzo, the part played by Lawrence Tibbett. In the scene to be rehearsed, Tibbett (as Guido) lunges at the father with a dagger while the old man is held securely by two of Guido's bandits. Guido means to gain Pompilia's fortune by killing her father. The whole bit of business was quite impressive; still, after forty rehearsals, Tibbett knew the routine in his sleep.

As he made his way from his residence at 120 East End Avenue (by the corner of Eighty-fifth Street) to the Metropolitan Opera House at Broadway and Thirty-ninth Street, he may have been considering the appropriate style of acting to be used for the scene. Tibbett was convinced that a broader, more dramatic theatrical style would attract an expansive audience and would help translate opera to a popular audience. The English language was particularly well suited for this demonstrative style. Defending his approach, he had observed that "the school of understatement is no more real than the school of overstatement. They are simply different sets of conventions."

I must comment here on how astute and insightful I find that hypothetical observation of Tibbett's to be: the baritone realized that opera—like all art—was a representation of reality and not itself real! Whether one mode of representation or another *seemed* more or less "real" was a matter of style or convention but not essence. There are many individuals today who have not learned this lesson. It is, of course, also possible that no such thought had crossed Tibbett's mind on *this very vivid morn* (though he had made the assertion in 1933). He may have been absorbed in a meditation on the particular vocal exercises he would use before the rehearsal (as a rule, he practiced on the vowel *a*, as in "May," believing that it was particularly well suited to his vocal needs). Or else, he may have been thinking about something entirely different: perhaps he was making a mental note of the weather; the day—January 26, 1937—was a Tuesday, so perhaps he was thinking that he enjoyed Tuesdays, or else abhorred them; he may have even been musing on the curiosity that (as he noted in 1933) his mustache "hair grew luxuriantly on the left side of [his] lip but hardly at all on the right." How much does this matter?

Arriving at the Met, Tibbett was undoubtedly welcomed by stage manager Defrere and composer Hageman, the two who had so insistently desired his presence. He took his place onstage thinking (it is tempting to surmise) that the English text of the libretto would allow him to sing naturally: he had learned from Basil Ruysdael many years earlier that natural singing was best—one must always, and especially in English, sing as if one were speaking the words to music. Distorted pronunciation, contrived enunciation: these prevented the vocalist from becoming a "singing actor," Tibbett's conception of his vocation. Natural singing allowed the baritone to achieve a heightened sense of identification with the particular character he depicted: "It was a tremendous relief," he had observed, "to find out that it was all right for a singer to be himself."

Similarly, in acting and stagecraft, he had agreed with the idea of natural depiction. As often as possible, props should be fashioned of the same materials as what they represented. The dagger, for instance, that he would use in today's scene was steel like an actual weapon but with its blade dulled. Eight years ago, during a performance of *Faust,* Martinelli had pierced Tibbett's side with a sword that had been analogously dulled, but the incident had not warranted the discarding of actual weapons as props: rubber or wooden daggers, he was convinced, would look ridiculous.

Tibbett, as Count Guido of Arezzo, could not fail to see that his colleague, John Gurney (as Pompilia's father, Pietro), was being held securely by Guido's two ruffian associates. One of these bandits was played by Joseph Sterzini, a bass and member of the Metropolitan Opera chorus. The other was played by Ludwig Burghstaller. The scene called for Guido to kill the father by plunging his stiletto into the man as he was held captive, hands behind his back, by Guido's two henchmen. In reality, this involved

Larry (as he was known to his friends and colleagues) lunging with his gilded, ornamental steel prop dagger at John, who was being held by Joseph and Ludwig.

As the scene was played, at 12:30 P.M., Tibbett struck out at Gurney and missed (as was intended). Let me be clear about this: it was intended that Guido kill the father; but since this was representation and not life, it was not intended for Tibbett (playing Guido) to actually kill Gurney (playing the father) in order for him to "kill" him (in the opera). So when Tibbett missed Gurney, this would have been perceived by the audience as a fatal blow. And there was an audience, of sorts, at this rehearsal. At least one hundred members of the cast were present, along with seventy-five musicians in the orchestra pit. Thus, on this forty-first repetition of the scene of the murder of the father, all would appear to have proceeded as intended: Guido "killed" the father, but Tibbett appropriately missed with the blow and averted the actual killing of Gurney.

What did not proceed as planned on that Tuesday afternoon was that Joseph Sterzini, in the guise of playing one of the bandits, unaccountably held up his hand in the path of the steel dagger that Tibbett was wielding so as to miss Gurney. Sterzini's hand, therefore, was brought up in the path of the descending weapon. Despite the dulled blade, a flesh wound was opened in Sterzini's hand; approximately two and one-half inches long, it ran from the left wrist up to a point between the thumb and forefinger.

How are we to account for this unforeseen occurrence? How is it possible to explain an event that seems to "just happen"? According to Mrs. Sterzini, interviewed by the *New York Times* after the calamity, her husband had been a member of the Met chorus for thirty years, since his arrival in this country from Ferrara, Italy. Opera had been the "one interest" in her husband's life. Was it not possible that Joseph had acquainted himself with the libretto—derived from Robert Browning—for the opera in which he was performing? Could he *not* have been aware that the most widely known poem by Robert Browning, "My Last Duchess," concerned itself with murderous deeds in Sterzini's hometown? In that poem, it becomes clear that the Duke of Ferrara has murdered his wife, the Duchess of Ferrara. It is easy enough, perhaps, for us to look back and decide that Sterzini ought to have been more careful! But wait: he was not, after all, in

Ferrara; he was onstage, in New York, acting, merely acting. Since opera was his "one interest" (Surely his wife exaggerated under the duress of the moment; more likely, she meant "dominant passion," or some such phrase—for how would it be possible to sustain a marriage if one had only a single interest and that one object was not one's spouse?), it is feasible that he found himself transported by the spirit of the role, carried away with the action of the scene, and his movements became animated to an extent that they could not be scripted, so to speak, by the text of the libretto. It is also possible that Sterzini, a fifty-two-year-old heavyset man, was simply clumsy.

Immediately upon realizing that Sterzini had been wounded, Lawrence Tibbett (according to his account in the *New York Times*) "stopped singing and took hold of his wrist." He told him to "get off the stage." Sterzini's reply (quite admirable, and yet, to be expected from someone for whom opera is his "one interest") was "oh, no, let's finish the scene." Tibbett "insisted and dragged him off the stage and turned him over to some others and told them to take him upstairs and put a tourniquet on and get a doctor." Apparently, Tibbett's instructions were followed. A local physician, Dr. Joseph Siegel, arrived at the Met from his 487 Seventh Avenue office. He tended to the wound and applied appropriate bandages. Sterzini then changed to his street clothes and went over to Manhattan General Hospital at Second Avenue and Seventeenth Street.

It would be irresponsible of me not to mention a fascinating and, no doubt, uncanny interaction. The part played by Tibbett in *Caponsacchi*, that of the dagger-wielding villain, the man who was, in the opera, to have murdered the father but whose depiction resulted in the affliction of the wound on the hand of Joseph Sterzini, was Count Guido Franceschini of Arezzo (known in the libretto as Guido, for short). In *The Ring and the Book* and *Caponsacchi* (as well as in life since Browning based his poem on an actual 1698 trial), Guido appears before the pope (in this case, Innocent XII) to defend himself on the charge of murder. An earlier Guido of Arezzo (ca. 995–ca. 1050) was a Benedictine monk whose scholarly efforts exerted a strong influence on the theory of music. He, too, appeared before the pope (in this case, John XIX) and persuaded him of the high quality of Guido's innovations and contributions on music and singing. We remember him today for the device that is named for him and thought to be based on his teachings: the Guidonian hand, the hand of Guido. This instructional system utilizes the human hand as an aid in the memorization of the musical scale. Each part of the hand corresponds to a particular tone of the scale. The student would point to these regions on the left hand in order to signify musical tones. The human body, in effect, would "act out" the creation of music. It is eerie to observe that the injury to Joseph Sterzini was received on his left hand and that—if his hand were taken as the Guidonian hand (not so unlikely, really, since his hand was injured by the figure of Guido)—the wound, running from the wrist to between the thumb and forefinger, would isolate and designate the lowest three notes of the scale, or, roughly, those that fall within Sterzini's own basso vocal range.

When Joseph Sterzini arrived at Manhattan General Hospital, he was examined and found to have sustained a wound that had punctured the area of the left hand between the thumb and first finger, penetrating about two inches. Since blood vessels of the deep palmar arch had been severed, the decision was made to operate. Sterzini was a man with high blood pressure. Nevertheless, it was felt that surgery was indicated. He was placed under an anesthetic, following the most current medical procedures of the day. Sterzini emerged from the anesthesia "in fine shape," according to his physicians; oxygen was delivered to assist his revival. According to all accurate modes of prediction, at or around 5:15 P.M., he ought to have rested for a time from the operation, risen, donned his street clothes again, and returned to his home: the upper story of a two-family house at 1859 Sixty-seventh Street in the Bensonhurst section of Brooklyn. Waiting for him there would be his wife, Augusta Sterzini, and his nephew, Peter Baier, who lived with them. Instead, he died.

Lawrence Tibbett, meanwhile, had returned to his East End Avenue residence, to recover from the turbulent events of the *Caponsacchi* rehearsal, no doubt, but also to rest and prepare for the evening's scheduled activity. He, along with the Italian section of the Metropolitan Opera Company, would be traveling to Newark to sing Verdi's *La Traviata* at the Mosque Theater. (The German faction of the opera company would be singing that same night in Philadelphia: a performance of Wagner's *Die Walküre*.) Four years earlier, Tibbett had written, "I don't sing well after a heavy dinner. My voice loses power and tightens up on the high notes, and on the day of a performance I never eat much until after I have sung." Thus, we may feel confident that, having already vocalized during the rehearsal, and after the distressing events at the opera house, in preparation for the Verdi performance he would not be taking a meal of any significance. More likely, he would be engaged in the challenging task of altering his mental frame so as to depict the evening's characterization: Germont, the father of Alfredo. It would be necessary for him to transform himself from Guido, the murderer of the father, into Germont, the father.

At 7:10 that evening, Mrs. Tibbett received a telephone call. It was Mrs. Earl Lewis, the wife of the Metropolitan Opera Company's box office treasurer. Mrs. Lewis notified Mrs. Tibbett of the death of Joseph Sterzini. Now Mrs. Tibbett had been at the opera house for the *Caponsacchi* rehearsal; she had witnessed, from the sixth row, all of the painful and peculiar events of that misguided run-through. Nevertheless, Mr. Sterzini had wanted to continue! It was her husband who had insisted that he seek medical attention. Watching Sterzini leave the opera house under his own faculties did not prepare her for this astonishing turn of events. She later told the *Times:* "I was so shocked that I blurted out, 'He's dead!' My husband heard me and then got on the telephone."

Lawrence Tibbett was devastated. He attempted to withdraw from the evening's *La Traviata,* but there was no possibility at such late notice. He was forced to leave for Newark from Manhattan in order to perform in the Verdi opera. I must intrude here to report my own astonishment at the navigational miracles that occur in this 1937 episode. The Met's general curtain time was 8:00 P.M. If we hypothesize a later Newark curtain time of 8:30 P.M., still it was necessary for Mr. and Mrs. Tibbett to both speak for a duration on the telephone. Leaving, perhaps, at 7:30 P.M., they were yet able to arrive at Newark's Mosque Theater in time for that evening's performance! The shock of the news of Sterzini's sudden, unexpected death was now compounded with the considerable tension of arriving on time for the curtain at a performance in another city.

When Tibbett arrived at the Newark theater, the officials of the Metropolitan Opera had reason to feel remorse that he had received the upsetting news in such an abrupt manner. The *New York Times* reported that Tibbett "was so upset that he had great difficulty in going through with his part." One friend of the artist described him as being "terribly shaken." At least one contributing factor in his distress was the presence of the various reporters and the need to provide them with appropriate statements! In our era of vulgar replies to intrusive questioning, it is impossible not to admire the patience and civility displayed by Lawrence Tibbett and his wife in response to the inquiries of the press. Mrs. Tibbett was interviewed while her husband was onstage: it would seem clear that her attention was divided! But Lawrence Tibbett's dilemma was still more profound: in the midst of transforming himself into Germont, he was forced to relive the events connected with his earlier depiction of Guido. In between acts of *La Traviata,* Tibbett, despite his turbulent personal feelings, allowed himself to be questioned by the *New York Times*. Thus, earlier that day, around noon, he had been Guido; later that afternoon (in preparation) he had been Germont; then, when he received the news, Guido again; during act 2 in Newark, Germont; in between the acts, Guido (during the interview); and then back to Germont—this was indeed an agonizing alternation: from patricide to patriarch!

Something of the disarray of the situation was communicated to the newspaper reporter. In the *Times* article, it is deemed necessary to provide accounts of the plots of both operas—*Caponsacchi* and *La Traviata*—in order to differentiate them from the "actual" events. (It is also possible, of course, that the plots of these operas were considered more newsworthy then than in our current day.) In a "news" article, we are informed that "Mr. Tibbett, as Germont, in his passionate plea in the second act to Violetta, has a role of penetrating poignancy, and last night that emotion was intensified."

And here we might well ask whether the poignance was being vocalized by Lawrence Tibbett as Germont, or Lawrence Tibbett as Guido, or Lawrence Tibbett as Lawrence Tibbett. Immediately before act 3, he said this about Joseph Sterzini: "I wouldn't want anything like this to happen. I have known him for fifteen years. He supported me in many operas. Of course, I feel horrible. This is the most terrible thing that has ever happened to me. I'm anxious to do anything I can for his people." Following this Guido-oriented conversation, Tibbett again ascended the stage to resume the depiction of Germont. The *Times* account corresponds to this chaotic interplay of role conflict, this tension between real-life events and represented occurrences, by engaging in a bit of aesthetic criticism in the midst of the news account: "Again at the end of the act, in his voicing of the great air 'Di provenza il mar,' with its consolatory import, there was an undercurrent of strain and anguish that accentuated the pathos of the music. The audience at the Mosque did not know why at that moment."

Is it so clear to us what demarcations should exist between art and life? Is there ever a point when the personal joys or misfortunes of the artist do not spill over, as it were, into the creative effort? "Mr. Tibbett has sung the role of Germont innumerable times during his career at the Metropolitan," noted the *Times*—"but never like this!" was the subtext, "and never under these circumstances." It is painful (and yet, tempting) to suppose that, as Germont, the father, Tibbett was assuming the role of he whom he was earlier meant to kill—the father, Pietro. Could Sterzini—the actual man killed in that representational scene meant to evoke the killing of a father—have inadvertently assumed the role of the father in the actual events of the day? It is intriguing, then, to meditate on the thought that Tibbett was, in a sense, assuming the role of the father (Germont/Pietro/Sterzini): precisely the role that confronted him with his earlier disastrous rendition of the patricidal Guido.

Mrs. Augusta Sterzini was described as a "quiet woman" by the reporter whom the *New York Times* sent to interview her shortly after the police told her the news of her husband's death. It is uncertain whether the quiet aspect of her demeanor was a result of her grief or whether it was a regular feature of her personality. The Sterzini nephew, Peter Baier, had traveled into Manhattan to claim the body of Joseph Sterzini. That quiet quality in Mrs. Sterzini could not suggest reticence since she managed to convey a good deal of information to the *Times* reporter. She had been expecting her husband at home that evening, she revealed, because he had not been booked to sing in the chorus of either the Verdi or Wagner opera. More significantly, perhaps, she disclosed that he had been grappling with an attack of influenza until only about ten days previous. Would Sterzini, a stalwart fellow who had urged Lawrence Tibbett to go on with the rehearsal despite his own injury, have called this influenza bout to the attention of the doctors? It seems unlikely. Would the physicians have modified their decision to operate had they known of Mr. Sterzini's possibly flu-weakened condition? In all likelihood, Sterzini would have deprecated his injury, indicating to the doctors that it was nothing—and, in truth, from his vantage point, how misguided could he have been? All of this attention concerned a cut on the hand: who could have anticipated that this cut would prove fatal?

For the police, however, a man had been killed under unnatural circumstances—and certain regulations and procedures had to be followed. By the time Lawrence Tibbett returned home to his East End Avenue apartment, it was 12:40 in the very early morning of Wednesday, January 27, 1937. He had completed his rendition of Germont and now was in the process of resuming his identity as Lawrence Tibbett; the *Times* reporter at the scene observed that the baritone appeared "worn and upset." Is this surprising? He could not have been pleased to discover assistant district attorney Sylvester Cosentino and seven police detectives—all waiting to question him. Seven police detectives? Were all of these men necessary? Also present in the Tibbett residence was acting police commissioner Harold Fowler; he was there, he told the press, as a friend of Mr. Tibbett's and not in any official capacity.

Lawrence Tibbett answered their questions for forty-five minutes; they did not terminate the exchange until 1:25 A.M. It must have been a hellish ordeal for the singer; tired (no, exhausted!), confused, wracked with guilt, concerned about the welfare of the Sterzini family, his head awhirl with Guidos and Germonts, it must have been an overwhelming strain for him to cling to his true identity as a performing artist, a provider of aesthetic pleasure, a man of generous and courtly instincts.

For, after all, what consolation could he derive from his conception of himself as an opera singer? Singing (as he had done the previous day) in English, his native language, singing naturally, without "pompous" vocal mannerisms, was, he believed, a way for the "singer to be himself." But being himself in this case meant being Guido, with poor Mr. Sterzini lying dead. Perhaps the "penetrating poignancy" of the role of Germont in

La Traviata might provide him with a measure of solace? The aria of "Di Provenza il mar" ("The Sea of Provence"), the *Times* news writer assured us, possessed great "consolatory import."

Ordinarily, a singer is able to draw sustenance from an audience. The vocalist, Tibbett had confessed six years before, "grows accustomed to the psychic influence which emanates from those thousands of heterogeneous units which combine to form that precious factor—*My Audience*. Their coldness can depress you, their enthusiasm buoys you up, and the feeling of contact with them makes you live more keenly." Standing before *his* Newark audience, dramatizing the role of Germont, why was Tibbett not able to fully lose himself in the role? Why was he not able to be, at least temporarily, supported and bolstered by those multitudes who had always demonstrated their unparalleled pleasure at his remarkable artistry?

It is important to recall Tibbett's significance as one of the very first of the American artists born and trained in the United States to break through into the front rank of featured Metropolitan Opera regulars. Certainly, Rosa Ponselle, also born and educated here, had debuted earlier; but her Italian background (she was born Rosa Ponzillo) provided her with a familiarity with the Italian language that Lawrence Tibbett did not have. Tibbett's enthusiasm for natural singing, American popular culture and music, popular artists such as Rudy Vallee, Al Jolson, and Duke Ellington, Hollywood films, and the plain drama of opera performed in English—all of this was closely related to his identity as a distinctively American artist. An oft-included detail in his frequent media portraits was the fact that he knew no languages besides his native English. One consequence of his not speaking any foreign languages was described in an article about him in 1930: he had to "memorize arias and lieder, word by word." Not even word by word: since, in opera, many notes are assigned to a mere portion of a word, Lawrence Tibbett learned his non-English-language roles phonetically, syllable by syllable.

The significance of this rote memorization might not be apparent unless we imagine the situation of Germont in *La Traviata:* the father sings to his son, Alfredo, of the joy that once existed for them in their home in Provence; it is Germont's attempt to bring his boy out of a state of grief (caused, in this case, by the father's meddlesome interference in his child's love affair). When Germont sings "God has guided me," why would not Tibbett escape momentarily into the respite of this soothing parental figure acting out a destiny prescribed by God?

How we learn and what we learn are connected inseparably. Onstage in Newark at the Mosque Theater, Lawrence Tibbett's greatness as an actor was no doubt working to conjure up the character of Germont in all his nuanced richness. But, as he was fond of emphasizing, "everything counts" in your musical depiction—who you are, what you are, how you came to be who and what you are. His Germont was a vessel that was filled with the richness of Tibbett's dramatic personality. And included in that totality was his phonetic learning of Italian aria. When Tibbett (as Germont) on that evening sang "God has guided me" in Italian, the sound of the words created a new meaning, a meaning that contaminated the meaning he had learned—those words, in effect, spoke him: "dee-oh me gwee-doe, *Dio mi guido!*" Pressing its imprint on the character of Germont, wrestling the actor from out of his role, there, on the stage: the hand of Guido!

II.

Assistant District Attorney Sylvester Cosentino was an exceedingly busy man. Later on that same Wednesday morning (during the very early part of which he had questioned Lawrence Tibbett for three-quarters of an hour), he interviewed the following highly significant individuals: Miss Helen Jepson, the soprano who played Pompilia, the wife of Guido, in *Caponsacchi;* John Gurney, the bass who played Pietro, Pompilia's father; Ludwig Burghstaller, who, as the second bandit, had been engaged (with the late Joseph Sterzini) in holding Gurney captive so that Tibbett could appear to slay him in the opera; Desire Defrere, stage director for the Metropolitan Opera Company—these were the principal personages who occupied the stage when Lawrence Tibbett inflicted the knife wound on the hand of Joseph Sterzini. During the questioning of the late morning, Tibbett was represented by a private attorney. Efforts were made, as well, to locate and interrogate the opera property man to discover why the dulled blade of the weapon had been able to inflict any sort of wound at all.

It is perhaps a truism to observe that the greater the importance of the participants in a case, the greater the possible notoriety of the events, then all the more swiftly is a junior executive replaced by a senior one. This was not the case with Assistant District Attorney Sylvester Cosentino, a fact that possibly attests to the high regard in which he may have been held by the district attorney. (It may also have been true that the district attorney preferred to shield himself behind the veil of his subordinate, Cosentino, in the event that a scandal might ensue.) On the other hand, Dr. Charles S. B. Cassasa, the New York City assistant medical examiner who had been originally assigned to the case—who had ordered the body of Sterzini to the morgue for autopsy and who had informed the *Times* that it was quite certain Sterzini had not bled to death—was replaced speedily and efficiently that Wednesday by Dr. Thomas A. Gonzales, acting chief medical examiner.

At the district attorney's inquest, Dr. Gonzales read aloud from the prepared text of his report. He reaffirmed the assessment of Dr. Cassasa that Sterzini had not perished from loss of blood. "I find," he pronounced, "after an autopsy that the cause of death was arteriosclerotic heart disease, hypertrophy and dilation of the heart, fatty infiltration of myocardium, cerebral and general arteriosclerosis." Just as we had inferred earlier from his actions and demeanor, Dr. Gonzales discovered from the autopsy that Joseph Sterzini was conspicuously bighearted; but, in this instance, his enlarged heart—weighing 720 grams—was not an asset to his continued health. In a winning attempt to translate his specialized medical language into plain speech, Dr. Gonzales suggested that Sterzini "had a chronic heart condition with hardening of the blood vessels. He might have died naturally at any time. The shock following the wound and the administration of an anesthetic for the repair of the wound may or may not have precipitated the heart attack."

"He might have died naturally at any time": Might not we all? Might not any one of us? On what grounds does the allowance that we might die at any time of natural causes absolve us from concerning ourselves with the consequences of a clear and decisive chain of events? The answer is this: the wound, the accompanying state of shock, the strain of the general anesthetic—all of these experiences "may or may not" have caused Joseph Sterzini's fatal heart attack. On the basis of the existing "may" in the report, continuing doubt and disturbance remain; on the basis of the "may not," however, there is no proof established for a conclusive interpretation of causality.

Assistant District Attorney Cosentino, acting for the district attorney's office, ruled—on the basis of the medical examiner's report and the interviews with the concerned participants—that, in the matter of the death of Joseph Sterzini, Lawrence Tibbett was "completely exonerated." The dagger used by Tibbett had been suitably dulled: it was only the "combined force of the two opposing thrusts"—Tibbett's thrust at Gurney meeting the oppositional (and entirely unexpected and unscripted) thrust of Sterzini's hand that enabled the dagger's "rounded point" to inflict a wound on the unfortunate Joseph Sterzini.

Complete exoneration would, if anything, provide a degree of comfort to the troubled soul of Lawrence Tibbett. But his comments to the *New York Times* reveal a measure of his deep feeling: "I am in a sense relieved to know that the wound was not the direct cause of death. But that is very little relief because of the poignancy of the situation and the tragedy visited on his family. I am terribly upset and grieved. There is no more I can say." However, the newspaper revealed that Tibbett was "doing everything he could to help the Sterzini family." Tibbett's mournful state of mind illuminates the dilemma with which he was grappling: years before, as Ford in Verdi's *Falstaff,* he had faced that enchanted Metropolitan Opera audience, singing the aria "E sogno? o realtà" ("Is this a dream? or reality"). It was indeed tempting to conclude that in "reality" he had been completely exonerated. Except: Had he merely dreamed that he wielded the dagger? Was it not his hand that meant to convey the impression that a dagger had caused a man to die? And that a man (although not the same man) had died at his hand ("may or may not" have: some consolation!): Was *this* a dream? Or a reality? No! The hand of Guido wielded the knife. But where, then, in the representational spectacle, had been the hand of Lawrence Tibbett?

It is conceivable that a period of rest and inactivity would have assisted Tibbett immeasurably in the endeavor of resuming his own identity in peaceful self-knowledge. Or, barring that, at the very least, he needed to experience the exotic variety of alternative roles, roles with a more comic, or at least more wholesome, fabric. But an opera was being prepared for a world premiere: in this instance, the representation took precedence over the reality—the show must go on, the opera must be performed. Officials of the Metropolitan Opera Company announced that the very dagger that had inflicted the wound on Joseph Sterzini—or else, a steel duplicate of it with a similar dulled edge—would be used in the final dress rehearsal of *Caponsacchi* to be performed the very next day. This ultimate rehearsal would take place on Thursday, January 28, at 11:00 A.M. before two thousand members of the Metropolitan Opera Guild. It was left unspoken that the dagger would be held by the hand of Lawrence Tibbett in the role of Guido.

At precisely the time when he least needed to be reminded of himself as the depicter of Guido, at precisely the time when the demarcation between art and life had become unclear, Lawrence Tibbett was called upon to be Guido: to convince an audience of his murderous intentions, to kill the father, to wield the dagger. There was even public musing as to who might be a suitable replacement for the late Mr. Sterzini: the role required a basso member of the chorus. Is it too much to imagine that there were some who hesitated before applying for the part?

The body of Joseph Sterzini was taken from the morgue to the Campbell Funeral Parlor at Broadway and Sixty-sixth Street. It is uncanny to observe that this location would become the home of the new Metropolitan Opera House a mere twenty-nine years later: a touching memorial to Joseph Sterzini, a man for whom opera had been his "one interest." The body lay in state on Thursday, January 28, and Friday, January 29, 1937.

On Saturday, January 30, 1937, funeral services were held for Sterzini at the Church of Our Lady of Pompeii, at 25 Carmine Street. The services were originally announced as taking place at the Church of the Blessed Sacrament, Seventy-first Street, near Broadway. Was this—the moving of the church services to facilitate a more public ceremony—one of the ways in which Lawrence Tibbett was acting to help the Sterzini family? Mr. and Mrs. Lawrence Tibbett were both in attendance at the funeral services, and it was undoubtedly a moving ceremony for the couple. High Mass was celebrated by the Reverend Albert Visci, and the absolution was given by the Reverend John Marchegiani. Verdi's *Requiem* was performed by Sterzini's colleagues of the Metropolitan Opera Chorus under the direction of

Fausto Cleva: a great honor, the Metropolitan troupe turning out to honor its own. But a few days later, on February 4, Tibbett would again become Guido!

Lawrence Tibbett could not have been pleased by the *New York Times* review of *Caponsacchi*. After all the effort, the forty-two rehearsals, the anguish, the heartsickness, the grief, the simple fact appeared to be that the critic Olin Downes was less than enamored of the opera's music. Composer-conductor Hageman was singled out for conspicuous disapproval: "Pretty and plausible sounds emanate from Mr. Hageman, but they are singularly unoriginal. The score, for all intents and purposes, is a compendium of the styles of other opera composers." Summing up the entire work on the basis of the deficiencies he found in the score, Downes blasted, "And at last, truth to tell, this thing of expert routine and outmoded convention becomes tiresome." The entire company must have been severely disappointed; having labored so valiantly to prevail in bringing the opera to the stage, they must have yearned (even secretly) for the validation of critical acclaim. There was, it is true, the gratification of knowing that the "large and brilliant audience" evidently approved of the production: Downes admitted (begrudgingly, one supposes!) that the audience "repeatedly called" the composer and principal artists "before the footlights." But this popular acclaim is dismissed sourly by Downes with his concluding line: "At the end of the performance there were repeated ceremonies of 'hail,' if not 'farewell.'"

As a tireless proponent of opera in English, Tibbett could not have been satisfied with the assertion of Downes that "it is surprising how English, which in most cases was clearly enunciated and distinguished by fairly effective diction, can help to destroy illusion, if the line is not itself momentous or poetic. And how, under the circumstances, did the poetical aroma of Browning evaporate!" Since Browning himself wrote in English, one supposes that Downes felt that the English language contributed in the opera to an effect of "melodrama."

Lawrence Tibbett's artistry was singled out for commendation, but in a way that suggested he had toiled heroically and desperately in a doomed venture: "Mr. Tibbett sang sonorously, venomously, uproariously, murderously and swashbuckled. What else could he do? How otherwise does

Guido Franceschini emerge from the poem onto the operatic stage? That Mr. Tibbett found no opportunity for a distinguished style cannot be laid to his door. He did what he might." Clearly, one takes the critic's meaning: Hageman's "stinker" of a score drags even the most dramatic performances down to its mediocre level. This could not have been the response desired by the baritone as he patiently had attended rehearsal after rehearsal!

But was not a premiere that was associated indelibly with the tragic and inadvertent death of the unfortunate Joseph Sterzini a problematic endeavor simply by way of its having to live up to the considerable toll of its production? Is there *any* opera worth the price of a single human life? "It depends on the life and the opera," you might quip, and I would understand, naturally. But let us say *your* life, and let us designate any opera you select: how would you respond now to this inquiry? Without question, Joseph Sterzini would not have hesitated: when wounded in the hand, he desired that the rehearsal go on, the artistic whole was for him far larger and more important than the small portion represented by his relatively inconspicuous life. But you: Is your life worth, say, *I Puritani*? *La Bohème*? Then how about *Don Giovanni*? Is your life worth—*Caponsacchi*?

What would be the human toll on your life as a result of your acting out the part of a murderer when—entirely by accident—a man happens to be killed at your hand? Are you able to say it was all a dream, all representation, all gesture? Or does something of the reality linger on? After all, is not representation a reality of sorts? Although the actor playing Hamlet is most assuredly *not* Hamlet, has not a part of his life been occupied with the experience of *being* Hamlet on the stage?

For Lawrence Tibbett, the hand of Guido left its discernible impression on his subsequent career. In 1933, he had reminisced that he had been "in bad health" when he entered high school; however, he had built himself up to "good physical condition," a state of health that had remained. But in March 1937, the month following the *Caponsacchi* opening, he canceled a sold-out concert at Constitution Hall in Washington, D.C., due to laryngitis.

In January 1938, while on a half-hour walk near his Connecticut home one afternoon, he fell on the ice and struck his forehead on a sharp stone— resulting in a cut on his head that required seven stitches! During that same year, he observed during an interview: "If my self-conceit ever begins to get the better of me, I put one of my own records on the gramophone. Listening to my own voice sobers me. Until I heard my first record, I thought I was a good singer. The gramophone is my severest critic and my greatest surprise." Does this suggest a diminishment of the pleasure he derived from singing?

His difficulties continued: while on board the SS *Monterey,* Mrs. Tibbett's jewelry was stolen—a cache worth fifty thousand dollars! More interviews, officials, questioning, the providing of burdensome accounts until Meyer Sopher, an attendant on the ship, was arrested and confessed. Jewelry valued at twenty thousand dollars was recovered from the culprit's room: the rest he tossed overboard! The varmint was sentenced to imprisonment for seven years.

Although he had always taken pride in his reliability and professionalism, Tibbett canceled, in September 1940, all his engagements for the rest of the year—this the result of a mysterious throat ailment that was never adequately explained. The effects of this throat debilitation haunted him for the duration of his life. In the current *Metropolitan Opera Encyclopedia,* one finds in the entry for Tibbett that "his theatrical powers remained intact after a throat ailment in 1940 impaired his vocal suavity." Various armchair "experts"—formal and informal—began to speculate on the reasons behind Tibbett's throat condition; a variety of explanations were put forward: his hard life; an enthusiasm for spirits; the consequences of overworking while battling a bad cold; the inevitable strain that results from a career of heavy roles such as Scarpia and Emperor Jones (might one here include the role of Guido?). Finally, in 1949, a physician hypothesized in *Newsweek* that Tibbett had experienced a severe case of "spasticity of the larynx muscle."

Were his vocal problems not enough, late in 1941, he was hospitalized for an emergency appendectomy that debilitated him into 1942. In July of that year, he suffered an injury—this time to his spine—from yet another fall. While at the Connecticut estate of Chester La Rouche, an advertising executive, the baritone, according to the *New York Times,* "slipped and fell on a stone while broad-jumping"; it seemed that "the male members of the party decided to 'be boys again.'" By 1945, many critics were of the opinion that Lawrence Tibbett's vocal abilities had deteriorated irretrievably. His operatic appearances dwindled in favor of concert and recital work. In 1947, illness canceled all but one autumn appearance at the Met. In early 1949, he was honored on the stage of the Metropolitan Opera for his twenty-fifth anniversary with the company, but in the summer, illness again forced him to cancel his commitments for a Cincinnati engagement series.

It was the conventional wisdom that Lawrence Tibbett's voice was never the same after the baffling 1940 throat malady. Caveats are issued to avoid recordings that were made after that year; some of those releases, in fact, are described as "tragic" and a "travesty." There are many who believe that Tibbett should have ended his career following the unexplained throat predicament. But he did not. It is worth remembering that his vocal problems did not originally date from 1940 but from 1937, when laryngitis followed close on the *Caponsacchi* disaster. In 1960, an automobile accident caused a flare-up of the 1938 head injury sustained during that midafternoon walk near his home; during surgery, he lapsed into a coma and died.

I prefer to think of him as he was on the stage of the Mosque Theater in Newark, as he sang the role of Germont in *La Traviata*. Let us imagine him singing the aria that so entranced the audience, "Di Provenza il mar" (as Lawrence Tibbett would have preferred, I will cite the lines in English): "From your native brilliant sunshine, what fate stole you away? Oh, remember in your grief that there joy shone for you, and that there alone peace can still radiate upon you. . . . Ah, your old father, you don't know how much he suffered." The images of sun, warmth, radiance: as he sang them, did they call Lawrence Tibbett back to Provence (a place he had never visited) or to Bakersfield, California, that hot and sunny town where he had been born? It is time that we return to that "native brilliant sunshine" and explore the memories Bakersfield may have held for him.

III.

Lawrence Mervil Tibbet was born in 1896 in Bakersfield, California, the youngest of four children in the family. The singer had been taught, he wrote, "to take great pride in the family name. My ancestors had come to

California in the gold rush of '49 and the name had never been sullied." Nevertheless, when a typographical error misspelled his family name by adding an extra *t* and his teacher advised him that the name was improved by this modest modification, he let the error stand. His "family protested furiously. It was sacrilege! Wasn't the name that was good enough for my forefathers good enough for me?" This is an intriguing question. Why did Tibbett, the plainspoken Americanist who had resisted the advice of many veterans that he change his name to Lorenzo Tibbetto to placate the Italian chauvinism of the opera world, need "just one extra *t* to feed [his] vanity"?

The mistake in his name initially occurred on the Metropolitan Opera program for his first significant role, Valentin in Gounod's *Faust*. Did Tibbett wish to begin his life anew as an opera singer by means of the symbolic modification of the spelling of his name? There would appear to be reason to support the idea that Tibbett compressed powerful statements into small gestures. As an adult he described how he had been reared in a deeply religious Methodist background; when he had been caught smoking corn silk, he was severely punished. As a result, he noted, he does not smoke, except "about once a year I smoke one cigar, and get great satisfaction out of the feeling that I am doing something terribly wrong and that the devil is patting me on the back." No smoking: except for one cigar; no name changes: except for "just one extra *t*"—would the devil (certainly a conspicuous presence in *Faust*) be "patting [him] on the back" for that slight name adjustment?

But why would he want to commit this "sacrilege"? Several years earlier, while acting in a Los Angeles production of the play *Othello,* he had felt once before that the name with which he had been born, his father's name, was insufficient: he had himself "listed in the program as Lawrence Mervil. Since Mervil is my middle name, my mother and sister didn't protest very much. They just thought it was silly." Tibbett, however, did not agree; he "thought 'Lawrence Mervil' was something very hot—a really distinguished name for an actor." I take this to mean that he did not see the name "Lawrence Tibbet" as being "really distinguished." Here there had been no typographical error, no act of fate: a willful decision had been made to change the name, to eliminate the "Tibbet." The problem was that, when the reviews appeared, "no one believed Mervil was Tibbett, so I went back to my real name"—with the exception of the addition of the secondary *t* a few years later. He had refashioned himself, thrown a part of his name overboard as ballast, but no one had believed it: he was who he was.

And who was that? He was the son of William Tibbet and Frances Mackenzie Tibbet, born in Bakersfield, "a tiny, raw, tough town in the center of a farming community." His mother sang in the local church choir, his sister played the piano, and others in the family were musically talented as well. His father, however—"I am sure that, had my father lived, he would have opposed my ambition to get into the theater"—was not perceived by Tibbett as being supportive of the arts. William Tibbet was, in his son's words, "a God-fearing man with a large blond mustache, who believed in strict law and order." He was the sheriff of Kern County (which included Bakersfield) and, according to Lawrence, was "a dead shot, a splendid horseman, and had killed two cattle thieves"—"of course," he recalled, "my father was my hero."

As a small boy, he and his friends would play "sheriff and rustlers"; but the game took on a decidedly representational component in that young Lawrence "was always the sheriff" while his friends took turns depicting Jim McKinney, a local outlaw who "had killed four men in cold blood." In this primitive specimen of backyard theater, Tibbett was playing the part of his own father; his friends acted out the role of the man his father had been charged in life with bringing to justice.

At the age of seven, while playing at this game as usual, acting as the sheriff in a battle with the rustler McKinney, he received word from an older boy: "Hey, Larry, Jim McKinney just killed your father!" In the midst of play, of representation, an event takes place that causes the relation between life and art to be held up to question; the boy's reaction exemplified this confusion: "At first I thought it was a joke, part of a game." Had he known Ford's aria from *Falstaff* at that early date, he might well have called out, "E sogno? o realtà" ("Is this a dream? or reality"). But it was no dream: having led a posse after McKinney for several days, Sheriff Tibbet had chased the outlaw back into Bakersfield where he was hiding out. "Father was too brave and too reluctant to kill. Instead of shooting on sight, he ordered McKinney to come out. McKinney killed my father with a shotgun." The outlaw also killed another sheriff until he was, in turn, killed, by Lawrence's Uncle Bert, "with a shot right between the eyes."

Freud called the death of the father "the most important event, the most poignant loss, of a man's life"; certainly, Tibbett's words about the death of Sterzini—"this is the most terrible thing that has ever happened to me"—could apply to that woeful day when representation became real. If we allow ourselves to imagine his reaction, the boy must have been devastated at this grievous loss. But Tibbett had this to say, in a 1933 account: "The emotions of boys are unfathomable. I cannot explain the apparent lack of grief with which I met the announcement. I have never been able to understand why I was not at once crushed. But I did not feel at all like crying. I was only very, very proud. Perhaps a psychoanalyst can explain my pride. I cannot. It was not until that evening that I realized my loss." Is it not likely that, absorbed in the act of playing, of depicting what exists in the imagination, the boy answered Ford's question by opting to remain, just a bit longer, in the dream?

With the life insurance policy left in Sheriff Tibbet's estate, Mrs. Tibbet moved the family from their frame cottage at 716 K Street "on the edge of Bakersfield" to Long Beach, California, where she opened a small hotel. Had his father lived, Tibbett felt sure, he would have resisted his son's desire to perform on the stage. But his father had not lived: Was this a reason why Tibbet chose to be Lawrence Mervil while acting Iago in *Othello*? Was this why "his vanity" required that "extra *t*"? And what relation might there be between the vanity of the name change and the "pride" at the news of his father's murder? Needless to say, these are powerful emotional materials! One would appreciate the ability to fix reliably certain memories and recollections as existing merely in one's own distant past—thus, when one mounted the stage, there would be the comfort and security of a dream, of pretending, of play. But for Lawrence Tibbett, this was not to be.

Years later, in 1929, he was assigned the role of Jack Rance, the sheriff in Puccini's *La Fanciulla del West* (*Girl of the Golden West*)! Sheriff Rance is charged to arrest the bandit Ramerrez, who has changed his name to Dick Johnson and is being pursued by a posse. Both men are rivals for the affections of Minnie, a saloonkeeper. (My mind is dizzy with the uncanny similarities between this opera and Tibbett's life: Rance and Sheriff Tibbet; Minnie and Frances [Mrs. Tibbet], who both ran public houses; and the outlaw who changes his name!) Perhaps because this opera was *so* close to the events he wished to consign to memory, Lawrence Tibbett bolstered himself against becoming too involved with its emotional contents. Much as he would later insist on the realistic depiction of weaponry in operas, he assumed an appropriate role of expert on Americana: he corrected the German director as to the posture, stance, and movements of "real" Western sheriffs and outlaws and, when challenged, informed the director as to the basis for his expertise. Thus, in a sense, he was able to play his father on the stage without crossing a certain line (crossing a certain *t*?)—that is, without becoming his father. But the director did not fully understand Tibbett's story: "He thought I was the one who had done all the killing I had told him about, and he guessed he had better be good to me or I'd run amok and shoot up the Metropolitan Opera House."

Yet during this play, like the earlier game, Tibbett was the sheriff and was able to play the father—his father—with a control that did not strain the question of reality or dream: he held the gun, he fought the fight. But remove the gun and place a dagger in that Guidonian hand and what might occur? What is it that prompted Tibbett to fancy that the director feared he might "run amok" at the Met?

But it was Joseph Sterzini's death—not his father's—that Lawrence Tibbett admitted as being "the most terrible thing that has ever happened to me." Despite the similarities between Tibbett's life and the plot of Puccini's *La Fanciulla,* even though he had been then playing his father, the sheriff, in a Western milieu not unlike Bakersfield, nevertheless the representation remained representational, the game maintained its existence as play, and the props, while being *realistic,* were never *real:* no one, in life, had been killed. In *Caponsacchi,* however, much had existed to lull Tibbett into a calm of exotic and faraway regions: the boy from Bakersfield was whisked into another time and another place. No longer a sheriff, or a father, he was the killer, he was the villain—a safe and enjoyable play of depiction that appeared to have no similarities whatsoever with the events of his actual life. Except: a hand moved, and in a split second, a weapon meant to imitate reality became itself real, a "just pretend" murder actu-

ally resulted in the loss of a life. So much had been different that it is conceivable one might not have noticed what now seems evident: once again,
a game was being played that involved the killing of the father; once again,
the imaginary leapt its boundaries and became life.

Only after the death of Joseph Sterzini, after the inquest, and the funeral, and the laryngitis, and the fall that inflicted his head wound—only
later did Lawrence Tibbett reveal, in a July 1938 interview conducted in
England, an intriguing element in the story of his father's killing, an aspect that he had not previously disclosed in earlier accounts. Several days
before his father's murder, young Tibbett had received from him a "hell of
a spanking for running home from school. I'd had a fight and got badly
licked. I went home, sobbing my heart out, thinking I'd get some sympathy.
Did I? I got another thrashing and was sent straight back to school." He
had gone to his father for fatherly concern and empathy—and he had been
soundly punished. He had been thrashed and spanked. Now, four days
later, playing "sheriff and rustlers," was his depiction of his father influenced by the sheriff's administering of justice on that young rustler who
had been fighting in school? If he—during his punishment—had imagined
terrible thoughts about his father, did they now intrude on this backyard
depiction in which he was cast as his father? Was his childhood depiction
of the sheriff more profound at that moment precisely because he was acting out of divided loyalties—both sheriff *and* rustler, both father *and* son?
Was this ambivalence what lay behind his "unfathomable" and confusing
"lack of grief" when he heard the news of his father's actual death? Was
this complex depiction what contributed to his feeling of "pride"? Lest we
become overwhelmed with the drama of the moment, it is opportune to
mention that the questions posed here are not fully answerable—at least,
not by me in this story; it is not clear that they are ever fully answerable
by anyone.

But on the stage of the Metropolitan Opera, playing Guido, the killer
of the father, was his earlier performance as the father lodged somewhere
in his memory? Did the killing of Joseph Sterzini transpose the key from
major to minor, from life to death, from the order and control of art to
the dangerous unpredictability of existence? Looking back, in 1938, at

that distant horrific childhood event through the gauze of his more recent nightmarish adult experience, Tibbett theorized, "That incident is like a theme running through my life. Someone always spanks me and sends me back to something I've been trying to run away from."

It may now be possible to understand why Tibbett's performance as Germont in *La Traviata* (in Newark on the evening of the death of Joseph Sterzini) was so poignant and affecting that it tore down the barriers between journalistic reporting and aesthetic criticism. Acting the part of the father, he was addressing himself as the son, the outlaw-rustler, the name-changer, the admitted "nonconformist": the father who disapproved of the theater was addressing his son the artist. As Germont, he sang "Di Provenza il mar" to the son who looked up to him as a "hero," to the Guido he had been earlier in the day. And in so doing, he sent himself back, "to something I've been trying to run away from," to Bakersfield: "Ah, your old father, you don't know how much he suffered. With you far away, his house filled with misery. But if at last I find you again, if my hope did not deceive me, if the voice of honor is not totally silent in you, [then] God has answered my prayer." Who was it who sent him back to that awful memory by means of this dream-turned-reality? "God has guided me!" *Dio mi Guido!*

After forty-two rehearsals and the death of Joseph Sterzini, Richard Hageman's *Caponsacchi* was performed all of two times at the Metropolitan Opera Company. Could that have been the normal scheduled run of the opera? Forty-two rehearsals for only two performances? Or did the death of Sterzini cast a pall over the subsequent scheduling decisions? *Caponsacchi* has never been revived. Who would dare risk a revival? Recently, I heard an old recording of Helen Jepson, the original (the only!) Pompilia, singing an aria from *Caponsacchi,* "This very vivid morn." Initially I heard only the music, from another room—I did not know the opera from which the aria came: hearing it was not a pleasant experience; on that basis, it might appear that the *New York Times* critic had been right. But then, listening again, with the libretto before me, I heard Pompilia sing: "This very vivid morn. Out of dead shadows up I sprang alive, light in me, light without me . . . everywhere change. . . . My heart sang: 'I, too, am to go away. I, too, have something I must care about.' Last night I almost prayed for leave to die. How wrong had I been dead! How right to live!" I felt a distinct chill pass through me. I thought of Lawrence Tibbett and Joseph Sterzini—now both dead—and I thought of how they live on, each one in his own way, in the history and the lore and the memory of opera.

Opera and life: perhaps they are two "simply different sets of conventions."

❧❧

Here, then, was that recording—remastered by me so that you were able to hear all of the passion and pathos of that remarkable voice. Are you able to hear the tremendous difference the remastering makes? As Lawrence Tibbett once maintained, "everything counts" in one's singing. Are you able now to hear it?

Do you hear what I hear? Or are you asking: What is it about this recording that bears remastering? What is it about this story that bears retelling?

Lawrence Tibbett lived a renowned and distinguished life and brought great pleasure to millions of people. This story of one facet of his life, one mere aspect of his long career, becomes a fiction: it becomes *my* story because it makes of that fragmentary part a whole, a theme, an encompassing unity.

I went out and bought the book *Lawrence Tibbett: Singing Actor*, edited by Andrew Farkas. I studied the library's newspaper archives and microfilm review files. I thought it would all be intriguing, pleasurable, exotic: appropriate material to control and arrange into a story.

But, while writing this story, I have twice cut my left hand with stiletto-like knives that I had wielded before countless times (preparing food) without mishap! I have even noticed that Lawrence Tibbett, the paternal figure in this story, was born on November 16, my own father's birthday!

What does it mean to play a game, to represent, to tell a story, to write? What does it mean for me? When is the fiction felt?

That *other* Guido of Arezzo, the inventor of the Guidonian hand, wrote (about 1025), "In our times, of all men, singers are the most foolish, for in any art those things which we know of ourselves are much more numerous than those which we learn from a master."

Singers? All artists, creators, wearers of masks: writers!

Am I yet another fool?

I know not whether this—all of this—be dream or reality.

I am writ by the Hand of Guido.

"YOUR SISTER
AND SOME WINE!"

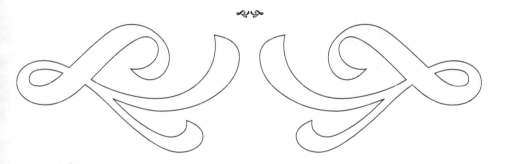

"*Le roi s'amuse* is the greatest subject and perhaps the greatest play of modern times. . . . In going over the various subjects, when *Le roi* came into my mind it was like a bolt of lightning, an inspiration. . . . The whole story lies in that curse which also becomes moral. An unhappy father who mourns the theft of his daughter's virtue is mocked by a court jester whom the father curses, and this curse lays hold of the jester in a dreadful way. This strikes me as moral and great to the highest degree. . . . I repeat that the entire subject is found in that curse."

After the Austrian censors had attempted to modify the curse:

"Without this curse, what scope or significance does the drama have? . . . But let me say this: why do [the police and the censors] think they know better than I do about this? Who is playing the maestro? . . . If anyone says to me I can leave my music as it is for this new plot, I reply that I don't understand this kind of thinking, and I say frankly that my music, whether beautiful or ugly, is never written at random, and that I always try to give it character. . . . My artistic conscience will not allow me to set this libretto to music."
　　—G. Verdi, 1850

I.

We hear a voice, amplified through a microphone, that sounds a good deal like Rod Serling on *The Twilight Zone:* "There is complete and utter darkness; nevertheless, it is yet possible to discern—by means of momentary flashes of lightning—an object, lying immobile on the ground. It is a large canvas sack, torn in several places along its surface. Protruding from the openings in the sack are a female arm and a head. Nearby lurk a few shadowy presences. Where are we? Some might say Mantua, in the sixteenth century. Others might be less certain. You be the judge."

　　A disheveled man steps forward, removes a flask from the copious pocket of a tan raincoat, takes a sip, lights a cigarette, and speaks: "I like to call it 'The Case of the Doll in the Sack.' That's not what they called it at Headquarters: it was phoned in as a suspicious act of homicide. Nobody even knew whether it was a man or a woman, at first, on account of the clothes: a riding outfit—male trousers, jacket, even spurs—but it was a babe, all right. On close examination, I saw that she was a beauty, and young, too, still in her teens. She had been stabbed in the heart. I hate like hell to see that. I've seen corpses of all kinds, killed in all sorts of ways, but what gets to you is when they die so beautiful and so young. Right away I knew I was going to keep the pressure on until something broke. Then I heard a sound."

A heavy figure is lurking in the periphery, partially obscured by shadows. The man in the raincoat removes a revolver from his pocket and cries out, "All right, freeze! You there. That's right. Get over here, slowly and carefully. Don't try any cute stuff! OK, sucker, now what's your name?"

As the figure emerges into the light, he is revealed as an individual with a disability: specifically, a hunchback. His handicap necessitates that his movement is awkward and difficult. He raises his hands slightly, but his face is contorted with emotion. "What does that matter to you? Tell you my name? That's useless."

"Listen, you deformed monstrosity, answer my questions or I'll take you in for murdering this girl here!" The man in the raincoat steps forward and gestures menacingly with his gun.

"Murder? Why would I murder my own daughter? Why would I take away my only priceless treasure?"

"I don't know, buddy. You tell me. I'm losing my patience here." A burst of thunder shatters the air.

"My daughter, my Gilda: she herself was struck by the arrow of my just vengeance!"

"Huh? I don't get you, pops. Start making some sense! You're the one who's hanging around the scene of the crime. If you didn't kill her, then who did?"

"*La maledizione!*"

"What's with the Italian, *padrone*? What are you, connected, or something? Speak English! Who iced her with the shiv?"

"The curse! It was the curse that took my only joy on earth!"

"I gotta hear this one. OK, *paesano,* let's take it from the top. Start at the beginning and don't leave anything out. This one sounds like a doozy!"

Music begins to play: low, ominous chords that create a horrific impression of doom and despair. As the volume increases, the two figures move gradually out of the light. Illuminated in their place is a large governmental hall. Abruptly, the music changes from thundering demonic sounds to the merry cadences of a festive dance. A host of characters rush in, wearing costumes of the sixteenth-century court. A few, however, are in modern formal dress—not unlike, for instance, a presidential inauguration. The attention focuses on one gentleman in particular; he wears a white tie and tails. He gestures in the air repeatedly with two fingers. Over the music is heard his voice practicing a speech, "My fellow Americans . . ." He is President James Fletcher Kilmartin. His friends call him "Duke."

Surrounded by his courtiers and associates, he "works the room," greeting guests and official visitors while engaging, simultaneously, those closest to him in intimate conversation. He sings out, "I will soon bring to a head my adventure with that unknown beauty in the town." Speaking with him is the English actor and libertine Philip Langford, his brother-in-law. At the mention by Langford of "some other lady" who might hear of his new infatuation, a face flashes before us, projected from behind: a comely brunette, looking very much like Judith Campbell Exner, the purported mistress of Chicago Mafia boss Sam Giancana.

Suddenly, he spots yet another temptress: a platinum beauty outfitted in an alluring gown. He comments, "DiMaggio's wife outshines them all." He is warned by an aide that he ought not to let Count DiMaggio hear him. "What do I care?" is the president's cocky reply. Stepping forward, he launches into a sprightly tune: "This one or that one, they all seem the same to me." His courtiers are captivated with amusement. "If one finds favor with me today, perhaps tomorrow it will be another," he sings. Between verses, he calls out: "Fair ladies, ask not what your leader can do for you, ask instead what you can do for your leader!" The melody is very catchy: "I mock at the jealous rage of husbands and the frenzies of lovers; I would even challenge the hundred eyes of Argus when I am roused by a beauty." A projection appears for an instant of the character of Argus from Greek mythology: in the pictorial image, Kilmartin is presented in the guise of Hermes (who challenged Argus and slew him) *and* in the guise of Pan (half man, half goat, a satyr and musician, the subject of the story Hermes tells to lull Argus to sleep before killing him).

Kilmartin brazenly approaches Marilyn, the Countess of DiMaggio, in direct view of her husband, the count. He woos her aggressively: "The flame of love, kindled by you, intoxicates, conquers, and overwhelms my heart." She advises him to calm himself. Everyone in the hall is watching. During this exchange, the hunchback appears, dressed now in the formal garb of a comedian—appearing as something of a cross between Frank Sinatra and Don Rickles. He addresses Count DiMaggio: "Yo! Joltin' Joseppi! Take a gander at the duke with your wife makin' whoopee over there. What's that growing out of your head, DiMaggio, horns?"

The hunchback now converses with Kilmartin about how he might make some time with the countess. He urges that the count be removed by making him the object of an FBI investigation—he'll lose his head (in a manner of speaking), for sure. The count (who overhears) is furious and plots revenge against the hunchback, along with the other courtiers who have all been similarly insulted. The hunchback, it seems, has been observed visiting a lovely young woman who is his mistress. Those who have been victimized by the hunchback's insults will pay him back through her. The president warns him not to be so abrasive: "You always carry a joke to extremes. The rage you inspire may be your undoing." The hunchback, however, is unconcerned: "What harm can come to me? I'm not afraid of them. No one would touch the president's favorite."

All at once, the music again becomes terrifying! Into the party strides Count Giancana, who insists on speaking with the president. "Let me speak to him!" he cries out. "My voice, like thunder, will shake you, wherever you are." The hunchback mocks him by imitating his voice: "Let me speak to him!" The president nods his consent, so the hunchback continues: "You conspired against us, sir, and we, in true clemency, forgave you. What madness seizes you to complain continually about the honor of a broad young enough to be your daughter?"

Singing like Marlon Brando as Don Corleone in *The Godfather,* Count Giancana thunders, "I'll raise my voice as long as the monstrous insult to my family remains unavenged. Go ahead, kill me—I dare you! I'll come back to haunt you, *cozzo!*" Then he flips the ends of his fingers against his chin in the direction of the president. He screams out, "Up yours! May you both be cursed!" But he isolates the hunchback for a special invocation: "You, serpent, who laugh at the fatherly grief I nurture toward the angel whom that SOB has turned into a whore—my curse on you!" Naturally, the president calls for his arrest on charges of income tax evasion, and he is carried away, hurling imprecations.

"Great! Wonderful! I love it! All right, people—let's take a break, shall we? Thirty minutes." An impressive woman steps briskly down the aisle toward the stage, followed at close distance by a reporter from the *Los Angeles Times* and a minicam team from *Entertainment Tonight*. "So the piece will make the deadline for the weekend arts edition? Good. Good. OK, so what do you need? Wait—what? You want me to stand here for the camera angle? Sure, sure. Listen, can you guys film me while I'm talking to the *Times* interviewer here and *then* I'll give you copy? It will save us all time. Super!" She positions herself near the stage for the minicam team and continues with her interview: "As you can see, this new 1990 production of *Rigoletto* is more than simply a new setting of a classic opera. Far more. It breaks new ground, I think, in being so contemporary, so fresh, so exciting, that people will want to see it just as they would a Beatles reunion or Elvis Presley returned from the dead."

She is Jane Triboulet, the director of this opera production. She carries in her Bree handbag the latest issue of *Los Angeles* magazine, with her face on the cover under the caption "Superstar Opera Impressaria." The feature profile describes how she overcame the debilitation of scoliosis to raise, as a single mother, a beautiful and talented daughter, Blanche; in addition, she has ascended to her current position as premiere producer and director of "pop op" (a deliberate palindrome!)—her term to describe "opera for the masses." As a result of a series of shocking, controversial, and outrageous interpretations of traditional operas, she is now able to stage opera extravaganzas in major sports coliseums and auditoriums that are taken seriously as important artistic statements. Rock stars Madonna and Bruce Springsteen were both turned down after auditioning for her productions: "They were just not quite right for the part" was the explanation she issued to the press. In addition, professors of music write scholarly articles about her work.

Her remarkable innovation is not confined to matters of theatrical production, operatic staging, music, and the like; she has pioneered new financial coalitions that challenge the prevailing generalizations about the nature of support for opera. This production of *Rigoletto,* for instance, is being jointly underwritten by a coalition of business, public foundation, and private investment support: she has obtained grants from the Chubb Group, the National Endowment for the Arts, and a consortium of wealthy Beverly Hills entertainers assembled by her *compare,* Ol' Blue Eyes himself, Albert Francis. Mr. Francis retains a fondness for opera from his youth in Newark; he is a national institution: the preeminent popular vocalist and planner of presidential inaugural balls. What Mr. Francis and his associates respect so much about Jane Triboulet is that her opera productions are not mere entertainment—they proceed from a deep and profound immersion in the score and libretto of each opera, a serious commitment to the artistic integrity of each musical project.

She is standing by the stage she has had constructed for this production of *Rigoletto* in the Los Angeles Memorial Coliseum (seating capacity, ninety-one thousand). The *Times* reporter transcribes feverishly as she speaks: "We plan on selling out each of the twelve performances. This should be bigger than the '84 Olympics! People will want to be there not just because it will be an incredible event, not just because it will be a knockout show with superb singing, drama, and excitement but also (and especially, I might add) because this staging will address serious questions about our country's recent history and where we are today: using deliberate and disruptive movements between the sixteenth century of Verdi's opera and our contemporary twentieth century, it seeks to confront nothing less than our national identity. Our presentation will be a sweeping panoply of American violence, chaos, and redemption. In all modesty, I am overwhelmed to be involved in such a staggering project!"

As the *Times* reporter walks off scribbling notes, Jane turns to the crew from *Entertainment Tonight.* "Thank you so much for waiting. But you know how it gets sometimes! Now, let's see: oh, yes, we have a firm commitment from Luciano Pavarotti, José Carreras, and Plácido Domingo to sing together during the intermission, backed by the Rolling Stones. Both the Stones and the tenors see this as a major milestone in their ability to reach new heights of musical expression. Yes, Katherine Hepburn will host the simulcast on National Public Television—her health permitting, of course. If she is indisposed, we'll use a team of Beverly Sills and Stacy Keach. What I'd like to convey to your television viewers is that opera is hot! It's sexier than *General Hospital* or *Dallas,* more thrilling than any blockbuster movie, with music more riveting than any megatour of the greatest supergroups. There's absolutely nothing like it. That's why Michael Jackson, the pope, Václav Havel, and Liz Taylor are all big opera fans!"

Excusing herself from the camera crew, she walks to the opposite side of the stage where a writer from *Opera News* awaits her. Jane recognizes him immediately: he is the very same columnist who did the article on her last year! "Ciao, Roberto!" she calls out, remembering his name. "You were so astute when you wrote me about the similarity of the *tessitura* in the vocal parts of Rigoletto and Count Monterone. (Of course, in our production, you remember, Monterone will be called Count Giancana, but not a word about that until your article is released after the premiere!) You see, that's exactly what Verdi wanted all along! Many opera companies use a bass for Monterone, but Verdi wrote his librettist, on February 2, 1851, asking for a baritone to sing the part. The ranges are quite similar as well: Rigoletto is B-flat to G, and Monterone is B-flat to F.

"As I see it, by deliberately incorporating twentieth-century American details into sixteenth-century Mantua, we universalize the conception of the curse: audiences will be able to perceive that dynamic musical malediction as something that involves history, crime, politics, rape, drugs, romance, and destiny! And what could be a more poignant and appropriate expression of the concept of fate (its apotheosis, really!) than the promiscuity of President Kilmartin (the Duke of our version) and the way his dealings with organized crime—you remember, of course, that his administration contracted with the Mob to assassinate Fidel Castro at the same time that they were carrying out an aggressive prosecution of gangland activities: talk about sending mixed signals!—set up an ineluctable process that resulted in his assassination! In that sense, *Rigoletto* is *our* story, as a nation, and as a people. So nice to see you again!"

In the time remaining during the break, Jane Triboulet rushes around the stage to her office trailer, where she anticipates receiving an important call. As a rule, she devises the conceptions for her opera interpretations in the strictest secrecy and does not reveal them until the opera is on the verge of production. But due to the unusual and historical nature of this production's public, private, and corporate support, she has released a prospectus of the new libretto and staging directions to the key financial angels: she has sent copies to Mr. Francis, to the Chubb Group, and to the National Endowment for the Arts. She is awaiting a message from her executive assistant disclosing whether there has been any response to her plans. Now, in her office, she greets her receptionist. "Cindy? Get me Howard on the line, would you? Thanks." She kicks off her heels, lights up a low-tar cigarette, and leans back in her chair. "Howard! Any word? Yes, I see . . . What? You're kidding! Really? No, I'll call them right back. The Endowment can wait, I'm sure, but I'll call Mr. Francis immediately. Bye." It seems that Mr. Francis and his people have read the prospectus and want to speak with Jane as soon as possible. With a twinge of excitement and anticipation, she turns to place the call.

"What?" She leans into the intercom. "Yes, this is Jane Triboulet, returning a call from Mr. Francis. Yes, I am quite sure that he called me! *When* did he call me? Why, my executive assistant tells me that he phoned us moments ago while I was out during rehearsal; Mr. Francis left word that he wants to speak with me as soon as possible! Yes, I'll hold." Jane calls over to her receptionist: "You know, Cindy, it really is true what they say about telephoning in L.A.: the lower the level of person with whom you speak, the longer you're kept waiting. Could you be an angel and get me something? Yes, I'd love a Chablis and papaya nectar on ice.—Yes, I'm still holding. Thank you—How much more break time do we have? Five minutes? Thanks, love."

Jane notices a file of contracts awaiting her signature that is placed conspicuously on her desk. She reaches for a pen and works her way through them. "Jane Triboulet here, still holding. What is my call concerned with? He called me! Mr. Francis called me! I'm returning his call. Yes, I'll hold." She presses a button on her portable tape recorder and nods her head toward it: "Have Fabrizio check on the timing of the overture in microseconds correlated to the lighting cues. Over." Taking a sip from her glass, she calls out: "Cindy? Please tell them I'll be right out. Thanks.—Yes! Oh, hello, Joey! I'm so glad to speak with a familiar person. Mr. Francis . . . oh, I see. He can't come to the phone right now. He's on a helicopter with Donald Trump, but he wants to talk with me as soon as he gets back. OK, here's what I'll do: I'm going into rehearsal right now, but I'll leave word that I should be called to the phone the *instant* Mr. Francis rings us back. Yes, thank you.—Cindy, beep me when he calls; I'll be onstage."

As she makes her way up the stage stairs, she views the singers and actors onstage waiting for her. One of them—the man in the raincoat—steps toward her: "Jane? Could I ask you something? I know we're just about to start, but I had a question. I'm a little unclear about my motivation in that last scene: what's going on in my subtext?"

His question is asked so sincerely, so needfully, that Jane decides to answer it. "Listen, people, gather 'round: now, Paul, when you ask about your character, you're addressing a basic idea of the whole production: a crime has been committed! Right? And who solves crimes? Do you follow me—a detective! Your character signifies the audience's desire to investigate the crime, to find a solution to the murder. The whole opera is, in a sense, a prolonged flashback to the murder. So, think Bogart in *The Maltese Falcon;* think Joe Friday in *Dragnet.* Does that help? Good!"

Jane walks around the stage, gesturing, while the singers stand in a half circle listening intently. "The first scene was tremendous! Now Rigoletto: it's impossible to overstate your sense of confusion, your cognitive dissonance, as you confront details from the sixteenth and twentieth centuries. You know, I love Peter Sellars's work—I truly love it!—but one of the many differences between us is that he keeps his characters motivated within their situation; he's also so faithful to the score: I mean, why can't the characters be as confused by the events as anyone else? Why not have shocking interpolations in the score? Doesn't that happen all the time? Our focus here is that we are willing to acknowledge—really deal with—the quantum leaps that take place whenever we listen to an opera that is set in another time period.

"In the second scene, Rigoletto is approached on the street by the assassin, Sparafucile. For our production, that role is depicted by the character of Jake Rubino, for several reasons: one, the part of the assassin's sister, Maddalena, can be made to correspond to one of Rubino's Dallas striptease girls; two, it was Rubino who killed Oster and, as we discussed yesterday, Rigoletto corresponds, in many ways, to Leo Horace Oster, the attempted assassin who is himself assassinated (remember that the death of Gilda is for Rigoletto equivalent to his own death); three, the milieu of the strip joint makes overt the implicit misogyny that surrounds the avaricious use of power, especially the actions of President Kilmartin—this is a central theme of the opera. Rubino asks Rigoletto whether he needs to put out a hit on anyone; Rigoletto turns him down but files away the information for future reference. Then he sings those magnificent lines about how he and the assassin are the same: one kills with words, the other with a dagger.

"Then Rigoletto enters his garden, where his world changes all at once: for there, before him, is his reason for being—his daughter, the beautiful Gilda, only sixteen years old. Now, here's another thing: why shouldn't our audience see Gilda as a typical contemporary sixteen-year-old? That's why she's dressed as Madonna in *Desperately Seeking Susan* and sings with that special Valley Girl inflection that we developed especially for this production. At the end of the scene, President Kilmartin, disguised as a poor student, sneaks into the garden and woos Gilda. Meanwhile, the courtiers, infuriated by Rigoletto's abrasive taunts, abduct Gilda (they think she's Rigoletto's mistress!) and bring her to the Las Vegas Sands Hotel—the very location where Kilmartin used to consort with his mistresses! When the hunchback is tricked into participating in the abduction of his own daughter (he thinks he's helping abduct Marilyn, the Countess of DiMaggio), he realizes that he has been victimized by the curse of Count Giancana against himself and Kilmartin. And that takes us to the end of act 1."

Suddenly, a repetitive beep is emitted from a cartridge attached to Jane Triboulet's bag. She speaks into the remote and then announces: "People? I'm sorry, but I must take an urgent call. Go on with scene 2 for the pacing, feel, and timings. I'll be back in a flash." With great fleetness of foot, she dashes from the set to her portable phone hooked up in a refreshment station a few yards off from the stage. She has notepad and cigarettes in place as she answers the phone.

"Mr. Francis! Hi! This is Jane Triboulet. It's so good to be speaking to you at last. Well. You've read the prospectus, so I imagine you're excited about the deal that was solidified for the recording rights of the special intermission concert of the Rolling Stones with the three tenors. Also the video of the entire production will be distributed around the world with very generous royalty arrangements. What? You have some particular questions about the conception? I see. Well, as long as we're talking, ask away!

"Why, yes, Mr. Francis. I knew that you were a close friend of President Kilmartin. I also am aware that the reason you pulled your film *The Cambodian Nominee* from syndication after his assassination had to do with your distress over that event—but Mr.—Mr. Francis, what is the connection of all this to our production of *Rigoletto*?" As she speaks, Jane lights a new cigarette with the butt of the one she has been smoking. She paces back and forth in the refreshment station. "Mr. Francis, I hear you, I *do* hear you. I was devastated myself by the Kilmartin murder. But doesn't it make a difference that President Kilmartin was the president? You know, a historical personage? What we want to achieve here is a direct connection on the part of the audience to the events of the opera. That's why we're using the most powerful, shocking event of recent years in order to involve the audience in a truly American experience. No, I didn't know that; I didn't know that you knew Marilyn, but I suppose I should have anticipated that. Uh, no, I wasn't aware that you are on cordial terms with Mr. DiMaggio. But Mr. Francis, with all due respect, why should that matter?"

A man rushes toward her at the phone station. She waves him away. "But, Mr. Francis, don't you think that your public connection with the production, combined with your historical involvement with some of the symbolically suggested characters—doesn't that make for a totally fetching postmodern interaction? I feel that, in this way, we're making a very exciting statement! Certainly, in the past, you've been most enthusiastic about that dimension in my work: how about your praise for my production of *Turandot* set in Jersey City or my production of *Pagliacci* based on the life of Fatty Arbuckle!"

She holds the phone away from her head and grimaces, then she speaks into it once more: "You needn't take that tone with me, Mr. Francis! We're both professionals, sir, I might remind you. If we remove the political material and the references to organized crime, how will the curse be brought to life for our contemporary audience? You opted to support my production precisely because I *don't* work in the old-fashioned way! I must say that I'm not wild to set the opera in a make-believe realm: that's what the *Ring* cycle is for! Mr. Francis, I will not be referred to by words of that caliber or vulgarity! I suggest we speak more on this later! Good-bye." My God, she thinks, it's just as Rigoletto sings in act 2: just one day and everything is changed!

Shaking her head in bemused discouragement, Jane hurries back to her office trailer for a moment's air-conditioned respite from the Los Angeles heat. Her secretary hands her a stack of pink message slips with no comment other than: "Blanche called, Jane." At the thought of her lovely and incredible sixteen-year-old daughter, Jane Triboulet is momentarily whisked away from the current frustrations of her complicated life. She is charmed and amused once again at the coincidence that her daughter, Blanche, and Rigoletto's daughter, Gilda, are the same age—it is this realization that confirms for her the rightness of her interpretation of the opera: she approaches it from the same space as Rigoletto—she knows what it's like to have a precious daughter. Cindy meanwhile knows from experience what Jane's priority will be in returning her calls and has already dialed a number: "Ringing Blanche, Jane." Jane reclines in her orthopedic desk chair: "Thanks, Cindy, you're a dear."

But there is no answer at the number Cindy has dialed. "Cindy? Where did Blanche say she was calling from? If she just called, why wouldn't she be at her apartment?" The apartment, in this case, is the pleasant flat Jane rents for Blanche near Mills College, an institution for women in Oakland, California. The apartment allows her daughter (a most diligent freshman student) the privacy to concentrate on her studies plus the option of participating in the stimulating female intellectual activities at the nearby college. Her secretary calls back over the sound of the rehearsal: "She didn't say where she was. I assumed she was at school. But, hey, don't worry: she said she's calling right back."

And before Jane is able to summon to her mind stressful thoughts about where her prodigious daughter might be, the phone rings and Cindy calls out: "Speaking of which, heeeere's Blanche!"

"Hi, Baby! Where are you?" A look of blissful contentment emerges on Jane Triboulet's face.

"Oh, Mother! I'll tell you in a bit. Aren't you going to ask how I am?"

Jane giggles softly; her daughter sounds fine. "OK, I will: how are you, honey?"

"I thought you'd never ask! Mother, I can't stand it: I'm in love! I just *had* to tell you. I'm in love with the sweetest man! He's a little bit older than I am—well, he's an older gentleman, really—but he's *so* handsome: he looks just like Albert Francis! He's a professional musician who's gone back to college. Isn't that terrific? I met him here at a Trump casino in Atlantic City. That's where I am, see? He said he's playing in the house band here to raise the tuition money for school!"

Jane feels the muscles in her body tighten up from stress. She affects a flighty tone: "Blanche, honey? What are you doing in Atlantic City? What are you doing in a casino? Remember, darling, why we decided to send you to Mills College? You could be cloistered there in a wonderful, gardenlike natural setting where your mind could be developed and stimulated in a pure and glorious way." Jane sounds as if she is reading from a catalog.

"But, Mother! It isn't *just any* casino: it's the new Trump Basilica! And I'm here for school. Don't you remember that research report I have due on the semiotics of religious iconography in commercial American life? Well, this is it."

Jane thinks to herself: Why am I so upset? Blanche has always been absolutely trustworthy—that's why she has been permitted to start college at sixteen. And Blanche has always been privy to Jane's bicoastal, globe-trotting lifestyle. She is troubled, however, by her daughter's neglect in not telling her in advance about her plans. "Darling, do you have a place to stay?"

"Of course, Mother. I have a room here at the Trump Basilica."

"All right, then. I'd like you to stay put for tonight—finish all your schoolwork—and then fly back here to L.A. first thing tomorrow morning, OK? We'll talk then about this love of your life and the whole situation. Oh, and Baby? Before you hang up, leave your number at the hotel and the name of your new friend with Cindy. Right. Bye."

As Cindy takes down the information from Blanche, Jane practices the deep-breathing stress-management technique she learned earlier in the year from Sonny Bono: Hands clasped behind her head, she leans back in her chair and inhales deeply to the syllable "la." Then, lips pursed out, she exhales forcefully, while shifting forward, to the syllable "ra." "La. Ra. La. Ra. La. Ra." Soon she is feeling a good deal better.

"Cindy? I'm sure there's nothing wrong here—Blanche is always falling in love with one adolescent crush after another—but I'd like you to call in Howard and see what he can find out about the guy whose name Blanche left you. The guy lives in Atlantic City. Right. Have him see what he can find out. And now: Is there time to ring back the National Endowment for the Arts? Let's see, there's three hours—yes, we'll just make it. Put it through, would you?"

Jane is suddenly starving. She opens the trailer's refrigerator and rummages around until she finds what she's looking for: the remnants of the scrumptious meal she had the night before at that new place that was so much better than Spago—venison-stuffed ravioli with a basil Gouda sauce and gourmet marinated eel pizza. She eats right out of the white food containers, using the chopsticks that she keeps on a string connected to the fridge. She finishes chewing as Cindy gestures that her call is ready. "Elliot? Hi, I'm so happy to have caught you. Yes, I've been in a whirl all afternoon—rehearsals and the like—and I've only just now had a moment to call you back. Did I forget to sign that silly oath *again*? I told you last time, didn't I, that all that stuff about obscenity and homosexuality really won't apply in my case, darling, I'm doing *Rigoletto,* so the question is moot, isn't it? Well, of course, I understand that you're in a position where you must observe the formalities. Naturally. I tell you what: fax me the oath and I'll whisk it right back to you with my signature."

As she speaks, Jane writes notes to herself on the calendar that is mounted on the trailer wall. All at once, she stops scribbling: "Yes, I *do* understand, Elliot. I've been funded by the NEA many times before; I know that all the awards must be approved by the advisory board. Now tell me exactly what objections were expressed by the Advisory Council about the project."

Jane, while listening, taps her pen against the wall to attract Cindy's attention; she holds the pen up to her mouth and inhales silently to show that she needs her cigarettes. "But that's so silly! Honestly, Elliot, it's hard to be patient with that level of absurdity! In act 3, when the Duke comes to Rubino's strip joint (you remember, that corresponds to Sparafucile's inn), he calls out, '*Due cose e tosto,*' and that means, in effect, 'I want two things—immediately.' OK. So far, so good. Then he says, '*Tua sorrella e del vino*': 'Your sister and some wine.' But Elliot, that's what it says! Look, I'll go over it for you: all the printed copies of the libretto say '*Una stanza e del vino*' (a room and some wine), and that's the way it's traditionally been performed. But it makes no sense! Why is this libertine checking in to an inn and requesting a seedy room and what will probably be bad wine? Remember, he's the president: he can get whatever he wants! It only makes sense if the Duke/president was lured to the inn/strip joint by the promise of an assignation with a woman: *that's* what makes him tick! Now, in this case, it's a stripper, and we know that, when he was in Congress, Kilmartin had this affair with Blaze Starr (or was it Tempest Storm?)—so it's perfectly logical. Now it was discovered that the original written score by Verdi contains the words, 'your sister and some wine.' Those words were crossed out, and, in a handwriting we know was not Verdi's, the words, 'a room and some wine,' were written instead. Don't you see: he was censored!

"Now, in 1851, Verdi was censored about all kinds of things: the King of France was changed to the Duke of Mantua, the century was changed, the names of the jester and the daughter were changed, I understand, from the Victor Hugo original—and that play was itself censored. Wait, hold on, I have this great quote in my notebook. Here! Victor Hugo wrote this, about his original play after it was banned in 1832: 'The ministerial suppression of a play attacks liberty by censorship and property by confiscation. The sense of our public rights revolts against such a proceeding. . . . To ask permission of power is to acknowledge it.' But you don't get it, do you? Your NEA Advisory Council wants to censor—in our modern day and age—the phrase that the Austrian censors struck out of Verdi's libretto well over a hundred years ago! What do they mean, 'it sounds indecent'! Well, of course it sounds indecent, it's meant to depict an indecent character! How does the Endowment expect an artist to create an impression of immorality unless it displays that immoral behavior? But the work of art isn't itself immoral. Yes, I know, Elliot, about the political sensitivity of the NEA, but, my friend, this is opera! Opera is not censored anymore! All right, give me the bottom line: the funding won't be approved without the change. OK, I've got it. I'll be back in touch with you soon."

Screaming out *"merde!"* Jane dashes out of the trailer to catch the end of the rehearsal she had planned on attending. She makes amends with the production team, sets up the schedule for the next series of rehearsals, and then, just as quickly, is back in the trailer, calling out to her secretary: "Cindy? Any word from Howard on that guy? Not yet? Keep checking." Jane's mind is in turmoil: she is distracted about her daughter, and that prevents her from concentrating on the issues at hand—would the politicians go for "sister-in-law" instead of "sister"? There's no blood connection there, but how would you say "your sister-in-law and some wine" in Italian? Why would you say it? How would you sing it? And then there is the whole question of the private consortium and the objections put forward by Mr. Francis: how can she persuade them that President Kilmartin and organized crime can be used in a work of art that deals with genuine issues of historical and social concern? Cindy recites: "Still nothing from Howard on this Walter Maldé dude" just as Jane, reaching for a cigarette, realizes—she's all out! "Just a minute, honey, I've got to get more cigarettes from the machine outside. Back in a flash!"

As Jane returns, a cigarette dangling contentedly in her lips, Cindy is excited: "Mr. Francis's chief of staff called! He says that Mr. Francis says that either you take out all the stuff about—wait, I wrote it down!—President Kilmartin *and* Count Giancana *and* Count DiMaggio *and* Countess Marilyn *and* Jake Rubino *and* the mob of courtiers, either you change the time period to the Middle Ages and change all the names or else they're pulling out all their funding! Then he said a whole lot of other stuff that I can't repeat for you." Cindy blushes a deep red. "Should I ring Mr. Francis for you?"

"Yes, thank you." Jane feels numb. She has always prided herself on her smooth demeanor under pressure. No time to show any strain now. "I'll make the call personally, Cindy." She picks up the receiver and, hearing the ringing, waits for a voice to answer.

"Hello?" It is a young girl's voice. "Hello?" It is the voice of Blanche! Could Cindy have dialed the wrong number? "Blanche? Baby, is that you?" The line goes dead. "Cindy? Show me the paper where you wrote down the number for Blanche's hotel room. Now get Mr. Francis's number from the address file: let's see—oh, my God!"

The two telephone numbers are the same. It is as if a blindfold were suddenly pulled from her eyes: "What is it with this *Rigoletto? 'Ah! La maledizione!'* Shit, I'm cursed!"

II.

Several days later, Jane Triboulet and her executive assistant, Howard, are discussing the situation while dining in the exclusive back room of Jambalini's, a new Cajun-Italian restaurant in Beverly Hills. Jane looks up from her muffuletta pizza: "The hell with them, Howard! I mean, who died and made Albert Francis king? I'm dealing with the most absurd bunch of fuddy-duddies in creation! And then Elliot and the NEA: can you believe them? If I didn't know better, I'd swear this was all a joke. This *is* all a joke, isn't it, Howard?"

Howard finishes chewing his portion of gumbo pasta. "No, Jane, I'm afraid not." He reaches over to light her cigarette: despite the city's recent no-smoking provision, they are allowed to smoke in the restaurant's private room since it is not open to the general public.

"What's the latest news, Howard? Does the Francis consortium show any sign of budging about all those changes?"

"They're holding firm, Jane."

"Well, then, I think I should go ahead with our revised plans."

Howard practically falls out of his chair. "But, Jane! How can you disband the production company? Won't that leave the Francis consortium financially liable for all the debts to date?"

"Yes, of course, Howard." She closes her eyes and smiles: "Isn't it luscious?"

"But what about the album and all the contracts you negotiated?"

"So what? I'm scot-free on that 'artistic differences' clause that we inserted in all the secondary provisos to the codicils. If they can't see what a major mistake they're making by tampering with a creative vision such as this—why, then, they deserve as much confusion and chaos as I can contrive for them! This is ridiculous, Howard! It's like the Dark Ages!"

Howard is nervously fiddling with his cigarette lighter. "Look! I would never tell you *not* to do this—you know, of course, that I love you and I'll always tell you the truth—but weren't you going to shop the project around first? Because, Jane, you're very well liked in this town! I thought the idea was, you pitch the project and get a network pickup for the whole gig, right? So what's the rush?"

"I *have* jobbed this deal all around town, darling, but no go: that beast Francis has real pull—even on television! But the time for action is now! I've got to move before they do. I can feel it in my heart what a tremendous vengeance this will be: a real payback! I'm sick of being used by these servile flatterers, these fawning flunkies and sycophants, these stooges, these jackals, these toadying parasites, these impudent, arrogant, obsequious, groveling worms—I hate their whole vile, damned race! All they care about is money! But, incredible as it may seem, Howard, some things are more important than money!"

"Do you think you might be overreacting—just a tad—on account of what happened between Albert Francis and Blanche?" Howard shifts the positions of his wineglass and his water glass on the table.

"I won't hear of this, Howard! What he did, what they did—his so-called associates hustling her off to Atlantic City so he could put the moves on my angel—it's impossible to forgive this. She's all the family I have, Howard. I have no one else."

"All I'm saying is that you might be acting—oh, what's the word, you know, too quickly, but I think it begins with an *s;* I don't know—"

"Precipitously?"

"Yes! That's the word! Why did I think it began with an *s?* I think you can do anything, I really do, but shouldn't there be the slightest glimmer of a plan here?" All at once, Howard notices a certain expression on Jane's face as she pours them more wine. "Jane? What's that twinkle, that flash in your eyes? You have something, don't you! I knew it!"

"Well, I did get one response: I think we can get the whole project packaged as a *Columbo*!"

Howard's mouth falls slightly ajar. He plays with his food silently. ◀

"Well? What do you think?"

"I love it, Jane, I love it! It's just—"

"Yes?"

"It's just that I'm not sure that I . . . you know, get it—now, the broad scope of it: that's inspired, brilliant!—but . . . the details: what *is* the connection of *Rigoletto* to *Columbo*?"

"The detective, Howard, the whole whodunit twist that I put on the production in the first place! The cop in the raincoat: why couldn't he be Columbo? Anyway, I made some preliminary inquiries and my sense is— we'll have to fiddle around with a few of the details, of course, and fine-tune the conception somewhat—that they're going to pick it up. I take a meeting with their people first thing in the morning."

"Jane, that's great! You're a genius!"

"The thing is, they can go to production absolutely immediately, and they really need good scripts. They can get this on the air in practically no time! I can just see it: when Albert Francis turns on his TV and there's the whole *Rigoletto* project he thought he killed, why, it will be like he was struck by a thunderbolt!"

"It's beautiful, really beautiful. And the show still pulls down those impressive numbers, doesn't it?"

"Well, I hear it's quite solid. Now listen: there's a few background details I need your help with so that my meeting will go smoothly. Here's a list of things I need faxed to me by later tonight. OK? Well, you've finished your dinner, haven't you? Haven't you?"

Howard is up and moving toward the foyer. "Dear Howard, have I told you what a sweetheart you are?"

Jane calls for a phone to be brought to her table. She sips wine while waiting for her connection. "Baby?"

"Yes, Mother."

"How are you?"

"I'm all right, I guess. Well, a little mixed up, I think."

"I can understand that, honey. I'm sure anyone who went through what you've been through would feel like a wreck!"

"It's not that, Mother. I feel happy and excited but also tired and depressed. I think I'm a little ashamed, Mother!" Blanche starts to cry.

"Oh, Baby, go ahead, cry, it's all right. You'll see: everything is going to be OK. Are you getting your schoolwork done?"

"Yes, Mother. But sometimes it's a little hard to concentrate."

"Don't worry, darling. I just have to finish a few things that are left here for me to do and then, you'll see, at your next break we can leave this crazy place: we'll sweep off to La Scala and sing and sip espresso and eat until we look like Pavarotti—actually, maybe Luciano will be there then: I can check! Would you like to visit with him like we did last year, Baby?"

"Oh, Mother, I don't know how you do it, but you make me feel better."

"I'm glad, dear. Now, have you thought about what I told you before? That this was all just a teenage crush, an infatuation? Remember, those who really love us don't lie to us or manipulate us."

"I know what you're saying, Mother, but—I still love him! I know you won't be happy about it, but that's how I feel."

"What? Weren't you listening when I told you about all those broken marriages? Not to mention those sordid affairs! What about that girl (What's her name?), she used to be on some soap opera and he swept her off her feet—she was just about your age!—and then she ended up with the Beatles and that guru and now she's with that comedian who makes movies? Well, you know who I mean. He calls all of us 'broads,' do you understand? Or 'chicks'—I mean, really! It's so insulting."

"I know, Mother, and I agree with you. But he didn't mean anything by it, that's just his way. I know he still adores me: I can feel it. Try to be a little more understanding, Mother. If I can forgive him, so should you."

"But he's not only been married, he *is* married! Right this very minute· he has a wife!"

"Does that have anything to do with love? You were never married."

"I always hoped that you would rise where I had fallen, that you would benefit from my mistakes. Well, enough of this, Baby, have a good night. Talk to you soon."

Jane thinks to herself: we'll see, Mr. Francis, which of us is the potentate and which of us is the buffoon . . .

Bright and early the following morning, Jane Triboulet parades into a conference room at Omniversal Studios, flashing a dazzling smile. She greets Mort, a senior producer of *Columbo,* as well as several other members of the editorial and production staff—Jimmy, Bruce, Tracy. Everyone sits around a glass-topped table on which rest platters of fruit danish, cheese danish, croissants, bagels, assorted cheeses, melons, and fruit; there are heated trays with scrambled eggs, sausages, bacon, hash browns; there are iced trays of smoked salmon and marinated herring. Coffee is served from a sterling dispenser, and Bailey's Irish Cream is available in a decanter for a discreet morning boost. Jane finds the arrangement most impressive. As she lights a cigarette, she senses a nervousness in Mort. "Oh, I'm so sorry! Is it all right if I smoke? I should have asked, actually."

Mort shifts on the couch. "Oh, sure, Jane. Please go right ahead. In fact, I'll join you." Mort lights up. "If I seem a bit unfocused, it's just because I'm not completely clear about why we're all taking this meeting. I thought I explained to you during that long phone conference we had—"

Jane interrupts: "I just want to say how really helpful you were on the phone and how much I appreciate all the time you took with me."

Mort leans forward and points with his cigarette. He is chewing, but Jane stops talking instantly. "Yes, well, I thought I made it clear to you then that your project script would not really work for us—even though there is a detective who wears a rumpled raincoat and who smokes. I know you said he could smoke a cigar instead of a cigarette, but that's not the point. You see, your treatment (which, by the way, I think is excellent, most impressive, really admirable, a first-rate piece of work; it's just not what we're looking for) is Bogie-esque, hard-boiled—how do you say it?—Raymond Chandler stuff, you see what I mean? Our show, despite the raincoat, and the cigar, and the unpolished speaking style, is really a variation on the classic murder mysteries: you know, locked-room stuff, Agatha Christie, *Murder, She Wrote,* lots of class conflict—you see my point?"

Bruce, who has been consuming his third fruit danish, jumps in with: "It's just not the same sort of thing!"

"Right," nods Tracy, "but be sure to call us the minute you develop something that we might use."

"Because we're really interested in you, Jane," continues Jimmy, "you're a superstar in this town, Babe."

Mort stands up and offers a tight smile. Jimmy, Bruce, and Tracy also rise hurriedly. "They're right, you know, Jane. All of us here have the greatest respect for you and your work: you're a pro, an absolute class act. Please, relax here as long as you like. They won't be using this room for another"—he looks at his watch—"thirteen minutes. Call me, we'll do lunch, really." They begin to move away from the table. Jane Triboulet remains seated in her cushioned chair; she refills her cup of coffee.

"*All the Marbles*." She speaks calmly but with confident authority. "Also known as *The California Dolls*. Before your series resumed production, Mr. Falk starred in that film to great critical acclaim. You remember, I'm sure, that the film was noteworthy as well for going on to post even higher numbers in the video market than it had in first release and regional theaters. In that film, Mr. Falk played the role of the manager of a traveling women's wrestling team. As he and the two women drive around the country, he plays tapes incessantly from Leoncavallo's opera, *Pagliacci*— 'The Clowns': the idea is that he sees himself and the young women as being nomadic clowns who entertain the audiences in town after town. Although the film is a comedy, when Mr. Falk sings along with the aria 'Vesti la giubba' ('Put on your costume'), there is an air of pathos to the whole performance, for he and the girls must transform, as the words say, their despair into laughter. Opera provided the soul for that film.

"And you all recall, I'm sure, the great success of the film *The In-Laws* (in which Mr. Falk also starred), which ends in that uproarious climax of Maestro Dragon and the Pasadena Symphony performing 'Here Comes the Bride' (taken from Wagner's *Lohengrin*) in a full classical orchestral arrangement. I don't need to allude to the numbers on that film: they are legendary in our industry. Nor do I have to remind you all of Francis Ford Coppola's newest *Godfather* project in which the latest Corleone sings opera and important scenes take place in the midst of opera performances. I shouldn't even have to mention to you the fact that opera and classical music are everywhere on television today: selling laundry detergent, marketing airline flights, European automobiles, soft drinks—they're even regular categories on *Jeopardy!* Let us, instead, consider the sound track used in the classic *Columbo* series and how crucial and memorable that music was in contributing to the overall effect of suspense and tension. Take, for instance, two episodes from 1978, 'Make Me a Perfect Murder' and 'Try and Catch Me': the music emphasized classically derived fugue patterns and variations. A masterful use was made of themes that recalled, to my ear, the second movement of Mozart's Piano Concerto in C, K. 467. My point, in all of this, is that I *did* listen very carefully to what Mort told me, I have studied your production needs, and I am convinced—absolutely!—that opera and a classical orientation can be brought to your program with great success. Will you hear me out?"

Mort, Bruce, Tracy, and Jimmy are all already back in their seats around the glass table. "Now let us forget all about the prospectus that you had a look at earlier. Let us discuss a new idea for a *Columbo*. What I'd like to do is talk you through the general features of it. OK? Oh, before we start? Could I have just the teensiest bit of Bailey's in my coffee cup? Thanks so much." Jane removes a notebook and a portable compact disc player from her briefcase. She cues up the player to the appropriate sequences and takes a sip from her accentuated coffee.

"As the credits roll, the first thing we see is a knife. What we are hearing all along is the overture to *Rigoletto*." She turns on the portable CD. "We see a pair of hands, sharpening a knife, then sheathing it in a case, and working to conceal that knife-in-its-case by sewing it inside the folds of a theatrical costume. Gradually, the camera moves back: we see we are backstage, in a dressing room, and we get a picture of the face of the man who is working over the knife. Now here, it's important to get a sense of this character. He will be playing the Duke of Mantua in the opera, and part of the point of the episode will be that this singer is very much like the character he creates. Think of a libertine, a promiscuous, really horny guy, nevertheless with a tremendous amount of dignity, grace, and charm: someone who is quite deceptive and manipulative in getting what he wants. Imagine an Errol Flynn type of guy, a Don Juan, someone the way we now know President Kilmartin was—wait!—here's a crazy thought: picture him in your mind as someone like, oh, I don't know, say, Albert Francis! Yes, the great Albert Francis as a famous professional opera singer—a tenor. You've never had a *Columbo* villain who was a professional opera singer: I checked!

"As the music changes to a lighter, more frivolous atmosphere"—she gestures to the CD player to call their attention to the music that has been playing all along—"we see him enter the dressing room of the leading so-prano and come on to her full throttle. We hear their conversation and—it's really so perfect!—the music in the background is taken from the sec-tion of the opera where the Duke tries to make time with a particular woman. The audience doesn't need to know that—it's really irrelevant!—I just wanted to point it out so that you see how effective the opera context really is. What they say to each other I haven't fully worked out yet, but it's not really that important: obviously, they get into an argument. Maybe they've been having an affair and she wants to break it off; or else, perhaps she has found out that he is having an affair with a young protégé who is underage and she wants to blackmail him; or—this is the best one yet—she won't respond to his coming on to her; she won't buy what he's selling and it drives him crazy! Anyway, something like that. We get a sense of this guy as being world famous, but that superficial charm conceals a really sleazy character who's involved in all sorts of garbage.

"Now we see the singers in full costume (it is just before the perfor-mance) and we get some shots of people entering the Coliseum—What am I thinking! I mean, the Dorothy Chandler Pavilion in the Music Center—and then we get some quick cuts that zip through the first act of the opera. We see that our knife sharpener is the Duke and that the soprano he ar-gued with is Gilda who, in the opera, will be killed in the third act. But not by our guy! That's the whole point: not by our guy; our guy, in the opera, is the one they were trying to kill but who escapes."

Jane stands up for emphasis. "We have reached the point of the cru-cial sequence. The Duke sings 'La donna è mobile' ('Woman is fickle, or changeable')—everyone knows that, right? It's the most famous aria in the world: 'Woman is as changeable as a feather in the wind, always a pretty, attractive face, but, crying or smiling, it's always two-faced.' Is he describ-ing women here or is he describing himself? He continues: 'He who trusts her will have his heart broken, but no man can be completely happy if from her breast he has never sipped love.'"

Mort leans forward. "Jane? Is that a literal translation?"

Jane frowns. "Why? I just translated spontaneously as the music played."

"I'm wondering whether that could be punched up a bit, you know, made a bit more direct, more perky? How about 'women are crazy' or something like that?"

"I'm sure that can be worked out, Mort. We could even use subtitles, right? The point is this high note at the end: I want you to listen to it again, *'e di pensier!'* Got it? OK. Now, a lot of things take place that need not concern you right now. The broad aspects are: The Duke is going to be paid back for what he did to Rigoletto's daughter, but the daughter, Gilda (the soprano), still loves him and offers herself to the assassin instead; the killer delivers the body to Rigoletto in a sack. Rigoletto thinks he's killed the Duke—whom he works for and hates!—but finds out at the last minute that it's his daughter dying in his arms. How does he find out? Here's the kicker: he hears the Duke singing in the distance, from backstage. He realizes he has been the victim of a curse as the opera ends.

"Here's the thing: in the opera, while Gilda gets killed, the Duke is offstage—and that's the tenor's alibi! He had to be offstage so that he could sing that very same aria, 'La donna è mobile,' and have it sound as if it came from a distance so Rigoletto knows the Duke is not dead. But the tenor—the killer—has just enough time to go downstairs, underneath the stage, and—while the soprano is in the sack lying onstage—stab her with his concealed dagger through a stage ventilation grate! He then rushes backstage and barely manages to sing his aria once more. But—and this is what Columbo will discover—when he sings it from backstage, he can't hold the high B on that last note. He cuts it off abruptly. Rigoletto opens the sack and finds his daughter. Here we'll see the audience, expecting to see a soprano pretending to die, stare in amazement at an actually dead woman! It will be a terrific shot—a real shocker!—and that would be the break for the end of the long opening sequence."

Jane switches off the CD player. "When Columbo enters the action, we'll be able to use a lot of his personal quirks to further the investigation. Since he's Italian, opera is a fundamental part of his heritage, his identity. He'll recall how, as a boy, his father sang the arias from *Rigoletto* for him. The tenor will be world famous (like Pavarotti or Domingo), and Columbo can fawn over the tenor and tell him that Mrs. Columbo plays his records all the time at their home. There's even the possibility of comic developments as Columbo investigates singing and asks the tenor to teach him how to sing opera. But: what Columbo will discover is that the trademark of the tenor is his vocal style—the way he sings is the way he is; it's his vocal personality. Let's see: Pavarotti's slogan is 'king of the high Cs'—maybe we can think of something like that for our killer. Columbo will realize that the tenor always, always, always hits that high note and holds it. For him to not hold that note, well, that's an unusual occurrence of the first order, and we all know that when something takes place in a routine that's not supposed to take place, that's when the lieutenant gets suspicious.

"At any rate, he asks himself, 'Why couldn't the tenor hold the note?'—you know, it's these little details that really obsess him—and he realizes that the singer couldn't hold the note because he didn't have the breath control; he was too tired from the strenuous activity involved in the murder: running downstairs, climbing a ladder to reach the stage grate, hiding the knife, running back up the stairs, and then having to sing! Columbo will see that the murder was theoretically possible and—on the evidence of the violation of the vocal trademark—actually feasible. The lieutenant confronts the tenor with a recording of him singing the aria and proves to him how he's given himself away. The tenor confesses that there was a little too much of the Duke in him, after all. The show ends as the two of them joke a bit, joining in on a chorus of 'La donna è mobile.'"

Jane steps over to the decanter of Bailey's and pours it, straight, into her coffee cup. She looks straight at Mort: "That's what I've got so far."

"You know, Jane, I've got to hand it to you: you really *were* listening to me when we talked on the phone! I think there's something here for us to work with. But, you know, I'm seeing the Duke in a different way. Not so much like Albert Francis. He can still be a Casanova, but since he gets so tired during the murder, I think it would be more convincing with him as a heavyset fellow. I'm seeing Dom DeLuise as the Duke. We can dub in his voice with the voice of some tenor."

Bruce chimes in: "And I think we could get Judy Light from *Who's the Boss?* to play the soprano!"

Tracy frowns. "Can we budget her, Bruce?"

Bruce slaps his forehead. "You're right, you're right! I know: we can get Genie Francis! She used to be on *General Hospital*. She'll be perfect."

Everyone starts talking all at once. Mort calls out, "We're really rolling with this one! Jimmy, take Jane down the hall and have Lester issue a feature writer contract."

Jane thinks, all right for you, my Duke: "The hour of punishment approaches that will sound fatally for you."

It is one month later, and Jane Triboulet is at a party at the home of Mort, the Omniversal producer, high in the Hollywood Hills on Mulholland Drive, to celebrate the beginning of production on her *Columbo* project. The champagne is flowing liberally and Jane wanders around the veranda, cigarette in one hand, champagne in the other, laughing and chatting with people involved with the show. Mort comes up to her with a small bowl of caviar linguine: "Jane, I had them do this up in the kitchen especially for you; I know how much you like it."

"Oh, Mort, that's so sweet of you."

"You know, Jane, I just want to tell you how great it's been to work with you. It's been so inspiring, you don't know! In those first moments, I'll admit, I never thought the show would come together like this."

"There *was* that nervous instance when I walked into your office and found you placing a call to Albert Francis—"

Mort hugs Jane and guides her over to the pool. "Oh, that, ha, ha! You remember, it was nothing, I was returning his call, remember? He was pressuring us, amigo, but I told him off: 'Sell out Jane? The devil you say! Albert—Babe!—am I a thief, in your book? Or a bandit, sweetie? When have I ever betrayed a client or a member of my team? Jane is with me and she has my one thousand percent fidelity!'" He points off in the distance. "Would you look at those stars? Wasn't it amazingly clear today? There was only that one small brown ridge of smog just above the horizon."

A group of people join them at the pool. They include Jimmy, Bruce, Tracy, Jane's executive assistant, Howard, and her secretary, Cindy. Mort addresses them all: "I want to tell everyone something. I want to embarrass this woman here for a moment—No, I can! It's my home—by telling you all how I love her. Jane, I just want to say that those vicious lies about you—that you're hard to work with, that you're sharp-tongued, that you're irreverent: none of that has been true! That rep was prefabbed by sick, ugly types who envy your talent and who were pee-ohed when your production company folded. Because, sweetheart, when we made all those changes and modifications, you were terrific!"

Jane shrugs her shoulders. "What else could I do but go along?"

"Well—to be frank—I thought you might walk when it turned out that Mr. Falk's favorite piece of music was that 'Send in the Clowns' number from *Pagliacci* which we then decided to substitute for that 'Woman Is Crazy' thing from *Rigoletto,* and then that top studio brass suggested that we would get a Fellini angle if we emphasized the clown motif, and then it was decided at that executive meeting that it would be much more exciting if we used elephants like in *Aida,* so we did have to stray just a bit from your original idea, but I think we all agree how much better off we are now as a result of all this great team input. I mean, it's now a complete romp, even better than that Coke or Pepsi commercial with Michael J. Fox. You know the one, Jane?"

"You mean the one where all the snippets from various operas are mixed up together for no reason in one compact commercial? Yes, I've seen it." Jane fusses with her linguine.

"Great! Anyway, that's why I love this woman. She's a real team player. She inspires us all to greatness. And that's why we moved her up into production as soon as we did!" All of a sudden, Mort turns around: he sees that people are rushing into the house. "What's going on? Did Mr. Falk finally get here? Why didn't anyone call me? Peter? Peter?" He hurries away.

Jane turns to Howard and Cindy. "I don't think anyone's arrived; it's just that it's starting to rain."

Howard jumps as thunder and lightning work their effects in the hills around them. "Whoa! Let's get inside. Wasn't Blanche supposed to make our shindig tonight, Jane?"

Jane calls out as they run into the house, "I've left messages for her, but I haven't spoken to her in a while: she's been burning the midnight oil on this college project, doing research all over the country; I encouraged her to travel, as a means of recovery, you might say—I expect she'll be here."

Inside, the party is noisier and more crowded for having moved indoors. A different CD is playing in each room: Jane has the sense that four different voices are singing all at once. In another room, some people are watching TV. Mort calls everyone into the living room. "Will you get a look at this! Here are some shots of the guest stars in costume and makeup that Tracy had blown up this morning." Jane drifts over and spies an enormous photograph of a character in costume—looking part Egyptian (*Aida*), part clown (*Pagliacci*), part Robin Hood (anyone's guess). Yes, Jane thinks, will you get a look at this. Who would have believed Jane Triboulet ever would have been faced with censorship, with insidious artistic pressure! That only happens to people with no verbal or public relations skills: performance artists and the like—really fringe types. In the nineteenth century, perhaps, during Verdi's time, sure, OK, but in our day and age? Now, in this party, surrounded by people, as an artist, she feels thoroughly and completely alone.

Jane reminds herself that more people will watch this operatic *Columbo*—even if it gets poor ratings—than ever would have seen her contemplated *Rigoletto,* even if it sold out all its performances at the Coliseum: that's the power of television! The success of this TV program will show the consortium, the National Endowment for the Arts, all of them (who should have known better!) that Jane Triboulet will not be played for a fool! For their attempted censorship, their affront to art, their outrageous deceit and arrogance, their name is crime, and mine shall be punishment!

As she looks at the large photos, Jane feels herself overcome by an annoying and unpleasant sensation. She wonders, why do I feel so odd? She becomes aware of a persistent sound—music, really—that is not quite opera; she hears it as if from a distance. Where is that coming from? What is it? She wanders through the house, in search of the music that so unnerves her. Finally, she finds it: on the far side of the house, in a small bedroom, emanating from a television set that several guests are watching. It is the late night rerun of *Entertainment Tonight*. Jane joins the others who are gathered around the screen. What is that voice? It seems like some nocturnal illusion!

Jane hears the voice clearly, at last: "She likes the theater but never comes late; she never bothers with people she hates: that's why the lady is a tramp!" It's Albert Francis, singing on television! Jane stumbles: "That voice!" The TV continues, "She don't go to Vegas in ermines and pearls, she shouldn't play craps with dukes and earls, she hates California, it's cold and it's damp: that's why this broad is a tramp!" Jane staggers onto the bed. No, she thinks, it's impossible! The song continues but she only hears isolated phrases: "she's broke, it's oke! . . . she's flat, that's that! . . . she's all alone when she lowers the lamp: that's why the chippie is a tramp!" Oh, thank goodness, she realizes, the dreadful singing has stopped.

But now there is speaking on the tube. Mary Hart is introducing, on tape, live from Las Vegas, an Albert Francis press conference! There he is, that weasel! What's he saying? "And so I take pride in announcing our plans for the immediate presentation of Pop Op—my kind of opera, opera for the people: all you phonies, stay home!—with the production of a New Age, swingin' *Rigoletto,* composed by that really brilliant Italian cat (you may have heard of him), Giuseppe Vur-dee. Starring in the title role will be that great, great singer (didn't he do a *Columbo* once?) Johnny Cash, the man in black, as Rigoletto. The part of the Duke will be played by yours truly. And now, ladies and gentlemen, I take pride in introducing— the greatest female talent since that Andrew Lloyd Webber cat turned out his Sarah Brightman chick for *Phantom of the Opera*—Blanche Tribou- let as Gilda! Here she is, isn't she lovely? Let's hear it for her, ladies and gentlemen!"

Jane sees her daughter, her angel, talking to reporters. "My daughter! God! My daughter! No, it's impossible, she was on her way here, from Mills College." On TV, Blanche is describing her reactions when she first met Albert Francis: "His sheer talent is so great, he's so fatally handsome, it was like a knife pierced me right here." (She points to her heart. The au- dience applauds.) "Mother, if you're watching, forgive me and him: I hope you'll be very happy for us."

"Blanche? My angel, you mustn't leave me! If you go away, I'll be left all alone." Jane is talking to the TV set, but she appears to be talking to herself. The other guests look at her quizzically and leave the bedroom. "Blanche! Baby!" Abruptly, Jane's mood changes: "That's it, honey, you're dead! You're dead, do you hear me?" And then again: "Oh, that bastard! I'll get him!" And once again: "Blanche! My baby! I'm cursed! I'm cursed!"

∼∾

"*Rigoletto* is one of the greatest operas ever written. . . . While searching in my mind for possible subjects for a story with an operatic theme, *Rigoletto* occurred to me and it was like a lightning bolt; it was tremendously inspiring. . . . The whole conception for me depends on the various degrees of censorship, modification, and change that occurred during the transformation of the original play—Victor Hugo's *Le roi s'amuse*—into an opera. Art is undoubtedly very personal; but it must also—necessarily—be able to communicate with as many people as possible. This process involves changing names, changing meaning, changing form, changing language: is this not yet another aspect of the curse? In modifying the play to the opera, the King of France, Francis I, was changed to the Duke of Mantua; the French jester, Triboulet, was changed to Rigoletto; the jester's daughter, Blanche, was changed to Gilda; the title was modified from *The King Amuses Himself* to *The Curse* to *Rigoletto*. The opera itself incorporated the idea of deception through names: the Duke disguises himself as Gualtier (Walter) Maldé, a poor student, in order to woo Gilda; Rigoletto operates in secrecy and won't disclose his background. Why should the process end there? Why shouldn't, for instance, Hugo's angry father, Saint-Vallier, who became Monterone in the opera, be transformed into a contemporary manifestation—for example, Giancana? The curse that inflicts the jester is a curse of change, recrimination, the failure to understand oneself. If the curse is conceived of expansively enough, it applies to the entire human dilemma."

After Congress voted to establish a loyalty oath that requires recipients of National Endowment for the Arts grants to certify that their art will be inoffensive in a variety of ways:

"Without this conception of the curse—as a plague of censorship, co-option, and loss of aesthetic integrity, what scope or significance can my story possibly have? Once the public censorship process begins, there is no easy matter stopping it. How will I gain any public support to write this story? Viewed dispassionately, it might be seen to offend everyone: opera lovers, especially; traditionalists; but also, and not exclusively (for I may have left some faction out), the handicapped; women; smokers; the city of

Los Angeles; actors; actresses; scriptwriters; opera singers; opera producers; politicians; organized crime factions; detectives, with or without raincoats; the makers of a wide variety of commercial products; prominent baseball legends; television producers; rock groups; restaurateurs; Mills College; religious groups who find the idea of a curse repugnant; people who find the allusion to sexual relations between an older man and a sixteen-year-old girl offensive beyond mention; popular nightclub entertainers; people who dislike my writing. . . . But let me say this: Why do these censoring factions think they know better than I do about this? Who is playing the maestro? Why do I even allow the possibility of censorship and recrimination to enter my mind? If anyone should say to me that I can modify the details of my conception 'just a wee bit' in order to accommodate this or that special-interest group—real or imagined, possible or fantasy—I reply that I don't understand this kind of thinking, and I say frankly that my writing, whether wonderful or disgusting, whether hilarious or offensive, brilliant or insipid, is never written at random; I always try to give it character, context, and a certain comic spirit. All around me I see possible interference to this project: the inability of my obtaining an NEA grant (let alone that my hand would not sign the oath); disapproving publishers; demagogue politicians; hostile audiences at public readings; people who may assail me on the streets at random; people who may, for no good reason at all, desire my autograph; the possibility of causing injury to my friends and loved ones and those whom I admire and respect. Censorship, prohibition, proscription, restriction, interdiction, exclusion, removal of permission: inside as well as outside, all around me is censorship! I am cursed, in truth. . . . My artistic conscience will not allow me to set this opera to fiction."

—G. Green, 1990

"SUCH DEAR ECSTASY"

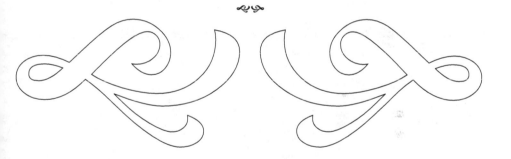

"To be popular doesn't necessarily mean to be the best. To be popular is nice. But what really is important for me is to be at the high point of a career as a singer, as an artist. We have an instrument to make art, not only to sing. To make art, to leave a documentation of what you did in your life, to be a piece of this chain from the past to the future, to maintain opera and help this continuity—this to me is what's really important."

—ALFREDO KRAUS

I.

Baron Augusto Ayme d'Aquino, a diplomat attached to the embassy of the Kingdom of the Two Sicilies in Paris, was concerned about his friend Bellini. He had lately vanished from all the best salons. Several days earlier, Bellini had sent his regrets *at the very last moment* to Mme Jaubert, canceling on account of illness his attendance at her dinner. The Principessa Belgioioso was sufficiently troubled so as to dispatch her physician, Luigi Montallegri, to Bellini's quarters at Puteaux, outside Paris, where he was residing at the home of the Levyses. On the very same day, the eleventh of September 1835, Baron d'Aquino journeyed to Puteaux to visit Bellini. The matter was of some delicacy in that he had not been invited, nor had Bellini announced hours of open reception; nevertheless, d'Aquino *had* visited his friend recently and was no stranger to the home of M. Levys.

Upon his arrival, he was shown up to the large room on the second floor of the villa that Bellini occupied. D'Aquino thought to himself how much more convivial and tranquil this room was, with its one window facing out onto the serene gardens below and its other window gazing onto the Seine, than the cramped and chaotic quarters Bellini occupied in town, in the Bains Chinois on the Boulevard des Italiens. He found his friend resting in bed, and, aside from a noticeable paleness to his always light complexion, in good spirits: very solicitous of d'Aquino's generous interest in his state of health. Bellini assured d'Aquino that he was just getting over a slight gastric malady and that he would be returning to Paris shortly. All at once, Mme Levys burst into the room! "Really!" she announced. "Is this the most appropriate way for the maestro to spend his time, knowing as he does that he has been told he requires absolute rest?" Baron d'Aquino found her manner to contain more than a nuance of insult toward his person: Who *was* this creature to take that tone with him? How dare she forbid Bellini to visit with his friend if that was what he found appealing? In any event, d'Aquino opted to withdraw. That evening, he reported to his uncle, the composer Michele Carafa, on Bellini's situation. "Check on him again tomorrow," Carafa advised.

The next day, d'Aquino returned to the villa at Puteaux. From a distance he was able to see that the windows on all three levels were open only to the slightest degree, suggesting that the house was not in a state of reception. D'Aquino could not help observing to himself the irony that Bellini, who was such an agreeable and original fellow, so refined and at the same time so utterly natural, should take up quarters with such an odd and curious sort as the Levyses. Did it not say everything about them that their principal (as opposed to their country) residence was here in Puteaux? Little of certainty was known about them. It was rumored that M. Levys was a colonel (retired) in the British army who had gone into investments of a disreputable nature in Iberia. Had not Bellini commented, in his own distinctively melancholy manner, that the thirty thousand francs he had invested with M. Levys had failed in their return by half? And that still a year had returned only half again on the original amount? There was no answer to d'Aquino's repeated entreaties at the gates of the villa. At long last, d'Aquino spied the squat, portly figure of the gardener as he trudged along from the rear grounds. This dreary man, whose name was Joseph, informed d'Aquino in imperious language that "nobody is being received."

Baron d'Aquino was more than a trifle disturbed: he was, after all, a diplomat in the international service. To be treated in this manner, to be "handled," as it were, and by this sort of individual, was not to be believed! But it was important not to take these slights personally. It was Bellini's well-being that was of significance; nothing else. Besides, all of Bellini's Paris friends had been subjected to the same degree of humiliation and abuse at the villa. The following day, d'Aquino returned to Puteaux with Francesco Saverio Mercadante, one of the maestro's oldest acquaintances. Again, they were refused admittance by that oaf of a gardener!

That evening, at Luigi Lablache's residence in Paris on the Rue des Trois Frères, d'Aquino and his uncle Carafa hatched a scheme to penetrate the ominous defenses of the villa at Puteaux. They were inspired by the extreme importance of their concern and their cause. Had not Bellini been made Chevalier of the Legion of Honor? Was not his opera *I Puritani* the most celebrated music to have been performed in Paris in ages? Certainly, the minister of the interior would be vitally interested in this case and in the state of Signor Bellini.

Determined and dauntless, d'Aquino and his uncle made the trip to Puteaux on September 14. This time, they were able to launch an ingenious subterfuge: d'Aquino needed to draw on all his skills as an attaché. To the gardener he bellowed, "What do you mean, 'Nobody is being received'! This is no social call. My good man, are you not aware that this gentleman on my left is a physician of the court? You *must* admit him in to the maestro. It is required and you are compelled to acquiesce!"

But Carafa returned from his visit with little of substance to report. Bellini was in bed. He was pale and resting. He found their masquerade touching and amusing, and he took pains to reassure all of his friends that he would soon be back in town. He asked that the principessa be thanked for her donation of Dr. Montallegri's services. D'Aquino and his uncle rode back to Paris in disgruntled silence.

For an entire week, no one was able to get in to see Bellini. The dissatisfaction of his friends broke out at Luigi Lablache's residence. Great emotions were expressed; wild talk circulated about the Levyses, about the gardener, about the precarious state of Bellini's affairs. "Do they not see," d'Aquino cried, "that as caretakers of Signor Bellini it is their duty to notify us of his welfare?" There was even talk of having the king's prosecutor intervene. Baron d'Aquino remained later at Lablache's than he had intended; he retired in a bitter mood.

The following morning, the twenty-third of September, the baron arose early in bright spirits. He had a new approach in mind. Obliged as he was to spend the day at his sister-in-law's in Rueil, he determined that he would leave on horseback and look in on Bellini. At the Pont de Courbevoie, he stopped in Puteaux. At the gates of the villa, d'Aquino mused that the quiet that had so nourished Bellini's creativity was now, for him, oppressive: Where was the help? Why was there no answer? He was startled by Joseph, the gardener, who came upon him unexpectedly. "As I have informed monsieur patiently and repeatedly each and every day he has banged at these gates, nobody is being received. And may I add, sir, with all deference and respect, that the monsieur, in particular, is not to be received—that is, especially after what M. and Mme Levys referred to as the broad and distasteful stunt that was perpetrated on the poor maestro—"

The baron struggled to maintain his composure. "Stunt, Joseph? Stunt? I am afraid that I have no idea as to your meaning! Now would you be so kind as to unlatch these gates and then explain yourself?"

The gardener brushed himself in the most annoying manner possible, raising a cloud of filth that left its dusty remnants on the baron's greatcoat. He retreated from the gate, adding, over his shoulder, "I am not obliged to inform monsieur of my meaning; my purpose merely is to see that monsieur and all other solicitors are not admitted."

"Solicitors! Solicitors! Why, I will have you know that—" But it was hopeless. The gardener had circled to the rear of the villa, and Baron d'Aquino was alone at the gates. He mounted his horse and resumed his journey to Rueil. The pity of it was that he was unable to meet the occasion of this family visit with his usual courtesy, grace, and courtliness. The encounter had left him in a foul and unattractive mood. The weather, as if in sympathy, changed abruptly: the most appalling storm broke out. D'Aquino lingered throughout the afternoon, hoping for a break in the atmospheric conditions. But there was no change.

The weather was not to be believed! Of all the days to have traveled on horseback! At last, the skies grew so dreary that the oil lamps were ignited. The baron bid his respects and set out on his return trip to Paris, by way of Puteaux. He arrived, at ten minutes after five, completely drenched by the driving rain, at the Levys villa. Aside from the turbulent storm, there was an utter and absolute silence in the vicinity of the Levys home. The air was cold and unpleasant; d'Aquino was thoroughly uncomfortable. Once again, he knocked at the house, but there was no answer. Looking all around him, he pushed sharply and suddenly at the gate, that solemn barrier to his sincere purpose: it gave way, with a hollow creak, and d'Aquino walked in carefully. Pausing to tie up his horse, he entered the house.

Inside, the villa seemed completely abandoned. The ostentatious decor and vile bric-a-brac that he encountered along his path had at one time been a source of gentle amusement as Bellini would nod at this item or the next and roll his eyes; but now, by himself, the presence of these objects was unnerving. His steps creaked as he proceeded up the stairs, his hand firmly on the balustrade. Outside, he heard the pestilent wind and the still fierce rain. The silence was heavy, encompassing.

He made the turn into Bellini's room and was relieved to see the familiar Sicilian accoutrements—so reminiscent of their sunny homeland. He found Bellini on the bed, sleeping. D'Aquino took note of his friend's noble and graceful person, his blond and curly locks, his distinctive placidity of expression; he was deeply touched at the serenity of this room despite the weather, moved by the presence of Bellini's grace and gentility. Outside the windows, the rain pelted the gardens unmercifully; the Seine roared by in turbulent abandon. An air from *I Puritani* entered his mind: "*Son salvo, alfin son salvo*" (I am safe, at last I am safe)—here in Bellini's room.

An elusive and delicate sense of airiness overcame d'Aquino: for the first time in days, his dark spirits lifted. He turned from the window and sat on the edge of his friend's bed. Smiling, he reached over to grasp Bellini's hand. It was ice-cold! D'Aquino veritably leapt from the bed! Incredulous, he was unable to accept the hideous truth: Bellini was dead. How could he have failed to observe this? The room, the rain, the singular, persistent grating of the shutter against the window in the wind, the uncharacteristic swirl of the spread that only partially covered his friend's figure as if in a tableau, the horrid, pestilent silence that was everywhere. Dead, dead, how could this be? And where in the world were the people of the house? In the silence, d'Aquino grasped the fingers of ice and tears coursed down his face. "*Son salvo . . .*"

"Ah, the monsieur has again insinuated himself into the residence despite the prohibition that had been so often explained to him!" It was Joseph, the gardener!

This time, Baron d'Aquino had not the energy or the pettiness to respond to his surly provocation. "Ah, Joseph! What has happened? Where are M. and Mme Levys?"

"As the monsieur may plainly see, Signor Bellini breathed his last; at five o'clock it was. Since M. and Mme Levys had departed for Paris, it was necessary for me to leave the villa unattended for the briefest instant so as to obtain candles and notify the appropriate persons. Since the monsieur has admitted himself, would he be so kind as to—"

D'Aquino could not listen to the gardener's drivel. He collapsed, in despair, into a settee: Bellini had died alone, with no one to assist him in his painful ordeal. He had been called from this earth in total and relentless silence and isolation—he who had created such captivating music. He had not yet reached his thirty-fourth year . . . and now he was gone.

II.

Paris was aflame with rumors! The young, handsome, virile Bellini could not possibly have died except by dastardly devices. The Levyses were to blame, of course! One theory popular in the salons was that Mme Levys (if indeed she was in fact Mme Levys and not some mere courtesan!) had poisoned the maestro out of jealousy: they had been lovers and her womanly ire could not tolerate his wandering eye. How else to explain why an apparently healthy man was now dead? There was something strange all along about those Levyses . . .

The king himself became involved in the controversy, issuing an order for a medical autopsy. Rossini, the only composer toward whom Bellini felt deference, cut short his country sojourn in order to take charge of the funeral arrangements. The eminent Dr. Dalmas, recipient of the Legion of Honor medal, was called in for the autopsy. There was, he declared, no justification for charges of foul play: "It is evident that Bellini succumbed to acute inflammation of the colon, compounded by an abscess in the liver. The inflammation of the intestine has produced violent symptoms of dysentery during life." If Dr. Dalmas had lived long enough, into the next century, he might have added the surmise that Bellini's illness was bacterial and chronic in nature and that the maestro had expired of the thickening of the blood and associated dehydration that accompanied severe dysentery. The maestro's blood, devoid of its necessary fluids, was unable to circulate to his brain and lungs.

The Levyses, therefore, under the advice of Dr. Montallegri, were guilty of nothing more criminal than the harboring of a fear that Bellini's illness was cholera (sweeping Europe at that time): to avoid having him removed by force to a public asylum, they may have forbidden access to his friends; to avoid a public quarantine and their personal contagion, they may have fled to Paris, leaving their houseguest to die alone. There had not been sufficient concern, evidently, to warrant the evacuation of the gardener, Joseph.

In contrast to the isolation of Bellini's death, his funeral brought out the most notable composers, musicians, and dignitaries of Paris. The Chapel at the Court of Honor of the Invalides was filled to capacity on October 2, 1835. During the funeral mass, a quartet of male vocalists sang the melody of the aria "Credeasi misera" (Arturo's solo from *I Puritani*) to the words of the Lacrymosa. Then, despite the driving rain and miserable weather, the large funeral party proceeded across the Seine to the Père-Lachaise cemetery and remained throughout the lengthy orations. Rossini, in a letter written after the event, described how he had been a pallbearer, and how the aged Cherubini, overwrought with grief and bolstered by Auber and Halévy—great composers all!—had tossed the first clod of dirt onto the casket. So Bellini was commemorated by his contemporaries, his friends, his colleagues, his audience.

The tenor Rubini, who had created the role of Arturo in *I Puritani*, was among the quartet of singers at the memorial service. Singing the music of the song Bellini had written for him to originate, did he not think back eight years to Milan, 1827, when he had been working with Bellini on the maestro's earlier success, *Il Pirata*? Rubini had achieved great success in the world of opera by means of beautiful, ornamental singing; now, for this role of Gualtiero, Bellini admonished him to sing dramatically, *as if he were the character he was representing:* an incredible concept! The maestro instructed him: "You are an animal . . . you don't put into it half the spirit you have; where you should be driving the audience out of its mind, you are cold and languishing. Show your passion; haven't you ever been in love? . . . Dear Rubini, are you thinking about being Rubini or about being Gualtiero? . . . It has entered my head to introduce a new sort of music which expresses the words very closely and to make a unit of the words and the singing. . . . Forget yourself and throw yourself with all your soul into the character you are representing." He had followed the maestro's instructions and had achieved unparalleled renown. Bellini had taught him to forget himself, to throw himself into his character, to direct his passion into his performance: all to "drive the audience out of its mind."

Bellini's favorite librettist, Felice Romani, was not in Paris among the mourners; instead, he devoted himself to writing a eulogy, for publication, to honor his "companion, collaborator, and friend." Through his anguish, did he not think back seven years to Milan, 1828, when he and Bellini collaborated on *La Straniera*? Faced with the composition of the heroine's culminating aria, Bellini had rejected Romani's written text. Romani had dutifully rewritten it once, twice, three times, four times. Then, despite his love and respect for the young maestro, he had requested some clarification. Were Bellini's words to him not still in his memory? "What do I want? I want a thought that will be at one and the same time a prayer, an imprecation, a warning, a delirium!" Then, Bellini had rushed to the pianoforte, and, afire with inspiration, performed spontaneously the completed aria that had, in that instant, appeared in his mind. "This is what I want," Bellini told him. "Do you understand now?" Romani, in an analogous flourish, had then produced the text, conceived by him during Bellini's wave of composition: "Have I entered into your spirit?" Bellini had rushed to embrace him.

Bellini's goal had been to achieve a state of release in which words and music were unified in a sense beyond sense. He sought to do nothing less than say that which is impossible to say. His devotion to the ineffable was a large measure of the inexpressible sadness felt by the mourners at his funeral. They mourned with the profound disappointment that inevitably ensues when the realization has set in that our expectation of receiving, say, an opera a year from a young and productive composer will never occur. All that we shall receive is what we already have.

Romani, in particular, bemoaned the loss of his future collaborations with Bellini. This loss was especially poignant since the two friends had been separated by a bitter feud and had reconciled only a short while before the maestro's unanticipated death. During their breach, Bellini had turned to Count Carlo Pepoli (a nobleman from Bologna who had been exiled for revolutionary activity) for the libretto for what would be his last opera, *I Puritani*. Bellini's hope had been that this fellow Italian, born in the same year as Bellini, would, if not duplicate the extraordinary rapport that had existed with Romani, at least be simpatico.

But Pepoli was not Romani; that is, he did not spontaneously embody those inexpressible elements of shared interaction: he did not immediately "enter into [Bellini's] spirit." The maestro had set out, therefore, to not only compose his opera, *I Puritani,* but to construct a semblance of a librettist that would do justice to his own high ideals of creative collaboration. Romani had been his alter ego, his second self, the words to his music: now, in 1834, Pepoli had to become the image of that image. The goal was not quite as impossible as it might seem. Pepoli suffered from a visual malady that caused him, at times, to be unable to write. Thus, the composition of the text of *I Puritani* often consisted of Bellini's attempts to inspire Pepoli to write in accordance with Bellini's spirit—his authorial essence and soul. Then, when Pepoli felt possessed of this soul, he would dictate the words and Bellini would inscribe them in his own hand. Bellini would infuse Pepoli with the essence of Bellini so that Pepoli could dictate—transmit, if you will—that soulful translation back to the pen of Bellini, transcribing as Pepoli. This partnership, if not precisely the same as that which had existed with Romani, was certainly an intimate association.

But Pepoli required further instruction. Bellini protested against Pepoli's rigid literary requirements; they had no relevance to what he wished to achieve in opera: "Your absurd rules . . . are fine talking points but will never convince a living soul who understands the difficult art of *moving people to tears through singing.*" The composer admonished the novice librettist, "Carve in your mind in adamantine letters: '*The opera must make people weep, shudder, and die through singing.*'" He urged Pepoli to throw away his accepted notions of preordained form: "Musical contrivances murder the effect of the situations, more so the poetic contrivances . . . ; to make their effect, poetry and music demand naturalness, and nothing else." The purpose of their collaboration, he maintained, was to create an opera that would please not "the sphere of the pedants" but "the heart." Two years earlier, when he had heard a performance of his *Norma* that had pleased him, he had written, "The trio could not be performed better, and so it makes everyone shiver." Could Pepoli be made to understand? Would he be able to "enter into the spirit" of Bellini? Elicit the chill, the shudder, the tears of sublime inspiration?

Describing their work together, Pepoli wrote that Bellini "had melody in his soul . . . [was] an excellent man for goodness, but sometimes eccentric by nature. At times he called me *an angel, a brother, a savior,* and at times, when he was altering the melodies of his music for the third and fourth time, to an observation of mine about the difficulty and impossibility of changing the composition of the drama or changing the verses, he would fly into a rage, calling me a man without heart, without friendship or feeling; afterward, we would go back to being better friends than before." What Pepoli could not understand—what he termed "eccentric"—was Bellini's profoundly artistic temperament. Believing as he did that art must achieve a sublimity of expression that, in a sense, transcends life and evokes an internalized and etherealized death, how could he express this concept to an amateur poet? How does one speak the words of a language beyond language? Pepoli, like Romani before him, would offer up words to be set, and Bellini would "fly into a rage": this rage of inspiration, of creative intensity, of living through art, is what epitomized Bellini's approach to artistic expression in everything he created. When he could hear his music performed to his satisfaction, he would be "seized by convulsive sobbing because of the internal commotion of so much satisfaction." When his music was performed badly, or inappropriately to his spirit, he would berate the guilty parties: "Don't compromise me." His mode of artistic creation required physical and emotional agony: like his performers, it was necessary for him to become what he sought to express. Only in this way could his operas cause audiences to "weep, shudder, and die." Repeatedly, he would demand the requisite time for his creative processes to work: "With my style I must vomit blood." Is this merely "eccentric"?

Nevertheless, Pepoli, serving as the medium through which Bellini-the-composer could be Bellini-the-writer, through which the words and the music could be united, enabled Bellini to complete *I Puritani.* Not only was this opera an unparalleled sensation in Paris, but Doca, a theatrical agent, wrote to Bellini of its reception in London, "Even in dreams one hears *I Puritani* being sung." Bellini, without Romani, was forced to create from the clay of Pepoli his own self-idealized Romani—and for that reason, *I Puritani* is Bellini's collaboration with himself: it is his most Belliniesque opera. It is his effort, in artistic form, to represent that contrived death that one witnesses and comments upon, as it were, from the audience. He desired an art so beautiful, so unique in sound, word, and sensation, that it would take people out of themselves and transmit them into a temporarily purer state of being. For an instant, for an hour, for three hours, one would cease being oneself and would live with Bellini in his realm. There, we would all "weep, shudder, and die" in appreciation of the celestial beauty, rage with eccentricity, and afterward, the images would live on "even in dreams."

III.

One hundred fifty-six years later, I found myself devoting isolated evenings to *I Puritani*. I had listened to this opera previously, but I ought to describe that interaction as having the music play in the background of my life, so to speak, while other more immediate sensations were in the foreground. It had been my prevailing assumption that, aside from *Norma* and *La Sonnambula,* all of Bellini's operas were nontheatrical vehicles for purely ornamental singing: operas, in other words, in which nothing happened; everyone would merely stand still and sing.

However, on this particular occasion, the recorded music filled the room and, unlike my previous experiences, *I heard* the music, the voices, the *sound* as never before. Evanescent and excruciatingly subtle sensations flooded my sensibility. On the table were the remnants of my evening's dinner—spaghetti with anchovy sauce, a green salad, a glass of wine—but all of that, along with the day's mail and the newspaper, were tangential, secondary to the whirl of music that tossed my spirits. The first words called out: *"All'erta! All'erta! L'alba appari"* (Awake! Awake! Dawn has broken)—and, in a sense, a new receptiveness to Bellini had emerged in me as if out of a deep sleep. It was as if Bellini were asking me directly, "Have I entered into your spirit?" And, without hesitation, my answer was yes!

For the moment, nothing in that room mattered. I stood, entranced, as a wash of sound cast itself upon me. The individual voices—so distinctive— were reassuring, calming, but also fiery, explosive, rising to divine heights of tremulous emotional excess and then resolving in serene and blissful quiescence. The sensations were overwhelming, theatrical, operatic, riveting. I was transfixed. Aside from the few isolated words or phrases, I hadn't the slightest notion as to what the voices were saying—nor did I care. I was listening to a sound that was somehow beyond meaning: and yet it conveyed to my spirit the essence of everything there was to say.

I asked myself: could it be the story and situation of the libretto that so moved me? And when I investigated, I found that Bellini and Pepoli had based *I Puritani* on a recent play of 1833, *Roundheads and Cavaliers,* by Ancelot and Saintine: a French historical drama documenting the situation in Plymouth during the English civil war. Right away, there had been a problem: the sympathies of the French play had been decidedly with the English Royalists; the political emphasis had been promonarchist and antirebel. Pepoli (who had participated in the revolutionary uprising of 1831 and been imprisoned and exiled) and Bellini (who had been involved in a brief revolutionary episode during his years at the Naples Conservatory) were both strongly prorebel. Thus, the plot of the play by necessity required an interpretive adjustment so that the political valences were reversed, so to speak. What remained, Bellini felt, were a series of scenes that "fill the soul with the most touching situations."

To be sure, the collaborators' radical sympathies remained: the monarchical play now contained a radical hymn to liberty which (when performed in its Paris debut) would drive the audience to frenzy. But the "touching situations" that Bellini emphasized were concerned with other elements: a heroine who lapses in and out of profound derangement; a hero who, on the verge of a lifetime of love and happiness, sacrifices (he believes) his future for the sake of humanity in an effort to spare his former queen from execution; a series of misunderstandings that cause two lovers to call out for an end to what seems to be an eternity of cruelty. But on none of these narrative elements could I attribute my intense emotional response to *I Puritani*.

Rather, it occurred to me that what was significant in the opera was the way in which it presented its themes in the margins. The revolutionary slant that had been effected could be perceived by what did *not* occur, by the ambience that had been dramatically altered. With the political enunciation blurred or obscured, the artistic expression—in supreme romanticist mode—was achieved by the sublime postures adopted by the principal characters. Everyone in Europe (and most especially, France) was familiar with the extremities of revolutionary fervor. Bellini's opera amazed because it devised situations that lured us to the brink of disaster and then brought us back to an acceptance of what is most beautiful in life: the human values of peace, love, harmony, fraternity, and mercy. In the simulation of death, we return—revitalized—to life. In the representation of the most severe reaches of human cruelty, we learn the virtues of mercy and forgiveness. The opera that Bellini inspired Pepoli to dictate to him so that he could then write its music—*I Puritani*—was (for Bellini and, I realized, for me) about art, about how we need art and beauty and passion in our lives, and about how all of us are humbled by what is most moving and poignant and ineffable in life.

Bellini's account of the opera's Paris reception (on January 24, 1835) may illustrate what concerned him in his art. He wrote his closest friend, Florimo: "I cannot find words to describe to you the state of my heart." Is this not Bellini's ultimate goal: to find a way to say what is unsayable? He wished to achieve the revolutionary crime of artistic greatness. The various musical numbers of the opera elicited from the audience "a very great furor . . . much effect . . . great pleasure . . . fanaticism . . . a huge furor." He noted that "the entire theater was driven to tears because [the musical tempo] lacerates the spirit." The audience "had all gone mad . . . [they were] carried away . . . it was an unheard-of thing." The cries of the crowd caused Bellini to appear onstage: the audience "shouted as though insane." He confided to his friend, "Oh, my dear Florimo, how satisfied I am! What bounds we have exceeded, and with what success? I still am trembling from the impression that this success has had on my morale and my physique. The impression was such that at some moments I am like a fool."

Reading these accounts, I felt strongly that my response to Bellini coincided with Bellini's response to Bellini performed. He wanted an art that would make audiences "weep, shudder, and die" through its musical vocalization. After the violent representation of artistic genius, after the revolutionary fervor of an art that dares to be "natural," to pull down the vanity of ornamentation in exchange for pure, passionate human expression, what more may an audience do than feel tears, terror, and the aesthetic equivalent of death? But after that "death" comes the realization that it, after all, is not real, is not actually death, but is only art—magic—the imitation and representation of an imaginary state of desire. We are not dead; we are alive: in relief, in splendid, ecstatic appreciation of what we are (alive) and what we are not (dead)—thus in spirited recognition of our ability to pull ourselves back from the abyss, we let out a rage of applause, insane approval, demented shouts and hosannas. And, of course, we feel a bit like fools. In the audience, we feel foolish for allowing ourselves the cathartic ritual of excess. And, I supposed, Bellini, as an artist, felt a bit of a fool for the humble and brief realization that he (with all his flaws and hubris) had been capable of creating something that so scaled (if only for a moment) the limits of our humanity.

I Puritani is an Italian opera based on a French play about the English civil war: it is thus about all war—and its abolition. Elvira, the daughter of the Puritan commander of a fortress in Plymouth, had been obliged to marry a Puritan leader whom she does not love. Her uncle persuades her father to allow her to marry the man she loves, Lord Arturo Talbot, a Stuart Royalist sympathizer. In the castle, on the eve of their wedding, Arturo discovers the queen of the deposed and executed King Charles I. He realizes that his personal desires are secondary to the call of history: he must save her from the cruel fate of execution. Passing the queen off as his bride-to-be, he escapes the fortress. Elvira believes she has been betrayed by Arturo and lapses into insanity. Arturo is condemned to death by Parliament. Elvira dives more deeply into madness as the countryside prepares for another onslaught of warfare and battle. Three months later, Arturo returns to the fortress and the two lovers, recognizing their authentic voices through their disguises, are reconciled, and this rapprochement reestablishes Elvira's sanity. The Puritan forces apprehend Arturo and seize him for his execution. Elvira, brought back to sanity, perceives in a perilous instant the deep and profound madness of which humans are at times capable: the realization drives her back to derangement. Is life itself sane or insane? Even today, a century and a half later, there is no easy answer: we hover in abeyance. It is at this moment—as he faces his own death and sees before him the wounded image of the woman that he loves above all else in life—that Arturo sings "Credeasi misera," the piece that was subsequently used in the 1835 memorial ceremony for Bellini.

In cadenced, expressive tones, Arturo sings out: "Poor miserable one! She believed that she had been betrayed by me. Her life was dragged out in such torment." Facing death, Arturo concerns himself with what matters most: love. He scoffs at his impending execution and emphasizes his enduring love for Elvira: "Now I defy the thunderbolts. I scorn and despise my fate if only I may die at your side." The voices of the Puritans call out for vengeance to be carried out on the traitor, Arturo. This is a premium tragic moment: the two lovers bid each other farewell and the hero is taken to his execution. But Bellini's purpose is to transcend the accepted expectations of artistic forms. He resists the typically exalted "tragic death." Arturo protests that the clamor for his death has denied him the ability to achieve final reconciliation with the woman he loves. She has been berating herself that he is now to die on account of her earlier mistaken belief that he had betrayed her. A multitude of voices are sounding, pulsating, resounding. Above them all, we hear, straining into its high, most emotional register, the voice of Arturo: "Stop! Stand aside! Cruel ones, cruel ones! *Crudeli, crudeli!*" All voices cease.

Arturo continues: "She is trembling, she is expiring. You perfidious spirits are deaf to all mercy. For a single moment, ah, restrain your wrath. Then sate yourselves with cruelty." In response to his words, the dissenting voices resume. Arturo is compelled to repeat his protest in the most urgent, poignant manner possible. *"Ella è tremante"* (She is trembling), he sings out, *"Ella è spirante"* (She is expiring): on the ultimate syllable of *spirante,* Arturo ascends to the high D-flat above high C. This is a remarkable sound, not merely for its high pitch and resonance but because it rises up, up the scale, toward heaven, at precisely the moment that the words bore into the earth. Typically, notes evoking death return down the scale, grounding them, so to speak, in a mortal descent to the lower registers. But Bellini's Arturo refuses to recognize this death, denies its ability to enter his consciousness. The brutes around him are treacherous because they are deaf to all mercy and human dignity. In an exalted irony, he calls on them to cease and desist for *"un solo istante"* (a single instant)—*then,* thereafter, they may satiate themselves with their cruelty. But Bellini's Arturo knows that one single instant is all that is necessary for humans to achieve self-knowledge: in that split second, mercy and restraint may enter the human soul. The quality of that redemption is absolutely unlike what humans are used to on this strange and glorious earth. Following the word *frenate* (restrain), Arturo on the word *poi* (then) ascends to the note of high F above high C, above the high D-flat he previously reached. Thus, the words say: stop for a single instant; then, you may proceed with your brutality. The music says: "restrain." Then; *then:* you will hear sounds never before heard; you will hear celestial harmonies never previously known.

The high F that Arturo sings is the highest known note in the tenor repertoire. It rises up beyond all sense of reasonable limitation. It takes the human voice outside itself into an ineffable and sublime dimension. It says that which is impossible to say. Bellini's music instills in us a moment that—in its ascendant grandeur, in its exalted aspiration toward that which is immortal and without end—transcends our small and sordid petty desires and characterizes the best of what is our human soul.

At that moment, as Arturo concludes his extraordinary appeal to human decency, word arrives that the civil war is over, the country is reconciled, the guilty are "already pardoned." It is as if Bellini's theme were that the mere suggestion of mercy already achieves it: representation becomes reality; we are synonymous with our highest and best inclinations. Arturo and Elvira sing together: "From sufferings to extreme rejoicing, this spirit is transported. This moment makes us forget the anguish." Elvira soars in song: "Blessed be the tears, the anxiety, the sighs, the moans. I shall rave in the tumult of such dear ecstasy." And with that, with love crowned supreme, the opera ends. It has taken us from "sufferings to extreme rejoicing" and has "transported" our spirit. Bellini's great art seeks to make us "forget the anguish." It is an art of tears, anxiety, sighs, and moans: it raves in the tumult of its dear ecstasy.

Is there any doubt that the Parisian audiences shrieked out their passionate cries of joyful appreciation? At the end of the music, I was transfixed, agape with wonder. The recording had concluded, but the sounds continued all around me. I had some difficulty returning to the humdrum details of my life—everything had been touched by this dear ecstasy. I picked up the dishes and washed them in the kitchen sink. I turned on the television set, went through the mail. But in, around, and through these activities, there was a special quality—a recollection of a small bliss—that remained with me.

On each successive listening, I felt myself drawn not merely to the overall Belliniesque artistry of the entire opera but to the particular culminating redemptiveness of the "Credeasi misera" scene—not least because it was selected by Bellini's friends and associates to serve as his memorial. What astonished me all the more was that what Bellini had conceived was so divergent from the operatic norm that—even today—there is real controversy as to how we ought to perform and "hear" the representation of the maestro's music.

It is known that Bellini wrote the part of Arturo for the tenor Giovanni Battista Rubini, the same Rubini that the maestro had earlier coached and who would later sing at his memorial ceremony. Rubini would have interpreted all notes above G with a falsetto approach—that is, with a tone that originated predominantly in the head rather than the chest. Today's tenors, however, sing high notes from the chest. We typically think of a falsetto tone as having a light, soft quality. Contemporary accounts of Rubini's highest tones, however, emphasized their power and commanding resonance. Thus, it is not clear how Rubini's high F (conceived for him to sing by Bellini) actually sounded. If we were to interpret Bellini's score in the performative style to which he was accustomed, we would achieve a result that would sound peculiar to our late twentieth-century ears. If the F were the only falsetto tone, this would cause it to stand out from all the other notes rather than have it emanate from the preceding notes. On the other hand, it is impossible to achieve a high F tone that is produced entirely in the chest. If we allow that Rubini's high F was actually a combination of head (falsetto) and chest tones, we still do not have a clue as to what proportion of head to chest tones the great tenor employed.

Individual tenors have attempted distinctive solutions. These include actual rewriting of the notes in the maestro's score to lower the highest ones (eliminating the D-flat and the F); singing the D-flat twice in full chest tones; attempting the high F in a light, pinched falsetto; and producing a mixed head and chest falsetto tone that nevertheless sounds more pronouncedly unusual than it would have in Bellini's day. Perhaps it is fitting that each attempt at the "Credeasi misera" culmination leaves one yearning to hear another. What looms just beyond our grasp is the dream of ever fully representing what Bellini wrote: stylistically integrated notes that ascend, ever higher, above and beyond the range of the expected and the appropriate. And this, I suppose, is as it should be.

Is there ever a stable sense of the expected and the appropriate? What sounds "right" for us today as a mode of stylistic elegance would not necessarily be always appreciated in the same light. When, two years after Bellini's death, the tenor Duprez created a Paris sensation by attacking a high C with a stentorian chest tone rather than a light head tone in Rossini's *Guillaume Tell,* our contemporary mode of tenor singing was born, but Maestro Rossini was not pleased. The new sound, he observed, resembled "the squawk of a capon whose throat is being cut." Today, however, the absence of such a "squawk" would fill us with the sensation that something was seriously amiss. Bellini's sense of art was profoundly interactive with his sense of his audience. How they responded and reacted meant everything to him, and he was willing to modify his conception to elicit that shiver from the audience that signified their intense emotional response. Bellini's profoundly human art was dependent on unlocking the nascent humanity of his audience. Ultimately, any tenor whose singing of "Credeasi misera" brings forth our tears, our trembling, and our dear deathlike ecstasy will be bringing forth an exuberant "bravo" from the spirit of the maestro. After all, it was Bellini who described his singers as "angels who enraptured the whole audience to the verge of madness."

I Puritani caused a sensation in Paris when it opened. The opera was performed widely and to conspicuous and consistent acclaim all across Europe and the United States throughout the nineteenth century—and on into the first half of the twentieth. After the Second World War, the opera lapsed into that category described as "occasionally performed with some regularity." And there it has remained. I could not account for this state of affairs. I searched the music shops for recordings of the opera: they were few. On the other hand, operas such as Puccini's *La Bohème* had been recorded again and again, sometimes by the same performers, with no apparent change or benefit in effect or interpretation. It appeared to me that, somehow, the public had lost the ability to "hear," to take in the spirit of Bellini's last opera.

There is necessarily some inherent essence in Bellini's music that is subtle, elusive, requiring a longer gestation period before it achieves its haunting totality of effect. This has always been the case—in Bellini's day as well as our own. His opera most respected by today's audiences, *Norma,* is also infrequently performed—although its signature aria, "Casta diva" ("Chaste Goddess"), is a fixture at operatic recitals. During rehearsals for *Norma* in December 1831, the great soprano Giuditta Pasta refused to sing Bellini's aria because it was "ill adapted to her [vocal] abilities." Bellini had great respect for Giuditta Pasta's abilities. In his mind, he could *hear* the way her voice and interpretive phrasing would make his music come alive: evoke its beauty for the widest possible operatic audience. His challenge was to convince Pasta of what he already knew she could do: *be* his Norma, assume her presence on the stage, sing the song he wrote for Norma to sing. Bellini tried everything possible to convince the soprano to sing that aria; desperately, he struck a bargain: she would study it for a solid week, working at it repeatedly each morning; if, at that point, she still did not care for it, Bellini promised that he would change what he wrote to suit her desires. Just as he demonstrated with Arturo's insistence on "a single instant," Bellini knew that a week's time would be enough for his spirit to enter into the great singer.

On the day of *Norma*'s premiere, December 26, 1831, Bellini received a lampshade and a bouquet of cloth flowers from the soprano: "Allow me to offer you something that was some solace to me for the immense fear that persecuted me when I found myself little suited to performing your sublime harmonies; this lamp by night and these flowers by day witnessed my studies of *Norma* and the desire I cherish to be ever more worthy of your esteem. Giuditta P., your most affectionate friend." She was acknowledging that his music had become a part of her, against her first judgment. It was Bellini's inner strength to recognize that his music required discernment, patience, and a period of inner development for it to wield its most powerful effect on any audience—and that observation would apply to our present-day listeners.

The more I listened to and studied *I Puritani,* the more intense grew my desire to see the opera performed on the stage. When I discovered that the San Francisco Opera had not performed *I Puritani* in well over a decade, I investigated the schedules of other opera companies in other cities. I was excited to discover that the Metropolitan Opera would be performing *I Puritani* in the spring. I immediately set out to obtain tickets and attend a performance of the opera.

In April 1991, my wife and I sat in the orchestra of the Metropolitan Opera House as the curtain rose on Bellini's last opera. As the production unfolded, I realized that Bellini's art did not merely depend on bel canto—"beautiful singing"—but, as he had always maintained, on the harmonious union of word, music, emotional intensity, and drama. When these elements were brought together, the effect was overwhelming. When even one ingredient was off, the effect was seriously deficient. Bellini's aspirations, in other words, were so high, so ambitious, that he counted on every participant, every nuance functioning at the zenith of its potential—just as he had worked arduously ("vomit[ed] blood") to achieve the overall unity and successful interaction of all the artistic elements in his operatic score. What pleased me in this new understanding was my appreciation that Bellini conceived of himself as an artist working in collaboration with other artists. These other creative talents were crucial in enabling the maestro's artistic vision to be evoked on the stage.

Bellini, writing about the problematic first performance of *Norma,* proclaimed, "I like telling the truth as much in good fortune as in adverse." Thus, he would approve of my candid response to the performance of his opera. The Arturo at the Met (to use a phrase of Bellini's in describing a deficient performer) was "a sausage on the stage." He had no feeling, no intensity, no dramatic fervor, no voice: when he completed his signature entrance aria, "A te, o cara" ("To You, My Beloved"), the audience, with the exception of the tenor's immediate relatives, was silent. The Elvira of Edita Gruberova, on the other hand, was the culmination of all I had envisioned about Bellini's designs. Her voice floated, soared, leapt in agile fancy; to use Bellini's phrase, she was an "angel"; in short, she "raved in dear ecstasy": she sang a paean of glory to the spirit of the maestro who spoke through her voice.

In the giddy moments after the wild applause had finally concluded, I thought about how wonderful Gruberova had been, how skilled had been the conducting of Richard Bonynge, what joy and delight I had felt to see and hear Bellini's opera. But how much greater still would the opera be with a tenor of the brilliance and artistry of Alfredo Kraus as the Arturo to Gruberova's Elvira? Why could I not accept the "well enough" of what I had heard? Why was I daring to conceive of an operatic performance, and a cast, that went beyond the best of what even the Met had been capable on that spring evening? This, I knew, was the spirit of Bellini.

IV.

In August 1829, shortly after the tremendous success in Paris of what would be his last opera, *Guillaume Tell,* Rossini arrived in Milan on his way to Bologna. When he heard that Bellini was living in the city, he made his way directly to call on him. When a servant announced the unexpected visit of the great maestro, Bellini wrote later to his uncle, "You can picture my surprise, which was so intense that [I] was all atremble with pleasure; not having had the patience to put on a jacket, I went up to greet him in shirtsleeves and therefore begged his pardon for the indecent manner in which I was presenting myself to him, justified only by the sudden pleasure of making the acquaintance of so great a Genius." Rossini, as was typical of his generous nature, added "many, many compliments about [Bellini's] compositions." That evening, Rossini attended a performance of Bellini's *Il Pirata;* he returned the following night for what would be its closing performance. Rossini told the composer nine years his junior, "You begin where the others have stopped." It is possible to imagine the immense joy that Bellini felt in this compliment: the greatest operatic master of his day, the man whose success he was surely seeking to emulate, had indicated to him that he was pursuing a unique and original path. Rossini assured Bellini that *Il Pirata* was "full of feeling" and "worthy of a mature man rather than . . . a young one," but its feeling was "carried to such a degree of philosophic reasoning that the music lacks some peak of brilliance." Rather than respond to this constructive criticism by a sincere reevaluation of his musical goals in the light of Rossini's observation (which certainly would be appropriate to the great honor that had been bestowed upon him by Rossini's visiting *him*), Bellini wrote his uncle, "That was his feeling, but I shall go on composing in the same way, on the basis of common sense, as I have tried it out that way in my wild enthusiasm." This was an amazing statement, issued by an artist whose most recent composition, *Zaira,* had been pronounced a solemn fiasco only a few months before. How many other young artists, in the face of their most serious failure, having received a suggestion from the greatest master of the day would yet cling resolutely to their already-charted artistic course? Bellini, in other words, had to be Bellini: his musical compositions were unequivocally *his,* and he could proceed in no other manner than the way he already created his art. Rossini, of course, was most astute, in that Bellini's work never etched out a line that would demarcate a peak of organic "brilliance" within any particular opera; rather, Bellini was always striving for a brilliance beyond brilliance, an eloquence that would exceed what he had already just achieved or what it might be possible for someone to envision—he could do nothing else and yet be true to his own artistic self. When, in 1834, he presented the score of *I Puritani* to Rossini for his advice, there can be no doubt he had decided that Rossini's modifications would take his masterpiece one step beyond. And so it was.

Rossini had been correct on another point that he had observed during his first meeting with Bellini. The young composer wrote his uncle that Rossini "told me that from my music he understood that I must love a lot, a lot, because he had found great feeling in it." It is impossible not to agree with Rossini on this point: such emotional intensity as exists in Bellini's operas proceeded from a deeply passionate and romantic nature. The woman toward whom Bellini expressed such passion (and with whom he was in love for over five years) was originally called Giuditta Cantu, but her married name was Giuditta Turina.

She was the wife of a wealthy silk merchant who was considerably her senior. She met Bellini in Genoa in 1828 at the inauguration of the Teatro Carlo Felice where Bellini's opera *Bianca e Fernando* was debuting. Bellini wrote his best friend Florimo that Giuditta was "beautiful, amiable, and strikingly sweet in manner . . . she received me with such generosity that she delighted me from that moment on." Indeed, he "dedicated the rondo from *Bianca*" to her. Six months into their love affair, he wrote to Florimo:

"In the end, we are in complete harmony, and I am quite the happy lover and go no more wandering about from beauty to beauty." In one fateful encounter, Bellini had discovered the love of his life and a major ambience for his operas: what better fuel to fire the operatic cauldron than an actual life of operatic intrigue? Giuditta's husband had to be kept in the dark, *of course,* and this necessity required an enormity of stratagems, duplicities, and faux chaperones. Giuditta's obligations as a married woman had the effect of stimulating Bellini's most tempestuous emotions: loneliness at their enforced separations, jealousy at her time spent away from him, romantic ardor at the imminence of their reunification. The very rhythms of operatic narrative were incorporated into their relationship. Bellini had written that before meeting Giuditta his romantic affairs in Milan had been unsatisfactory, and this was because, in relationships, his desire was "emotion as well as sex." With Giuditta Turina, he met his match. During their love affair, he wrote six operas: *La Straniera, Zaira, I Capuleti e i Montecchi, La Sonnambula, Norma,* and *Beatrice di Tenda.* Variously, Bellini was a guest at the Turina home in Cassalbuttano, or Bellini and Giuditta were guests at the home of Giuditta's parents in Milan, or they stayed at the home of friends in Lake Como, or else they were "chaperoned" by Giuditta's brother. Over time, Bellini achieved a romantic and artistic balance, a stability that enabled him to compose operas at his most productive pace. He had always derided those of his colleagues who lacked the fortitude and strength of purpose to insist on fees that would support sufficient time for measured composition. With Giuditta as his companion, he composed to his own time signature, not the beat of the impresarios. When their relationship ended, in 1833, there was only one opera remaining for him to write—the opera that would, in a sense, exemplify and justify him: *I Puritani.*

In May 1833, while Bellini was in London basking in the celebratory accolades that the English were bestowing on his operas, Giuditta Turina's husband discovered a series of letters that Bellini had written her some time earlier. The letters gave the lie to the pretense that Bellini was a mere friend to Giuditta or a traveling companion or a loyal friend of the family: Ferdinando Turina had his wife removed from their home and applied for formal separation. The expected behavior, the appropriate thing, would be for Bellini to send for Giuditta to join him either in London or in Paris where he arrived in August 1833. But Bellini took no such action. Rather, he wrote Giuditta of (as she explained it) "his [love] having cooled." He continued to correspond with her but discouraged any suggestions that she might join him in Paris—or even in Switzerland.

Giuditta's emotional anguish requires no explication; she expressed herself with great eloquence to Bellini's friend Florimo: "Destiny willed it thus, but Bellini will not be able to avoid feeling remorse. In Paris, he will find women more beautiful than I am—but never, never will they love him with the strength of the love that I still feel." But Bellini's motivation is intriguing: why did he not send for Giuditta when at last he had the opportunity to live openly with the woman he loved? Giuditta's statement to Florimo is persuasive: at precisely the time Bellini claimed his affections had "cooled," he was conveying the opposite emotional register to Giuditta in the letters that her husband found—at the very least, he only realized after the fact that his feelings had changed. No ultimate answer is possible: many of Bellini's letters were destroyed, and there is no way to know what he was thinking. But he wrote to Florimo, in June 1834, that Giuditta's recent "letter is most affectionate, and if it weren't for my duty to pursue my career, I'd be resolved to take up again the relationship that linked me to her; but with so many engagements, and in various countries, such a relationship would be *fatal* to me, as it would cut short my *time,* and even more my *peace of mind;* for that reason, I shall send an evasive letter in reply, without hurting her if I can avoid it."

Bellini, by his own admission, still harbored feelings for Giuditta, as she did for him. But he believed that the intensity of his emotional relationship would detract from his ability to concentrate on his work and rob him of his creative time and peace of mind. On what was he at work during this period? He struggled to compose an opera called *I Puritani.* It was an opera about a man and a woman who fell in love despite the greatest obstacles; just as their love was to be made official, a misunderstanding and a higher duty resulted in their arduous separation. Is it possible to see a certain situational resemblance between Arturo and Elvira and Bellini and Giuditta? Did something of Bellini's own personal nature enter into his description of Arturo's "Song of the Troubadour"?

"*Tocco l'arpa e suono duolo,*
(He played his harp and sounded sorrow,)
Sciolse un canto, e fu dolor!
(He sang a song, and it was grief!)
Brama il sol allor, allor ch'è sera;
(He yearns for the sun when it is evening;)
Brama sera allor, allor ch'è sol;
(He yearns for the evening when there is the sun;)
Gli par verno primavera,
(Spring seems winter to him,)
Ogni gioia gli par duol,
(Every joy seems to him sorrow,)
Ogni gioia gli par duol!
(Every joy seems to him sorrow!)"

Bellini did not send for Giuditta because to send for her would, in some sense, fulfill the romantic expectations of his day: he would be "writing" in accordance with prescribed aesthetic expectations. This Bellini could not do, either in his life or in his art—he needed to "begin where the others have stopped," as Rossini observed, and as a result, he was *all the more* representative of a primary romanticism in his most essential realm of expressive creativity: his art. The "Song of the Troubadour" is part of Arturo's "Son salvo" ("I am safe") aria that precedes "Credeasi misera." He hears Elvira singing the song of sorrow that he earlier had taught her, and in response, he sings it again—both lovers brought together by the common thread of art bridging their loneliness. I wonder which statement is more indicative of Bellini's pure sense of his soul: his "actual" letter of tactful evasion to Giuditta or his "imaginary" song of sorrow to Elvira? But even as I ask, I know what I take for the answer: Bellini's sense of shared sorrow and transcendent art leads into his insistence on the restraint of wrath for a "single instant" (*un solo istante*): only someone with a profound knowledge of human transgression—including his own—could make such a passionate appeal to human decency.

In Paris following the great success of *I Puritani*, Bellini, in need of intimate friendship and funds, encountered a variety of matchmakers eager to present him with a financially beneficial marriage; in response to the rumors that ensued, he reassured Florimo, "I don't like playing the Don Giovanni or the Don Quixote, and therefore I hope to die in my bed as the most peaceful of men." He was no Don Giovanni; nor, finally, was he the type to enter a loveless alliance. Perhaps he was still more than a little in love with Giuditta. Perhaps his operas—each one featuring a strong female heroine and which he described as "sisters" each to the other—necessitated his chaste, "fatherly" attentions. At any rate, he wrote, in April 1835: "Perhaps I should be enamored of my wife, but I don't think that I shall ever find her as she is pictured in my thoughts." Is that goal ever possible? What mortal being could rival Norma, Amina, Beatrice di Tenda, Elvira? Do we search out objects of love and compare them to an ideal prototype? Or do we allow ourselves merely to love—and discover to our joy that the ideal is now reality? It is then, as Elvira says, that "Ogni duolo andra in oblio" (Every sorrow will be forgotten). For the maestro, the veil between art and life was effaced, and he dwelt—in sublime love—with his operatic creations.

V.

The Principessa Cristina di Trivulzio Belgioioso took great pleasure in the knowledge that her salon was the toast of Paris. Regular visitors to her abode on the Rue de Montparnasse included Victor Hugo, Alexandre Dumas père, Alfred de Musset, George Sand, Frédéric Chopin, Heinrich Heine, and Franz Liszt. Lately, however, she had nurtured the young Maestro Bellini as her special favorite. She prided herself on her ability to recognize genius long before the (how would one put it?) popular acclaim of the audience had arrived. Now, of course, after the tumultuous success of *I Puritani,* Bellini's name was a household word; but the principessa had recognized his preeminence years earlier, in 1828, in Milan, when she had had him sit for his portrait at her Milan salon: in those *ancient* days, the music on everyone's lips had been from Bellini's *Il Pirata.* Now that she as well as Bellini were émigrés in Paris, she delighted in providing what assistance she might in the service of his art. When it became known that Bellini and Romani were no longer collaborating, hadn't the principessa introduced the maestro to her friend and fellow émigré Count Pepoli? And didn't the maestro signal his appreciation of that act of patronage and friendship by telling her that *I Puritani* would not, in a sense, exist had it not been for her resources?

Thus, she was attentive to his circumstances and took note when he had reported, earlier in the month, that he had been "slightly disturbed" by a gastric malady. Nevertheless, on the face of things, he had appeared to revive and was seen around Paris looking into arrangements about his opera box. He had even responded to Mme Jaubert's invitation to dinner. The principessa, naturally, was a guest at that affair, and she was most seriously attentive when Bellini's lateness became an absence with the commencement of the dinner service. When, in the midst of the service, the doors abruptly opened, the principessa had looked up with a smile: without a doubt, it would be her countryman, Bellini, apologizing for his delay in that *charmant* manner everyone found so endearing—but no, a message was delivered to Mme Jaubert, a mere two lines from Bellini in which he "expressed his displeasure at being too ill to join us." The principessa turned to the faces at Mme Jaubert's table. "That worries me," she announced. "That he has given up coming must mean that my poor Bellini is very unwell. He was so pleased about this dinner."

The principessa tormented herself as to what she ought to do to help poor Bellini. Finally, she determined that she would send her physician, Luigi Montallegri, out to Puteaux to assist the maestro. Bellini would remember the doctor: he was from Faenza, was a friend of Count Pepoli's, and had been likewise imprisoned for his revolutionary activities. The principessa recalled that, at her home, Bellini had been captivated by the doctor's stories of his service in the army of Napoleon in Italy. Montallegri would be discreet; he would tend to Bellini's care with all the subtlety and sympathy that the principessa knew he brought to her own medical needs. She made the necessary arrangements.

When Montallegri arrived in Puteaux on the eleventh of September, he found the Levyses frantic with worry. It was difficult enough to tend to the care of the patient, but to have to fend off the patient's caretakers— that was too much! As a result of the principessa's largesse, Montallegri had been able to reassign his other medical obligations and devote himself absolutely to the care of the maestro. In all candor, he was rather concerned about this dear fellow with whom he had enjoyed many pleasant hours of conversation. He was able, by degrees, to establish a regimen of treatment. The most arduous detail had been the removal of the constant distraction of the visitors. Bellini had felt obliged to see his friends (such as that Baron d'Aquino and Michele Carafa!) and this visiting had exhausted him unmercifully: it had to be stopped, and he stopped it. The Levyses were charged with responding to the various inquiries by post and messenger. Montallegri hoped that these measures might enable the maestro to achieve at least a modicum of rest.

At the end of a week of care, Montallegri developed a more serious concern for Bellini's well-being. To be sure, he had seen far worse—during the Napoleonic Wars and in prison—and he was always inclined to maintain hope in God. Nevertheless, he decided that some word truly ought to be sent back to Paris if the condition of his patient did not abate. With the expectation of an improvement, Montallegri opted to employ vesicants— topically applied blistering agents—in order to induce a recovery. It would be a splendid thing indeed if those enervating excremental evacuations might be reduced! But the patient must first, unfortunately, endure the intense pain of the blistering itself. For how long had these arduous lower intestinal evacuations been continuing? Montallegri did not know, but he wondered how—if they had been continuing, as the principessa had informed him, since late August and perhaps earlier—the maestro had been able to function at all. On the face of it, it did not *appear* to be cholera, but who could be sure absolutely? Montallegri had seen a good deal of cholera and believed it to be contraindicated by the longevity of the disease and the appearance of the feces; he suspected, instead, a dysentery of a pervasive nature.

On the tenth day of his attendance on Bellini, Montallegri wrote to Carlo Severini of the Théâtre-Italien: "There has been no appreciable improvement in our Bellini. His condition is still alarming; nonetheless, tonight he has had six fewer evacuations of mucous and blood and has slept a little. The vesicants promise to work, and I await a beneficial crisis from them. With esteem, I am Montallegri." Immediately upon sending off the message, Montallegri felt an improvement in his personal spirits: perhaps this was a good sign, he considered. He resolved to write to Severini regularly. That evening, Montallegri returned to his Paris office to check on his affairs. Profoundly exhausted from the ordeal of fighting Bellini's disease, he allowed himself some medicinal Bordeaux before dropping off to sleep.

Montallegri's examination of the patient the following morning rewarded his optimism: the bowel movements were less constant and voluminous, and the maestro appeared to have rested somewhat. The doctor believed that, in cases such as this, the medical arts mandated that the body be systematically irritated so as to achieve a spontaneous sloughing off of the disease: it was necessary to stimulate a physical catharsis that would be beneficial to the patient. After all, even those untrained in the science of medicine knew the maxim that a "cloudy morning brings in a sunny day"—that is, the body must be antagonized in order to fight off its disease. In vastly improved spirits, Montallegri wrote again to Severini: "The vesicants have begun to bring on a crisis of perspiration. During the past night, our Bellini was less restless and agitated. The slightly less frequent evacuations have permitted him sufficient rest. Montallegri."

The following day—the twelfth of his attendance on the ailing Bellini—Montallegri allowed himself a measure of relief: there was an additional degree of improvement. In the recesses of his mind, the doctor fondled the hope that the maestro would recover and resume his composing: Montallegri had seen more remote miracles accomplished in his lifetime! He scribbled off the following lines to Severini, knowing that Bellini's friends would receive the good news swiftly as a result: "Bellini's beneficial crisis continues. The matter has diminished enormously and the consistency has changed. We hope to declare him out of danger tomorrow. Montallegri."

The twenty-third of September ushered in a change in the weather that accompanied a deterioration in Bellini's health. Montallegri felt a chill in the air and the definite likelihood of precipitation. He knew now that this was no medical skirmish but a war in earnest: he and the Levyses must redouble their efforts in order to save Bellini. On the basis of his patient's condition, Montallegri could no longer be so sanguine that the maestro was suffering from a profound dysentery: cholera could not be ruled out! He focused his attention on maintaining his senses and continued his efforts. During a rest, however, he took a few moments to write again to

Carlo Severini: "The thirteenth day has come, and has been alarming. Bellini passed a very restless night because the crisis of perspiration did not occur as on the two preceding days. I remained with him all day and all night so as to see the fourteenth in. I'll write you something more definite tomorrow. I am, with esteem, Montallegri."

In the moments after the doctor had sent off his missive to Severini, he closed his eyes briefly. He was awakened abruptly by a desperate sound from Bellini's bedside: the patient had lapsed into convulsions! There was not a second to be lost! Montallegri dashed off a note to Bonnevin, the pharmacist on the Rue Favart near Severini's Théâtre-Italien (he knew his French was rancid, but there was no way around it!): "Monsieur Bonnevin, Get this note to Monsieur Bianchi at once and tell Monsieur Severini of the approaching end of the unhappy Bellini. A convulsion has left him unconscious, and he may not live until tomorrow. Montallegri." But what if his French were worse than even he imagined? It was better to write a chaotic communiqué than for it to fail to reach its receiver. The doctor penned across the margin in Italian: "Our [friend] is lost, a convulsion has put his life in danger." There was nothing further to be done but to dispense this last letter to the post and go have a conference with the Levyses to advise them of the urgency of the situation. Montallegri was ready to remain with the maestro to the end, but, in the event that this *was* an instance of cholera, the Levyses needed to be informed of all the contingencies: quarantine, public hospitalization, epidemic infection . . . or else, flight from the premises. The doctor breathed deeply and walked down the hallway. As his steps led him toward the receiving room, he heard the most violent contortions and agitated writhing from Bellini's chamber. Montallegri grimaced and mused to himself that it was not entirely impossible—even now—for dramatic and incredible reversals of fate to occur. Montallegri recalled how inspired he had felt during the maestro's *I Puritani* when Sir Giorgio and Sir Riccardo had together voiced a song of rebellion and gainful struggle:

> "*Suoni la tromba, e intrepido,*
> (Let the trumpet sound, and fearless,)
> *tu pugnerai da forte.*

(you will fight strongly.)
Bello è affrontar la morte,
(It is beautiful to face death,)
gridando: libertà!
(shouting: freedom!)"

That was what Bellini needed at this moment: the sound of the trumpet and the intervention of the Lord.

On the morning of September 23, Henry Greville, a friend of Bellini's, awakened to receive a communication from Monsieur Levys in response to his own letter of inquiry. Bellini, he was told, "having been better the preceding day, his night had not been good, and he was less well, but [Levys] hoped to be able to send Greville better news shortly." Greville recalled how he had journeyed recently to Puteaux: Levys had "assured him that there was no danger, but would not permit [him] to go up, as [Bellini] was forbidden to see anyone." Greville shook his head as he wrote in his diary: "Those Levyses have much to answer for, as they not only kept away and in ignorance all his best friends, but neglected to call in fresh advice."

In another part of Paris, the Principessa Belgioioso awakened in a refreshed state, having spent a night more considerably restful than in many a long while. The note of September 22 that Montallegri had sent to Severini had been read to her, and she had experienced great solace and relief to hear that the maestro would soon be out of danger: how wise it had been to arrange for Montallegri to assume the charge of Bellini's care! At the precise moment that the principessa entertained that reassuring thought, the Baron d'Aquino, afire with earnest intentions, rode furiously toward Puteaux: he had a new approach in mind to see Bellini.

VI.

Vincenzo Bellini awoke abruptly, as if from a deep but distressing sleep, to find himself in his bed—alone, in his room in Puteaux. He called out in a weak voice for assistance, but to no avail. He was truly alone. His brow was feverish; pain wracked his body: nevertheless, he found he was able—for the first time in many days—to sustain a degree of concentrated thought albeit alongside the woeful anguish of his perturbing illness. Vincenzo turned his head so as to be able to look out in the direction of each of the two windows of his room: first, the gardens; next, the Seine—from the two vistas, he ascertained that the weather was changing. The uneasy heat that he recalled as if from a profound dream appeared to be breaking in favor of a cold front. There was a distinct chill in the air. Vincenzo shivered, called out for assistance to cover himself; then, smiling grimly, he realized that there was no one to call. He grasped feebly for the quilt that had been placed at the foot of the bed; after covering his leg and half torso, he gave up in exhaustion.

To mark the passage of time since he was last awake, Vincenzo took mental inventory of the sensations in his body: the fever had not abated—he felt intensely hot and cold simultaneously, as it were. His very skin ached: it felt dry and parched, but also raw as if freshly scraped. Difficult as it was to focus on specific regions of his body in the midst of an enormity of affliction, he nonetheless isolated a mortifying gnawing in the realm of his liver. His entire intestinal area was in agony: the morbidity in his groin tormented him. Despite the open windows, the air in the room was fetid and repugnant.

He thought to himself: you must rise above this . . . ailment. Vincenzo struggled to imagine his Paris rooms in the Bains Chinois: if he could only see them in his mind's eye, as it were, he would, for that moment at least, be free from this dreadful reality of suffering. His body writhed in an agitated convulsion. In the first . . . room, you have a pianoforte and two chairs. The apartment is tiny. The second room . . . contains some of the Italian furniture that you had Giuditta send from her apartment. A bureau, a settee, candlesticks, silver, sheets, towels—all from Milan. In the bedroom, there is . . . ha! a bed . . . and a writing desk. The view from your apartment is . . . charming, looking out on the Boulevard des Italiens: it is possible to gaze upon the operagoers on their way to the Théâtre-Italien down the street. Concentrate a bit more and you may see the four-cornered tower of the Bains Chinois and the prospective bathers on their way to the public baths in the buildings. Vincenzo remembered the time that Ferdinand Hiller had come up to his rooms and he was at work at the piano on the tenor's final cantilena from *I Puritani*. He had not been feeling especially well that day and yet he was afire with the inspiration of composition. He sang then the beautiful D-minor passage that precedes the last resolution. Why could he not work now, despite his pain, despite his weakness?

Vincenzo shuddered involuntarily: he labored to recall how he had composed *I Capuleti e i Montecchi* in Venice during the icy winter of 1830—then, despite his illness, his cold, his fever, he had worked ten hours at a stretch during each day and another four hours in the evening. For twenty-six days, he had worked at this pace, sometimes with stinking breath from his poor digestion. But his efforts had justified him. Vincenzo resisted a swoon and called into his mind the crowd of cheering Venetians, holding aloft flaming lanterns, that had escorted him back to his quarters from the Fenice after the opening of the opera. Once inside and looking down upon the square from his window, a band had serenaded him with highlights from his earlier operas as the masses released ovation after ovation. The sound of their exultation had been like a palliative to him immediately thereafter when his health had collapsed entirely. His appetite had vanished for nearly two months, and then, what his doctor had called a "tremendous inflammatory gastric bilious fever" had attacked him. The physicians in Milan had prescribed bloodletting and then induced vomiting—despite it all, however, he had conducted his correspondence and had completed the negotiations for what would become his *Norma* and his *Beatrice di Tenda*!

The weakness had continued throughout that year, but how pervasively should a twenty-nine-year-old man allow himself to be crippled by a mere malady? "I am still alive," he remembered writing to a friend back then, and he mused that the sentiment was more relevant than ever at this precise moment. Vincenzo had always believed that the fierce satisfactions of musical composition were that much sweeter when taken to the limits of one's mental and physical capacity. But something ominous most definitely had occurred during that winter of 1830: ever since, he had experienced severe gastric difficulties during the warm months of summer. And progressively, Vincenzo realized, his health had deteriorated throughout the year: in Venice again in 1833, at work on *Beatrice di Tenda,* his health, he had informed his friends, was at the "breaking point." But was it not his very weakness, his profound enervation, that had enabled him to set so poignantly Romani's verses to music at the culminating moment of Beatrice's execution?

> "The death to which I walk
> Is victory and not torment.
> I leave behind my chains
> On earth, and verily all pain.
> To the throne of supreme justice
> That yet I see
> Of which I dream,
> All I carry from this life
> Is your abounding love."

No, it was nothing *in* himself, no banal bodily state or sensation, that had resulted in the exquisite beauty of Beatrice's finale; it was his ability to achieve a state *outside* himself—to move beyond Vincenzo to become Beatrice—that had highlighted his composition with an ecstasy that had then swept the audience away into a state of enthralling rapture. The more feverish his trembling, the more fervently he had vanquished his pain—that trivial realm of perception!—to earth, while he had soared into the angelic heights of the music that sang in his soul!

But he had paid a price for these heightened glories of divine creation. Each taste, as it were, of musical heaven would enact a bodily toll on earth. Periodically his strength had failed him and he had spent a week or two in bed recovering his resilience and his determination. But never, never, *never!* had he so completely lost track of the time, the place, the events as he had just now. When had all this commenced? He had been sick, when? When he first began work on *I Puritani,* early in 1834, and he had experienced a crisis as a result of the flurry of activities in Paris: a gastric fever that had overwhelmed him absolutely—but still he had proceeded to work on the opera. How had he done it? He had focused obsessively on the music within him to the exclusion of all other sensations and distractions. But *I Puritani* was done, completed, this was 1835, and he remembered—all at once—that he had written to Florimo earlier in the month: "For three days

I've been slightly disturbed by a diarrhea; I am better now, and think that it's over." Had he written to Florimo since? He could not recall. Nor could he bring to his mind whether he had recovered from that illness: no, the nightmare that now tormented him was still that illness!

At what point in this dream had *I Puritani* occurred? Or was it *I Puritani* itself that was the dream? He remembered, throughout the recurrent intestinal traumas he had endured, sitting in that squeamish place most likely to remind us of our lower recesses, our human failings, how he had insisted on thinking of soaring melodies, sequences of notes that rose ever upward toward the limits of the heavens: only in this way had he been able to work despite his pain, to make of his agony an imaginary thing, a fiction. When he would return from the outhouse, the music he had devised was real—everything else was temporal.

A sudden burst of thunder shattered Vincenzo's concentration. And with this lapse of attention, his bitter and unwelcome affliction returned to his senses vividly in all its wretchedness. He stifled the tears that came into his eyes: weeping would help no one, would do nothing to change his condition, would, in fact, prevent him from flying outside himself in order to relieve his suffering. Think of one of your melodies—those long, voluptuous, lingering melodies that penetrate the psyche and haunt the soul: that is what provides respite from your ordeal! Vincenzo heard in his mind the culminating aria of Amina from his *La Sonnambula: "Ah! non credea mirarti / Si presto estinto, o fior"* (I hadn't thought I'd see you / Dear flower, perished so soon): Giuditta Pasta had created that role for him, and the majestic Rubini had originated the tenor role of Elvino. Pasta had been so heavenly, so exquisite, that he all but died along with the audience. He, Pasta, and Rubini had been called to the stage for encores (Was it twelve, fifteen, or twenty times?) and he had been overcome with an intensity of joy that had overtaken his physical senses and transported him to a world of cherubim.

The sweeping acclaim for *La Sonnambula* reminded Vincenzo of the waves of applause and tumultuous excitement that had greeted *I Puritani*. The wondrous Pasta had not been Elvira, however; instead, there was the quartet of incomparable singers—Rubini, Giulia Grisi, Tamburini, and Luigi Lablache—that had driven the Parisians to the summit of human enchantment. After the dress rehearsal, he remembered writing to Florimo, "I never felt more pleased in all my life." Following the celebrated opening, he again wrote Florimo, "Lablache sang like a god, Grisi like a little angel, Rubini and Tamburini the same."

Vincenzo felt safe and secure in the refuge of these captivating memories. ("*Son salvo, alfin son salvo.*") He closed his eyes in momentary respite. All at once, the painful demons returned: his body was convulsed with excruciating pain. Oh, no! It was as if he were his own creation, Arturo, prevented from enjoying the peace of his loved one and being pursued by his frightful enemies: "*Ancor di me in traccia! Oh Dio! Ove m'ascondo?*" (Still on my trail! O God! Where shall I hide?). These invisible specters— these hellish apparitions—had invaded his consciousness: they overcrowded his thoughts, they drowned out his delicate songs. "*Arrestatevi, scostate! Crudeli, crudeli!*" (Stop, stand aside! Cruel ones, cruel ones!)

"*Egli è tremante. Egli è spirante!*" (He is trembling. He is expiring!) Vincenzo looked around the room as if to trap the deathly spirits that surrounded him: "*Anime perfide, Sordi a pietà*" (Perfidious spirits, Deaf to all mercy). The pain, the pain: it was unendurable! Deny it, forbid it entry: "*Un solo istante, Ah, l'ire frenate*" (For a single moment, Ah, restrain your wrath). He could hear, floating, hovering above him, that sublime, ethereal high F that Rubini had emitted angelically over the Paris opera house. That celestial moment had seemed to sustain itself for an eternity—"*Poi . . .*"

. . . *Then* I reached over to help my wife, returning after a long evening of work, into the house with her briefcases. "I know it's late, and I know you must be very tired, but would you listen to this music—just for a moment?"

I switched on the stereo and an exultant wave of sound flooded over us. Awash with the sublime harmonies, we turned to each other and heard Giorgio and Riccardo sing out: "*Esultate!*" (Rejoice!). Then, we could hear Elvira and Arturo sing:

> "*Dagli affanni al gaudio estremo,*
> (From sufferings to extreme rejoicing,)
> *Va quest'anima rapita!*
> (This spirit goes, transported!)

Quest'istante di mia vita
(This moment of my life)
L'angoscia obbliar ci fa.
(Makes us forget the anguish.)"

Tired, but uplifted and inspired, we could hear the voices sing: "*Ah, volutta, ah, volutta!*" (Ah, delight, ah, ecstasy!).

Deeply moved, both of us were in tune; both of us could hear as one.

In the same instant, we said to each other: "*This* is Vincenzo Bellini."

CREATURES OF THE MIND

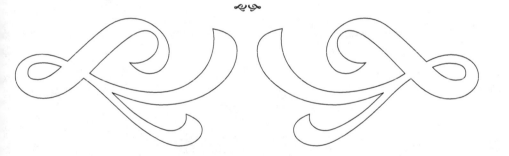

"In the end, we are dependent
Upon creatures we have made."

— GOETHE, *FAUST, PART 2, ACT 2*

Truth, so it is said, came from a well. What kind of well? An inkwell? What difference does it make? With your permission, *voilà!* here I am before you: *La Muse,* The Muse, one of the nine daughters of Zeus and Memory. Usually, I don't employ my Christian name, principally because for a great many years, especially during my Greek and Roman incarnations, I was not a Christian. But since my father is long deceased, or else sleeping the sleep of the formerly virile, and since my mother is invisible to the current younger generation and has not been a presence on earth for an eternity (I, of course, as The Muse, am still in touch with Mother Memory!), and since names are of great significance to what I am about to tell you, I shall confide my own to you: M. (for "Marcia") Muse, derived from the male Latin name Marcus, or Marc—possibly meaning "hammer," a reworking (some might say) of the name of Mars, the god of war. It may be said of me at least that I am decisive and that I persevere in my desires. (Also, I may be said to inhabit figurally both male and female forms: note the ambiguous "M.") According to Edith Hamilton, my voice is "lovely beyond compare." (I agree with her, naturally, but it is so much more seemly to cite the praises of another, don't you agree?) I am also charming, talented, and beautiful. Please, do not hate me because I am beautiful: I have no control over it whatsoever—it is my nature.

That is the truth, direct from the well. I know this because I have been a close associate of Apollo, the god of truth and light (although he, too, is dormant in these peculiar times) and am still possessed of my memory. I remember that Hesiod, a Greek back in the eighth century who lived near one of our mountain residences, always said that the muses "are all of one mind, their hearts are set upon song and their spirit is free from care. He is happy whom the Muses love. For though a man has sorrow and grief in his soul, yet when the servant of the Muses sings, at once he forgets his dark thoughts and remembers not his troubles." Lovely words, Hesiod, most becoming and astute.

I should like now to tell all of you about my great friend Green whom I love. You may have noticed that I refer to him by his surname rather than his given name even though I love him. This is because I am ageless: eternally youthful and yet a sublime manifestation of the wisdom of all eras. I decry this trendy tendency to achieve instant informality and intimacy by means of the given name! You, for instance, may refer to me as "The Muse." Even though I have favored you with my given name, I stipulate that you refer to me more formally, as it were, not out of any trace of disapproval or arrogance but rather out of a sense of appropriateness or self-respect: *amour-propre,* if you will. My great friend Green is a poet and musician. He dwells among notes and letters, inkwells and staff signs. Someday, but not today, he will write the book that you are now reading; he will dedicate it to me and cover himself with my praise and the absolute happiness that it brings. Right now, however, he appears forlorn, rather seedy, perhaps washed-up. Previously fastidious, he has grown a beard. He spends much of his time among the wine casks and beer barrels. For example, I have seen him, a classically trained poet and musician, abiding in a tavern devoted to the highly contrived representation of the late years of the previous century's previous century (when I was more prominently esteemed!). In this tavern, near the Civic Center in San Francisco, he does not create poems or songs but rather ingests a strange brew called "Irish coffee" in a subterranean room surrounded by the desolate and the homeless. I have witnessed him, in dissolution, smile in nihilistic pleasure as a sumo wrestler at this tavern croons the songs of a Mr. Cantor and a Mr. Jolson. He is under my protection and yet I am urgently concerned.

Much of his difficulty may be derived from his reluctance to name names appropriately. The name bestowed upon him is the name that appears on the jacket of the book you now hold: Geoffrey Green. "Geoffrey," a Teutonic form of "Godfrey," meaning "God's peace." Surely, this godly peace will enfold him by producing art, by following his Muse, by devoting himself to his calling. In this way, he justifies his name and becomes worthy of it: the verdant peace of God. But while he has called himself "Geoffrey" intermittently throughout his life, he has not consistently employed this given name. Instead, under the dictates of this oppressive and widespread informality, he has allowed himself to be called (even *suggested* that he be called) "Jeffrey," a bastardization of "Geoffrey," as well as "Geoff," and "Jeff," diminutives of that worthy appellation. These nomina dubia, these nominal names, serve merely to confirm him in his inclination to be a diminished, smaller, or more casual version of the destiny preordained by his cognomen.

Of late, my great friend has become infatuated with the facile charms of a demon, the singer Floria Tosca, an entertainer at the Met Lounge in New York, originally from Rome . . . or Milan. She has recently relocated to San Francisco where she sings in a new Italian/Persian club called Lotfi's Tavern. (At this latter location, she has been known to utilize the sobriquet "La Stella," indicating, presumably, that she is some sort of luminary.) Green's enthusiasm for this witch, doubtless inflamed by the beer and wine he has consumed, is particularly excessive when she sings the part of Donna something-or-other, Donna A., or—yes!—Donna Anna from the divine Mozart's *Don Giovanni*. The crowd cheers her (and my great friend is among them) when she steps out on the stage and Mozart lends his strains to her fiery lies and deceptions. What kind of Muse am I? Am I a madwoman to desert the heavenly realms in order to compete with the starry eyes of a superficial beauty over the love of a fool? Vanish, you Siren, phantom of the opera, ghoul of his nights! You pursue my great friend in vain, for I shall shatter the chains that bind him to your pseudocharms.

Whether I am Muse or Fate, I shall rescue his heart from that harpy who wears him as if he were a trophy or a jewel (albeit tarnished). Destiny decrees that at this hour Green must choose between our two loves: La Stella or La Muse! Will he belong to my rival or will he be forever mine? I confess that I am unable to pine away on the sidelines: I must enter into the fray! I shall transform myself by assuming the guise of the faithful Nicklausse—a variant of Nicholas, a name reflecting my Greek origins, meaning "the people's victory." But hold your hosannas: my victory will require struggle and strategy. You, invisible spirits who hover over these graven images, assist me in my work! I shall adopt the facade of a loyal scholar, Marcus Nicklausse, a real trouser role, and so guide the wayfaring heart of my great friend toward his Muse and his Fate and his destiny!

With your aid and approval, you, the people, shall achieve your blessed victory: Green, through his dissipation, will grope his way to the redemptive choice—*me!* At this very moment, Green labors to write a story about E. T. A. Hoffmann and his tales and the opera by Jacques Offenbach, *Les Contes d'Hoffmann,* that dramatized and evoked those stories. But lo! a shadowy presence intrudes on these creative enterprises. Whether this countenance lurks within my great friend's spirit or exists as some alien ambience outside his noble soul, I know not. (My godly powers are intact, but festering pollutants within the air cloud my fabled abilities to anticipate the future.) Look: there he is—adrift among the kegs and bottles, in the Nuremberg Room of Lotfi's Tavern next to the opera house. Kind kegs and bottles, casks and barrels, I invoke you! Assist me in my labors: your intoxication brings oblivion. Fare thee well: when next we meet, I shall be Nicklausse and you may not know me. *Adieu.*

♫ ♫

Hello, my friends! A stool, a glass, and a pipe! Be quiet, damn you! I've gotten up on the wrong side of the bed, alas, into a world blasted by an icy north wind! Nicklausse, why are you singing that damned snippet from Mozart's *Don Giovanni: "Notte e giorno mal dormire"* ("No rest by night or day")? Ah, that's the opera being performed next door, at this very moment, by . . . This evening, a little while ago, at the theater, I thought I saw . . . But forget it! What's the point of reopening an old wound? No, Nicklausse, I'm not having a nightmare! Life is short! We must brighten it up as we go. We must drink, sing, and laugh in fortune's face . . . for tomorrow we cry!

What's that? You'd like to hear the sorry story of that moral dwarf? Very well, then! But I've changed it: poetic license and such—from a clod called "Rock" to "The Almond Tree" to (its German translation—I am multilingual, you know!) "The Song of Mandelbaum!" It's another version of the well-known favorite I've performed often for you, "The Song of the Rat"—from old country to new, from East Coast to West, from northern California to south: an old-fashioned assimilation. You shall all be my chorus.

Once upon a time, at a sunny, sylvan court of high renown,
    (A court of high renown)
There was a sawed-off runt by the name of Mandelbaum!
    (By the name of Mandelbaum!)
The top of his head was bald like a clown,
And his lies were notorious all around town. Around town!
Voilà, voilà, Mandelbaum!

He picked his ethics up at the lost and found.
    (His ethics from the lost and found.)
Like Byron's Don Juan, he was known as a whore all around!
    (Known as a whore all around.)
Deceit had elongated his nose like a hound,
And his voice made a hideous, sniveling sound! Sniveling sound!
Voilà, voilà, Mandelbaum!

As for that face, as for that face . . . Ah, that charming face! I can see it, beautiful as the day I ran after her. Like some mad fool I left my father's house and fled across valleys and woods! The dark braids of her hair cast a warm shadow across her elegant neck; her deep brown eyes stared out with purity of expression, and as our taxi smoothly carried our hearts and our love along, so her vibrant, gentle voice raised to the attention of heaven a song of triumph whose echo resounds eternally in my heart . . .

    (No, damn it! I'm not speaking of Mandelbaum, that swine! I speak of her! Uh, no one! Nothing! No, my mind was wandering: it was nothing, nothing, confound it! And Mandelbaum is a more valuable fiction, grotesque and misshapen as he may be!)

When he had talked too much with ingenues uptown or down,
    (Ingenues uptown or down,)
What a sight it was to see his clothes all in a mound!
    (His clothes all in a mound!)
Just like sordid rabbits rutting around,

And his voice made an unctuous, sickening sound! Sick sound!
Voilà, voilà, Mandelbaum!

Do you see, my friends, that I am still able to entertain you with my great artistic stories? And now, for my reward: Lotfi, Lotfi, once more for me, yes, fill it again, this time with feeling! But I have more serious business at the moment than these absurd, meandering tales. I am in the midst of a grand conception—perhaps the most significant of my career: it will justify me as a great artist and it will pull me out of the sewer of my temporary insignificance. I refer to my Hoffmann project!

Ah, yes! My majestic fictional dramatization of the persona and stories of the great German romanticist E. T. A. Hoffmann, including the opera about Hoffmann and his stories by the French composer Jacques Offenbach. Friends, you may recall that I have always been concerned with questions of: What did that author mean by such a passage? What significance does that melodic theme have to the composer's design or conception? Are we able to discern in any reliable way what the creator may have meant? Such meditations were thrust upon me at an early age when I learned the details about how I had received my middle name.

I had always been told that my middle name had been given me by my maternal grandfather. This man had himself been duly named in the distant land of his birth; but during a severe childhood illness, his mother had prayed to God that if her son survived his ordeal, she would name him anew, this time in praise of God's mercy. When this grandfather with the new given name emigrated to the United States, the immigration agent could not read his surname properly and thus issued him an entirely new and different surname. Thrice named, toward the end of his life, in his adopted country, my grandfather was asked by his dutiful daughter to assign a middle name to her firstborn son. Decisively, and with no hesitation (his mind made up, his conception clear), he informed her of his decision as to my middle name: "Denny."

In those distant, formal times, it was believed that a name ending in *y* (for instance, Willy, Billy, Jimmy, Teddy, Harry, etc.) was itself a diminutive for a proper formal given name. It was assumed by my parents, then, that my grandfather, an expert in names, a grand master of names, had issued me the diminutive "Denny" to stand for the actual, formal name, "Dennis"—"Dennis," from Dionysus, the Greek god of wine, Saint Denis being the patron saint of France. (Lotfi, if you will? Another bottle of this superb Châteauneuf-du-Pape! Thank you, my friend; put it on my bar tab.) It will be clear, I trust, how aptly my grandfather assigned me a name that fits my current nature: I *am* my name, if you will, and it is for that reason that I expressly have my closest friends—all of you, for instance—refer to me by my middle name, "Dennis," a name of the highest intimacy since I never use it when I sign any of my stuff.

Imagine the shock and dismay of my parents when, having filed the papers that named me, they brought me over to meet the patriarch who was responsible for my middle name. They held me up, a beaming, bouncing baby boy, for this veritable Adam to survey among all the animals he had named. "So this is Denny," he smiled. "Yes," my parents replied, "Geoffrey Dennis." My grandfather frowned; his expression changed profoundly: "Dennis? What's with this 'Dennis'?" (He was mightily displeased.) "Dennis, from Denny," my mother offered, "exactly what you told us." My grandfather boomed: "Denny! I named him Denny! For Den-iel!"

All at once, my grandfather's meaning was evident; his authorial intention had become clear: his only grandson was to be named "Daniel," a biblical name taken from one of the great prophets, Daniel, meaning "God is my judge"! Could my grandfather's aesthetic spirit be made more obvious? He had not been consulted as to my first given name. Now, in the matter of the only name over which he had say-so, his design was stentorian: an elderly man, in poor health, presented with the only male grandchild he would ever know, inscribed his personal, authorial touch on the second given name of that boy, your humble servant—"God is my judge." The extensions of this sentiment are not obscure: who are you to judge me? God is my judge! Or: what do you know as to what I am doing, or making, or creating? God is my judge! This lad, his grandson, was to walk through this earth with an attitude toward life endowed by his grandpapa—an attitude that provided for colossal self-confidence, inner direction, and steadfastness of purpose. What a gift to bequeath to an individual! Friends, foes, *this* is who I am! I stand before you—Daniel: God is my judge!

Whoops! But what was I named by my parents (who were operating, all the while, on their sincere interpretive understanding of what they be-lieved to be my grandfather's authorial intention)? Dennis. A variant of Dionysus, pagan god of wine. From "God is my judge" to "hooray for wine"? A numerologist of my acquaintance confided to me his theory that one is, one becomes, one's name. It is clear that my second given name has exerted an influence on me that has brought me to my current Diony-sian state: Am I not irrational, orgiastic, or ecstatic enough to warrant my name? Is this the name that launches a literary work of grand conception? If I never use the name Dennis, am I not nevertheless "dennised" forever?

But look here: Is it not blatantly obvious that somehow, somewhere, a mistake has been made? Has it not been sublimely revealed that it was my grandfather's creative intention to name me Daniel? Is it not clear that, on some primal, basic, inherent level, I am Daniel? This is the truth! This is my truth! God is my judge! But why do all of you persist in calling me Dennis? Does the mistaken, coincidental act of writing down my misinter-preted moniker constitute some act of making or shaping that transcends my own ability to change as a person? Are you, by calling me Dennis, asserting that you prefer me as Dennis (rather than Daniel), even as you know that I was (by design, by intention) meant to be Daniel? Knowing that I am Daniel, why do you refer to me as Dennis? Is it that you, too, are fond of wine? Or is it that you prefer not to think about being judged by your immortal creator?

(I am afraid that, in the midst of explaining my Hoffmann project to all of you, I may have become a touch overwrought. Is it not ever so when an artist is involved with the object of his creations? Did not Flaubert say of his most famous creation, *"Emma Bovary c'est moi"*?)

I confess it! I am ineluctably attracted to the figure of E. T. A. Hoff-mann! I am fascinated by that author-composer-critic who was christened Ernst Theodor Wilhelm Hoffmann on the twenty-fourth of January 1776. But it is not Ernest Theodor Wilhelm Hoffmann—E. T. W. Hoffmann—who fascinates me. I am absorbed in the example of E. T. A. Hoffmann—that is, Ernst Theodor Amadeus Hoffmann, the name that he named himself in 1804. What is involved in Hoffmann's change of name? In 1804, Hoffmann decided to change his third given name from Wilhelm—the Teutonic form of "William" (meaning "willful helm or helmet: resolute protector")—to Amadeus—as a sign of tribute to his favorite composer, Wolfgang Amadeus Mozart ("Amadeus" derived from the Latin nominative "Amadis" or "Amade," and meaning "beloved of God"). At a certain point in his career, then, Hoffmann determined to cast aside his nominal protection—his helmet, bestowed upon him from birth—and place himself in the realm of ethereal beauty: he chose to create art, to walk down a road that would enable him to be "beloved of God." Is there any question but that it is easier to waltz through life as a Wilhelm (armed with a helmet) than as an Amadeus? Who, after all, gives a break to the "beloved of God"? When Hoffmann changed his name, he created himself in a very real sense. To say the least, he changed the way in which his meaning would be named. He exchanged the military protective helmet for the protection of God. How many of us as artists are able to do the same thing? I, a Daniel-who-has-been-named-Dennis-but-who-yearns-after-all-to-be-again-Daniel, am filled with admiration and empathy for such an audacious gesture!

Who among us is able to declare what intentions, what motivations were behind Hoffmann's decision to name himself as Amadeus? After all, Mozart did not refer to himself by that name, except (according to his biographer, Wolfgang Hildesheimer [Did *he* name himself after Wolfgang Mozart?]) in jest: "Wolfgangus Amadeus Mozartus." More typically, he called himself "Mozart" or "Wolfgang Amade Mozart," although he was christened "Joannes Chrysostomus Wolfgangus Theophilus Mozart." According to biographer Wolfgang, composer Wolfgang's second given name is not "in the baptismal register; it is the product of the biographers' desire to smooth out rough edges." Did Mozart give himself the name "Amadeus" (rather than "Amade")? Or was it a name assigned by posterity? If Hoffmann wanted to emulate Mozart—to *be* Mozart, in a sense—he already had a doubling of names that allowed him to occupy the same-named space as his musical hero: they were both Theos! Theodor Hoffmann and Theophilus Mozart. Perhaps it is for this reason that Hoffmann preferred that his friends and associates call him "Theodor." I prefer to believe that it was not a coincidental overlapping name that intrigued Hoffmann (or me, for that matter: Who shares my name? Dennis Day? Dennis James?); rather, it was his assumption of an artistic destiny, an artistic calling, that marked his decisive name change: "beloved of God" is an artistic moniker, an appeal to heavenly recourse as opposed to popular resources—like "God is my judge," the individual so named is assuming a level of existence or production that transcends his time on earth, or at least his contemporaries.

I have nothing but admiration for Hoffmann's determination to pursue multiple callings, to be any number of things—all artistically: musician, orchestra conductor, lawyer, painter, music critic, writer of fiction. He was drawn to a variety of affinities, and to each he said yes (or, rather, if we were to emphasize verisimilitude, *ja!*). How different was Hoffmann's willingness to express himself multiply from our contemporary obsession with singular pursuits: specialization, obsession with the particular, the "thing that is not all other things but is itself unique"! (Often am I asked, "What do you do?" and I am forced, like Hoffmann, to take a moment to decide: "Do" in what sense? At what time? Under what circumstances? The novelist Vladimir Nabokov, when he was asked whether he was indeed Nabokov, would reply to his inquisitor, "Why, yes, and what do you do?" I am my name, my identity: I am what I am and who I am—I am all things that are me.) It is perhaps for this reason that Hoffmann was inclined to describe himself as one or multiple characters within his stories while retaining his actual role (simultaneously) as author of the story. The basis for this stylistic device would appear to be located in his multifaceted nature: describing himself as a musician, he is nevertheless detached as a literary man; neither description would include his critical sensibility so, again, he would stand curiously outside himself, observing as if an outsider the blueprint of his own design.

In Hoffmann's story "Don Juan," for instance, the narrator is addressed by other characters as being the composer of several operas—doubling, in other words, Hoffmann's own situation as a preeminent operatic composer. But then this fictional Hoffmann, created by the author, E. T. A. Hoffmann, exclaims, "How would I like to repeat to you, dear Theodor, every word of the remarkable conversation that now began between the signora and myself." To whom does narrator Hoffmann speak? Why, to himself—to none other than fictional character Hoffmann since we know that "Theodor" was Hoffmann's designated form of intimate address! Hoffmann, in his stories, is both character and creator! There is a demonic tendency to all of this. To exist in nonexclusive form—to see oneself again as one's double, to occupy multiple space on this earth: these are sensations that are designed integrally to give us pause. Not only was Hoffmann an expert on doubles, on the phenomenon known as the *doppelganger,* but he is credited with inventing the entire representational device. Jacques Offenbach, the composer who would represent Hoffmann, was caught in the doubling of names in that he was born Jakob Offenbach in Cologne and changed his name so as to make it appear more French. It is no doubt significant that his name means "the supplanter"—that is, one who takes another's place: after all, his opera, *Les Contes d'Hoffmann,* would rewrite the romantic image of E. T. A. Hoffmann and supplant (at least partially) the central role of Hoffmann's writing in our aesthetic memory. The psychoanalyst Sigmund Freud would devote an essay to the uncanny tendencies revealed by Hoffmann's doubles. He, too, was caught in the web of inspired (imitative?) doubling: named Sigismund Schlomo Freud, he dropped the second given name and assigned himself a first name that was both an abbreviation of his given name and a new designation: Sigmund, of Teutonic derivation for "victorious protection."

Friends, you may recall that I am not immune to this demonic inclination. Do you recall the evening spent in my reading aloud to you my story about the tenor Enrico Caruso and that wonderful opera of Puccini's? (You, Nicklausse, will remember more vividly than most.) Well do I remember—in the midst of that "Flood of Memories"—the confused and disoriented response of many of you listeners. It had caused you some dismay that I was the narrator of that story. You, Dennis, commented to me after my reading that I had depicted myself as being even more arrogant and haughty than I am in life. (Do you remember? I thought that you would.) I remarked in response that it was not I who had been depicted as arrogant and haughty in the story, even though the narrator referred to himself as "Geoffrey Green" throughout the fiction. No, I was the Geoffrey Green who had been responsible for creating the fictional depiction of "Geoffrey Green" as being arrogant and haughty! Is it any wonder that I am now obsessed with E. T. A. Hoffmann?

And even then, when does the recession cease? When E. T. A. Hoffmann represented himself in his stories, wasn't he in some sense also representing himself in his life? If Hoffmann was the one who had doubled himself throughout his fiction, who was it who had named him E. T. A. Hoffmann? Wasn't he—even then—standing outside himself as a character? To provide you with a glimmer of Hoffmann's temerity, it would be as if I were not speaking to you at this very moment but instead were being depicted as speaking to you by a shadowy double of myself who was the "real" author of your author. Nonsensical, you say? (Nicklausse, you are laughing hysterically.) I could not agree more. Nevertheless, this is what Hoffmann achieved, and I am, hundreds of years after his death, resoundingly in awe of him!

But what I feel is more than awe: it is a deeper and more profound obeisance. For, you see, my initial decision to become an artist, my early inspiration to devote myself to the arts and creativity, was based on the portrait of the artist depicted in the first opera I ever attended in performance, *Les Contes d'Hoffmann*! This representation of E. T. A. Hoffmann in song inflamed my imagination absolutely: I recall vividly that I was sixteen years old . . . the production was the world-famous Cyril Ritchard staging (Do you remember him? From the TV version of *Peter Pan* with Mary Martin? He played both Captain Hook and Mr. Darling?), and the opera was performed at the historic Old Metropolitan Opera House at Broadway and Thirty-ninth Street. I could not sleep for weeks thereafter, so transformed was I by this aesthetic awakening! (Or was it my preoccupation with that girl—what was her name? her name?—whose leg caressed mine throughout the performance? I was, after all, sixteen years old! What would have made the greater impression on me? Even now, I can see her face, beautiful as the day I ran after her; like some mad fool I left my father's house and fled across valleys and streams . . . but what was I saying? Ah, yes! My first opera!)

Imagine my shock and extreme puzzlement when I discovered, quite a few years later, while researching a story about the baritone Lawrence Tibbett at the Old Metropolitan Opera House, that the final season at the Old Metropolitan Opera House was 1965–66, after which it was destroyed! Thus, I could not have been sixteen years old at this performance of *Les Contes d'Hoffmann,* I must have been fourteen or fifteen years old. (Such minor variations of recollected detail are not uncommon and may well be universal.) But then, when I researched the performances of the 1965–66 season at the Met, there was no *Les Contes d'Hoffmann*.

What in the world was happening? Could I be mistaken about this very crucial, highly pivotal memory? I distinctly recall that this expedition to the Old Met took place as a field trip from my school: it was a dark and dreary day—or was it evening?—so I presume that it was winter. Could it have been the New Metropolitan Opera House at Lincoln Center? No, absolutely not: I recall the darkness of the balcony where we sat, the steep incline of the seats in the auditorium as they viewed the stage—all so utterly unlike the New Metropolitan Opera House. This sense of vertigo I so vividly recall after gauging my sight line from the heavens of the balcony is far more appropriate to an old historic music hall, one that would soon be torn down, than a new, splendidly modern, and illuminated theater such as the New Met.

If I could not possibly be wrong that the opera was at the Old Met, then it follows that I was merely in mild arrears as to the accuracy of my own age when this significant experience took place. I must have been even younger when this extremely influential memory was formed. My research revealed that *Les Contes d'Hoffmann* was performed during the 1964–65 season. (Ha! Aha! Do you see where you end up when you doubt me? I am not mad, but a genius: God is my judge!) The first performance entry during that season was December 18, 1964. The Hoffmann was Nicolai Gedda: wonderful! I admire, I esteem, Nicolai Gedda: how absolutely right that he should be my guide to the musical portrait of E. T. A. Hoffmann! At this performance, all of Offenbach's villains were depicted by William Dooley. I must admit that I have no memory of William Dooley as a singer (although he has a wonderfully catchy name) but I have this enduring impression of the villains—so demonic, so grandly malevolent!

But wait: it is a distinct aspect of my recollection that the opera was viewed in the company of fellow students and not with my own family. Does it seem likely that a field trip for thirteen-year-olds would take place at night? I think not. Some minor detail requires rectification. Returning to my research, I discovered a performance on December 28, 1964, but no, the school would be closed for Christmas vacation: a field trip would be impossible! On January 9, 1965, another performance occurred with

J. Alexander as Hoffmann: who the hell was J. Alexander? Deeper digging reveals John Alexander, but does the disclosure of his full name alter my reluctance to admit him into this formative memory? No, who the hell was he anyway? Besides, January 9, 1965, may still have been our Christmas break, and if not, wouldn't there have been insufficient time for the teacher to have organized a field trip to the Old Met so immediately after class resumed from a vacation? The date is out of the question. But there must be other dates.

On January 27, 1965, Giuseppe Di Stefano played Hoffmann: yes! Of course, he did not have the natural affinity for the French language and repertoire as did Nicolai Gedda . . . and he did have the mistaken judgment to sing with Maria Callas during that disastrous recital tour, but still, he is an important, even legendary singer: didn't Al Pacino play a Di Stefano recording in the movie *Serpico*? I think he did, I think he did! How wonderful to imagine Di Stefano depicting Hoffmann in a way that would so inspire me for a lifetime! But then again, there is still the problem of the evening performance: thirteen-year-olds at night? Unlikely, I should think.

In February, J. Alexander is back as Hoffmann (damn!), but Morley Meredith depicted all the villains (hmmm: Meredith was well known—perhaps he is worthy of inhabiting my memory), but again it's night on the eleventh, and on the eighteenth, and—wait! On the twenty-seventh of February, a matinee performance with J. Alexander—this could be it (I don't care for the tenor, but still, a matinee, the field trip, the Old Met, this could be the reconstruction of an accurate memory)! But what day was that matinee? How the hell do I find out what day it was on February 27, 1965? At any rate, it is sadly clear to me that the Met's matinees take place on a Saturday; would it be likely, even reasonable, for a school field trip of thirteen-year-olds to take place on a Saturday? What teacher would schedule a field trip on a day off from school? Think of the scheduling problems that would occur in attempting to compel student attendance on a Saturday!

When I returned to the performance listings, I discovered that the role of Olympia was played by someone named Jeanette Scovotti; Giulietta was someone named Biserka Cvejic (I like that name: Biserka! What an in-

spired, passionate name for a soprano!); Antonia was Lucine Amara; Stella
was played by a dancer named Sally Brayley—all of this is wrong, wrong,
wrong! Not only are all these singers (with the exception of Biserka) not
in the forefront of musical history and therefore inappropriate for so significant and hallowed a memory, but I recall with scintillating clarity that
all of the female parts were created by the same diva; furthermore, all of
the villains were depicted by the same male singer: this, we were taught,
was in keeping with composer Jacques Offenbach's original intention.
When I rechecked the archives, I discovered that none of the performances
of *Les Contes d'Hoffmann* in 1964–65 at the Old Met were so cast or
performed!

When did such a production take place? Aha: on November 29, 1973,
with Plácido Domingo as Hoffmann, Joan Sutherland as all the heroines,
and Thomas Stewart as all the villains: what a cast! And I could have seen
it: on November 29, 1973, it was Thanksgiving vacation, most likely, I
could have been home from college . . . but then, I now no longer have my
school field trip recollection and this could no longer be my first opera and
we're talking about a performance at the New Met—damn! However, if
we are willing to look backward in time, back, say, to 1961 (still possible
in terms of the overall accuracy of my memory: I would have been ten years
old), we discover that on November 11, 1961, there was a performance of
Les Contes d'Hoffmann that fulfills the stipulations of my memory: the
great, the very great, diva Anna Moffo played all of Offenbach's heroines
(Olympia, Giulietta, Antonia, and Stella), the renowned George London
depicted all of Offenbach's villains, and Nicolai Gedda played Hoffmann
in the Cyril Ritchard production: yes! *This* is what I remember: this is the
stuff of which memories are made! Who could avoid being permanently
affected, deeply moved for life, by such a historic cast? A mere lad of ten
years old, I was beyond myself with the emotional profundity, the vast
enormity of this expansive operatic event!

What's that, Nicklausse? The performance was at night? A field trip
for ten-year-olds at night? All right, all right, there was another performance with Moffo as all the heroines, Meredith as all the villains, and
Gedda as Hoffmann on January 3, 1962! That was during a vacation, so
it could be at night! What? Oh, the field trip aspect: damn! How do I pre-

serve the accuracy of what I know *for certain* must have been the details of my memory? I have it! It must have been a rehearsal! Since it has to have been Moffo, London, Gedda, at the Old Met, during the day, on a field trip, at an early age, we simply must have attended a rehearsal of the opera during the day before the opening. That's it: I remember it all so precisely now—we even studied the details of Moffo's career, and Gedda's previous roles, and London's makeup as the villains (the instructor must have had some sort of press kit or pedagogical package from the Met), and we discussed the appropriate audience etiquette for observing a rehearsal. It is all so clear to me now! My first opera: and I have not been the same since!

There is no question in my mind that this memory has now been salvaged and preserved. Imagine the effect on a young boy of such a momentous experience: on that dark, overcast day in November, I would have been a mere lad of nine years old; it is impossible to overestimate the powerful impressions that would proceed from that initial encounter with Hoffmann's magic, mystery, and mayhem—all musically depicted by the glorious artistry of Moffo, Gedda, and London! To this day, I find Anna Moffo's singing thrilling and inspiring; undoubtedly, my continuing pleasure in the recorded sound of her voice derives from that initial exposure to her virtuoso elegance. But my senses—heightened as they are by my elevated artistic inspiration—perceive a minor impediment in your reaction to my tour de force re-creation of my remembered experience: Does my emotional investment in Anna Moffo proceed from that formative memory, or am I "authoring" my memory—creating it, if you will—to suit the prerequisites of my consummate aesthetic taste? Is my memory so "right" because I have reached a state of sublime accuracy, of historical arrival? Or else, have I succeeded in convincing myself that what I wish would have happened has happened, not because it actually did occur but because I need for my "authored" memories to coincide with my artistic taste?

Part of my difficulty, friends, is that it has not always been easy for me to tell the difference between my aesthetic desires for life and the life I live as an aesthete. Take, for instance, my love for La Stella: who would not love her? She is dark, beautiful, as deep and intriguing as the sea, and her voice is as alluring as a mythological Siren. She is, in a sense, Anna

Moffo—except that she is Floria Tosca. Am I entranced by her charms because she reminds me of Moffo, whose loveliness I found so delightful when I witnessed her depiction of Offenbach's heroines as an impressionable nine-year-old? Or is it that, as an adult possessing supreme artistic elegance of taste, I admire Anna Moffo and thus project my infatuation with her, first, onto La Stella (who, I must admit, bears more than a passing resemblance to her), and second, onto the shape and contour of my most hazy and elusive memories? Have I succeeded in rescuing my recollection of my first opera performance, or have I created a spurious memory—to order, to my precise specifications—to suit the sort of life I wish I would have lived? These considerations grow difficult: why, for instance, did I comment a few moments ago on Nicklausse's singing Leporello's part from *Don Giovanni*? "*Notte e giorno mal dormire*" is what Nicklausse sang as we heard the notes from the opera house next door. But the character Leporello actually sings "*Notte e giorno faticar*": I exert myself night and day. Why did Nicklausse sing "no rest by night or day"? And why did he sing in Italian and then in French? Is it because that is how Offenbach's libretto reads? If so, am I, at this moment, writing a story, living my life, or listening to an opera? How are we ever able to tell?

What's that, Lotfi? The curtain is about to rise for act 2? Aha! Well, what say you, my friends? Do you wish to return to the divine Mozart's *Don Giovanni*? I confess that I have spent a good deal of time pondering Mozart's "Keeper of the List." And there is no question but that you will hear La Stella as Donna Anna sing brilliantly, exquisitely. However, there are considerable delights in other forms of listening: Nicklausse is correct in what he has just said—it is, indeed, a pleasure to drink while a foolish tale is told. It may be that such pleasures are comprised equally of moments from life, writing, and opera: who can say? I have no doubt that much of my life is lived internally—within a profoundly inner realm. There, life itself is perceived by means of writing and opera, precisely as both art forms are envisioned and created from life itself. Is it any wonder that I became enraptured with Floria Tosca when she sang, "*Vissi d'arte, vissi d'amore*" ("I have lived for art and for love")? Do you wish, then, to hear the story of my foolish loves? The tale of my three mistresses—writing, music, and love? Go ahead, my friends, smoke! In the interval between finishing a pipe and lighting it again, you will come to understand this drama of my heart. Before this opera reaches its conclusion, you will be wiser as to this drama of my soul. As you watch the smoke's white cloud rise into the air, I shall begin.

In 1877, Jacques Offenbach—composer of operettas, freshly returned to Paris from a triumphant tour of the United States, in ill health from gout, and deeply concerned as to the verdict posterity might decree on his life's work—began to consider the idea of writing an opera. He was in his late fifties. Despite the great success he had enjoyed in France, his adopted country, and around the world, he was motivated in part by his deteriorating reputation since the Franco-Prussian War of 1870–71 and in part by his receding fortune. It had been said of him that he had authored a series of impressive popular entertainments but nothing of eternal artistic value. Offenbach, a contemporary of Flaubert, sought to create that work of immortal art that would justify his life, transcend his earthly existence, and provide the world with a divine validation of his time on earth.

Twenty-six years earlier, in 1851, a play had been produced at the Odeon that had impressed him deeply. *Les Contes Fantastiques d'Hoffmann* was a drama by Jules Barbier and Michel Carré that attempted to evoke the life of the great German romanticist E. T. A. Hoffmann. Based on several of the writer's stories, the play utilized the conceit that Hoffmann was—at one and the same time—the author and the subject of his fictions. Offenbach felt, one may suppose, a great affinity for the figure of E. T. A. Hoffmann: as an émigré from Cologne, Offenbach might well have identified with the marginal status that accompanied Hoffmann throughout his career and travels. Like Hoffmann, Offenbach had changed his name (from Jakob to Jacques) and his nationality. In addition, he saw himself, like Hoffmann, as an artist of the highest degree of refinement, an artist of such seriousness that his popular success, while welcome, did not do justice to the brilliance of his talents or his potential. His desire was to create an operatic work that would be, in a sense, about art itself: it would concern itself with the career of a writer-composer; it would dramatize some of that writer's stories as episodes of disguised biography; and, situated as these events would be, in the interval between the beginning and end of Mozart's

Don Giovanni—imitating the form of Hoffmann's own story, "Don Juan" (which is itself set during the performance of the opera *Don Giovanni*)—the opera would be an opera that is about opera.

Offenbach had flirted with the idea back in 1851, but one commission or another had always appeared to distract him. Now, desperately aware that there was little time left, he committed himself to the project. There was only one problem: Barbier and Carré had already completed a libretto that they had assigned to Hector Salomon, the chorus master at l'Opéra. Salomon's score was nearly finished! Undaunted, Offenbach succeeded in convincing Salomon to step aside from the project in his favor. (On some level, Salomon must have known that Offenbach needed to write this work, must have known that O.'s claim to E. T. A. Hoffmann was greater than his own—that Offenbach, was, in a sense, the epitome of E. T. A. Hoffmann: why else would he have relinquished a nearly completed composition?) While still engaged in other projects, Offenbach signed a contract for the opera with the Théâtre de la Gaîté-Lyrique. In the twilight of his life, Offenbach envisioned a narrative scheme that would demonstrate Hoffmann's multiple deteriorations—ethical, spiritual, artistic. The opera would be framed by the appearance of Hoffmann's muse: she would be transformed into his friend and companion, Nicklausse, and then reappear in her natural form at the end of the opera. Under the original negotiations, Hoffmann was to be a baritone; the four loves of his life were to be depicted by one lyric soprano; there would be no spoken dialogue. Offenbach launched into his creative enterprise. And then the theater went bankrupt.

Naturally, labor on the opera was delayed. But Offenbach found that work on the opera, despite the agony of his gout and the financial difficulties of his life, filled him with energy and passion. He discovered a source of inspiration in himself, in his own previous creations: just as the opera would be about Hoffmann as an author and character, so would his composition be a grand new work that included in its material tunes and airs from Offenbach's earlier scores. No matter how rewarding, work did not proceed swiftly: Offenbach was forced to take time out for new operettas and revivals in order to pay the bills. He offered the project out, and it was accepted at both the Vienna Ringtheater and the Paris Opéra-Comique;

Offenbach opted to keep the opera in Paris. But changes were in order: Hoffmann became a tenor, the female a lyric coloratura, and the dialogue was spoken.

Following a May 1879 private performance of the work-in-progress in the living room of his home on the Boulevard des Capucines, Offenbach labored to make the requisite changes in the opera. It is possible that he saw in his main character—Hoffmann—an image of himself: a composer who was chronically lured away from his most congenial projects in order to slave away at temporarily remunerative potboilers. How does one view oneself as an artist under such circumstances? Is one the artist who produced mediocre *X, Y,* or *Z?* Or is one evaluated by the work of genius one feels oneself capable of producing—judged for eternity by the aesthetic goals that were nurtured, if never fully attained? Perhaps, by his artistic representation of himself-as-Hoffmann, Offenbach was freed of his own Hoffmannesque inclinations toward delay; perhaps he was merely haunted by his mortality and ill health and the awareness that there was not much time: at any rate, Offenbach was toiling on a sustained project as never before. The premiere was scheduled for autumn 1880.

Seeking a cure for his ill health and the opportunity to work more productively, Offenbach journeyed to Germany. But there was more to his trip than a mere cure: he was also returning to the land of Hoffmann, his protagonist and creative alter ego (perhaps in order to depict him more clearly), doubtless reminding himself of the peculiar French-German perspective in his opera. Offenbach was also returning to his own native land, narrating for himself the story of his own life in much the same way that he was planning to depict Hoffmann relating the history of his art, his life, and his loves. How better to work on an opera about a composer who describes his old stomping grounds than to revisit one's own?

When he returned to Paris, his health had not improved, but he applied himself to his prospective masterpiece with great ferocity—with only a few sidetracks for operettas that he composed simultaneously. Redoubling his efforts for the autumn opening, Offenbach traveled to Saint-Germain in the spring of 1880 to complete his work on the Hoffmann opera. Is it not apt, for an opera about a nomadic composer, that the compositional process would be achieved by means of travel and relocations? When he was not engaged in composing, Offenbach absorbed himself (as did Hoffmann before him) in the life of Mozart: there is evidence to suggest that Offenbach was deeply moved by Mozart and his fate—there is so much to say and so little time in which to say it. And of course, if one devotes all of one's time to saying what one has to say rather than living one's life, how does one arrive at anything to say worth saying in the first place? Mozart solved this problem, struck a balance that enabled him to live and work, and then he died. Throughout the summer, Offenbach toiled on the final preparations of the opera. He wrote to the director of the Opéra-Comique to "hurry up" with the production of his opera: "I haven't much time left." Nevertheless, the premiere was postponed until winter.

Offenbach, however, was an old hand at the complexities of producing operas and operettas. He knew that there were countless delays resulting from vocalists, orchestra members, staging, costuming, scenery, direction, production, rewriting of the score, and the like: it was necessary to cultivate a grand perspective, a sense of the ultimate, a belief that one's opera indeed *would* be produced in one's lifetime. With this confidence nurtured within his sickly frame, he journeyed back to Paris in September 1880 in order to listen to the rehearsals of *Les Contes d'Hoffmann* at the Opéra-Comique. Watching his opera performed onstage, no matter how tentatively, and listening to his music performed by singers and full orchestra, even to an empty auditorium, must have been thrilling sensations for Offenbach. It is difficult enough to create art when the world is interested, is awaiting your vision, but when the world clamors for something other than what you wish to create (operettas, say, when you yearn to produce a grand opera), then it is a vindication of your inner strength to see and hear on the stage before you the realization of your artistic conception.

In early October, still basking in the contemplated aura of his imminent masterpiece, he performed the piano score for several of the major cast members. During the experience, he may have envisioned himself as a Moses, high atop Mount Nebo, staring off with clear vision at the land of Canaan just beyond his grasp: there it was, his opera, his masterpiece, his promised land, the culmination of his life, stretched out before him in perfect order and clarity. Did he hear a voice saying to him, "I have caused thee to see *it* with thine eyes, but thou shalt not go over thither"? And if so, was it his voice, or the voice of God, or the voice of some muse with whom he had never before spoken? Shortly thereafter, surrounded by his people, his tribe, his family, his friends, holding before him his testament, his body failed him—his breathing deteriorated and he lapsed into unconsciousness. In the first hours of October 5, 1880, Jacques Offenbach passed away.

What he left behind was his written piano score, detailing the conception of his grand opera: the theme was the deterioration of Hoffmann—creative, spiritual, ethical, psychological. This deterioration would be represented by Hoffmann's tales, recounted as if they had been actual life experiences. First would come Hoffmann's innocent and starry-eyed fling with the automaton Olympia; then would proceed Hoffmann's serious, passionate, and tragic love affair with the creative Antonia; then the cynical and decadent desire for the prostitute Giulietta—culminating in his stagestruck yearning for the diva Stella. This conception was Offenbach's covenant with posterity. But on February 1, 1881, a closed dress rehearsal of the still-delayed opera took place: it lasted from eight o'clock in the evening until twelve thirty the next morning. Afterward, the word *supprime* was inscribed on the pages of the score: suppress, abolish, quell, eliminate, cancel.

It is not known what those in attendance—Offenbach's family, officials of the Opéra-Comique, select guests and experts—murmured in response to that evening's long performance. Suffice it to say the group determined that what they had witnessed—a scant four months after the death of Maestro Offenbach—required cuts and modifications. Earlier, it had been decided that the act representing Hoffmann's true love (Antonia) should occur *after* his love for the courtesan (Giulietta)—a marked opposition to Offenbach's conceptual design. In this posthumous revision, Hoffmann would first experience innocent infatuation with the automaton, then would fall in love with a whore, and only then would he be ready for the mature love of his life: Does this make sense? Does true romance follow deep cynicism? But it is easy to suppose that those custodians of Offenbach's heritage rationalized that he, too, would have made similar changes: after all, he had customarily made changes during the productions of his operettas, but those operettas were not his designated masterpiece! For those initiating cuts and suppressive modifications, all that is necessary is for them to cultivate a posture of creativity: they are not destroying, so to speak, the masterpiece of the artist; rather, infused with the deceased master's inspirational spirit, they are making the constructive alterations the artist would have approved had he lived to consult with them about the need to make such modifications. Instead of following what they knew to be Offenbach's plans, as he had written them, they applied an "Offenbach principle"—understood only by themselves—to revise and rearrange the composer's designated score. Why bother to transcribe one's art under these circumstances? Why not use telepathy or telekinesis? (I am thinking of an opera from one to a million. How do you like it? Isn't it wonderful?)

At long last, the first public performance took place on February 10, 1881. The act in which Hoffmann wooed the prostitute was eliminated; but since its best number, the barcarole, is a song from Venice, that song was inserted into the act in which Hoffmann falls in love with the virtuous Antonia. The characters who sing the song are no longer in the opera, so we substitute two unknown voices heard through a window. But wait: why would they be singing a Venetian song in Munich, where the Antonia story takes place? No problem: simply change the location of the Antonia story from Munich to Venice. And what about that great duet between Hoffmann and the courtesan from the suppressed act? Fiddlesticks! Merely insert that piece into the epilogue and have Hoffmann sing the same song he would have sung to the prostitute to his artistic muse. What difference could it possibly make? There is as much art to arrangement, to assembling what artistic materials you have, as there is in creating the stuff in the first place. Under these circumstances (the composer dead, his creation expurgated, then shuffled and cut like some tawdry deck of cards) the opera made its first appearance—to great popular acclaim!

What's that? Why, yes, Nicklausse. Perhaps I am becoming a bit overwrought. It would make sense to explain why all this distresses me so much. After all, on a recent trip to Venice, I did hear the gondoliers (citizens, after all, of northern Italy) crooning the songs of southern Italy! And, of course, this musical lapse made no difference whatsoever to the tourists who were their principal audience. Moreover, expecting to hear the musicians in the square of St. Mark's perform selections from opera, the glory of Italian culture, I was astonished to hear instead Viennese waltzes! So why should it so offend me to have Munich be changed into Venice? Why? Because art, for me, is the ability to designate that it should be thus and not otherwise! We do not possess this ability in life: myriads of events take place about which we have no say, no control, no opinion, no alternative. But in art the artist is able to choose: x and not y or z; a over b and c! The artist labors for hours, days, sometimes years, over precisely such choices: brown or black? charge or advance? delay or defer? The assumption is that it all matters—it matters, dammit! The way I represent my choices is central to what I call my art: central to what I call myself. But what do we hear? That the 1881 Parisian audiences, faced with a production of a bastardized Offenbach opera, were enthralled—they loved it! What difference did Offenbach's obsessive, Herculean labors make to this audience? Did they know? Could they tell? Did they care?

Now it might be supposed that this enthusiasm for the corrupt version was peculiar to the French: even today, they express highly unusual—even shocking—affinities (for instance, for Jerry Lewis, Sylvester Stallone, and Mickey Rourke, to name a few). But the opera was performed in its early years not only in France but in Berlin, London, Monte Carlo, New York, and Chicago. Some restorations occurred: for instance, the Giulietta act was restored—but it was placed *after* the Antonia act! In other instances, new material was added: from other Offenbach operettas, from other composers, from mysterious sources. Progressive rearrangements took place: Why the hell not? What does Offenbach care? He's dead! Significant portions of the opera were penned by unknown sources. Offenbach's conceptualization was repeatedly violated. In some productions, Hoffmann was an artist; in others, he was a degenerate drunk. In some performances, the muse transforms herself into Nicklausse; in others, this was omitted. At the end, the muse is transformed back from Nicklausse to her original guise—or not. In some versions, the loves of Hoffmann were depicted by one singer (as Offenbach intended); but in other versions, there were many singers. Ditto for the villains, who might be represented as being one demonic presence—or else not: is not variety the spice of life? In each and every and all of these changes, there was a universal response from the audiences throughout the world: they loved it! Expurgate the hell out of Offenbach's opera: we love it to death!

Still, I wonder to what extent *Les Contes d'Hoffmann* may yet be considered Offenbach's opera: sure, *most* of the music is his, but does the conception hold? If Offenbach meant for the opera to be a portrait of the artist, an evocation of how the writer came to write the tales that we see dramatized before us, of what possible similarity is there to a production in which we smirk at the alcoholic author collapsed in a drunken stupor? If we see Nicklausse changed into the muse at the end but not at the beginning, doesn't this raise all sorts of questions about either transvestism or bisexuality that Offenbach never intended? (Mark you, I am not alluding here to the myth of authorial intention—that is, my imagined certainty of what I think the author or composer meant; I mean instead the specific unambiguous manuscript designations that Offenbach as composer notated.) If, for instance, we know that Offenbach meant for Hoffmann to experience a sort of aesthetic epiphany when he falls into the reverie of inspiration at the muse's direction, how are we to respond when we experience a production in which Hoffmann sings to the muse a song that he previously directed to a whore? It is certain that Offenbach considered the muse to be of stalwart moral character. But if the same song is appropriate to both whore and muse, is this not at least an inadvertent insult to the muse? Is this not claiming that the artist's muse is a kind of prostitute? Surely I am not the only one who sees this? Who is disturbed by this? Is there anyone else who has anything to say? Silence. Well, I, at least, assert that *my* muse is not a whore: I value and cherish my imagination and creative abilities.

But what of the public? What of the audience? Does it matter what they believe? To me, it makes a tremendous difference when Hoffmann is represented as rousing himself from disappointment in love, transcending the physical frailty of intoxication, in order to begin the stories that form the basis for the opera we are witnessing. But audiences, it would seem, observing Hoffmann as a degenerate dipsomaniac, are uncritically approving. What if Hoffmann were depicted as a child molester? Or a drug addict? Would audiences still approve? I cling to the belief that a discriminating audience is able to discern the difference between the elevated and the mundane. But on what do I base this belief? (Recently, in Milan, I inquired about tickets to an opera. "Ah, yes," said the desk clerk, "a good choice. I will obtain tickets for you." As he processed my order, he mouthed, in English, the words to the song playing in the background on a radio: someone named George Michael was singing, "I Want Your Sex.") Is the public so indiscriminate that it will accept anything that is presented to it? (How else to explain the American presidents of the last few decades? How else to explain the success of that fraud, that preposterous Puccini appropriator, Andrew Lloyd Webber?) In heaven, I imagine Jacques Offenbach looking down at the productions of "his opera," saying: "For this I labored during sickness unto death? At what price this glory?"

At what price, indeed? For what the months and years of sacrifice, of solitary toiling despite the gout and the physical deterioration? Quite simply, he had labored to effect the masterpiece that would justify his life; his efforts had been to achieve the transcendent realm in which art is hallowed. But on that February evening of the premiere, four months after his death, observing his work performed for the living, standing among the ghosts and shadows of the dead, the unliving, and the immortal, did Offenbach's specter view the audience's acclaim and hosannas as his just reward? Or was he infuriated by the lapses, the adjustments, the trifling with his grand conception? One imagines a fellow phantom complimenting him on the response of the house: "Is it not a most gratifying reception, Monsieur Offenbach? Are you not overwhelmed by such validation?" And yet one dares to suppose that the faintest shudder passes across the maestro's mien: "One appreciates the ovation, but of course! Still, there is the sense of engaging an apparition that is not my own. Who is this stand-in for whom they applaud? What does this musical composition—this opera—have to do with me? Does it reflect my conception, my design, my music, my arduous creative process? I am troubled by this: deeply perturbed, monsieur!" The artist yearns for glory, yes, but a glory that proceeds from the artist's own work—complete and unabridged.

On the other hand, is there not an aspect of applause—loud, oceanic waves of voluminous sound—that supersedes any and all irksome exceptions one might have noted? Hearing the bravos accumulate ad infinitum—directed at oneself—is one not inclined to become slightly philosophical (somewhat forgiving?) about the disparaging elements that so annoyed one in the moments before the adulation began? Yes, yes, there is that idiotic matter of the discarded act, but still! will you listen to that applause:

extraordinary! Under the charitable hypnosis of the applause, would the shadowy Offenbach not recall that his opera had resituated the location of the Giulietta tale in the first place? Might he remember that E. T. A. Hoffmann's "The Story of the Lost Reflection" (a tale within his "A New Year's Eve Adventure" upon which the Giulietta episode is based) was set in Florence, not in Venice? Would Hoffmann—the *real* Hoffmann—not be as disturbed by Offenbach's change on his work as Offenbach was by the alterations effected on his operatic composition? Furthermore, was it not possible to conceive of an artist's relation to art as embodying elements of a dissipated interaction with a prostitute: that is, taking one away from life, from the world, from one's overt behaviors into a murky alternative realm, stimulating a sense of two personalities—an artistic secret uncompromising self and a mundane public accommodating one? Thus, could it not be said that the song to the muse and the song to Giulietta were—and ought to be—the same song? Could it not be said that when Hoffmann falls over drunk, he is not incapacitated but drunk with creative inspiration from the divine touch of the muse?

And what of the muse claiming Hoffmann for her own higher artistic purpose? When she stipulates that she loves him, is she not seizing him from the world and preserving him for art alone, is she not destroying his other (human) relationships? Is the muse in league with the so-called villains of the opera—Lindorf, Coppélius, Dappertutto, and Dr. Miracle? They are the demonic presences who foil Hoffmann's love affairs and again and again produce tragic results. But—and here's the rub—if all of this tragedy results in Hoffmann turning to art in earnest (as the muse desires), might it not be said that the dastardly deeds of the villains had, as their end, a virtuous goal? If we honor Offenbach's original conception of the muse framing the opera, are we hallowing the role of art? Or does that design craft a dark irony? There is a price to be paid by every artist who puts life on hold in order to live through art.

E. T. A. Hoffmann understood this thoroughly. When he named himself, when he created himself as an artist, he accepted that art was (in his words from "A New Year's Eve Adventure") a "strange magical realm where figures of fantasy step right into your own life." His narrator in that fiction he describes as having "not separated the events of his inner life from those of the outside world; in fact we cannot determine where one ends and the other begins." His narrator declares to Giulietta, "You are my [higher] life! I don't care if I am destroyed, as long as it's with you. You set me on fire!" Could not this apply to Hoffmann and his art, to Offenbach and his art, to any artist and that artist's muse? But if Giulietta is art, there is a price that enables one to be enthralled with her eternally: "Leave me your reflection, my beloved; it will be mine and will remain with me forever." To which her lover replies, "How can you keep my reflection? It is part of me." Art, in other words, ennobles our highest impulses and steals the reflection of our lives.

And Hoffmann saw himself as trapped: pinned between those two contradictory desires. On the one hand, he lived for art, producing literature, aesthetic criticism, music, music criticism, painting, and every conceivable other form of artistic expression. On the other hand, he wrote himself into his stories, inserted himself as a real presence within the shadowy realm of fiction, as if to acknowledge that there was a vacuum in his life, an emptiness, resultant from his artistic enterprises. Time devoted to art is time lost to life. Such time is precious and is achieved by believing in its value: would such a creator advocate the idle wasting of time in order to foment an "art" that would be indistinguishable from garbage to the common audience member? No, no, a thousand times no! In fact, Hoffmann penned a story ("Ritter Gluck") in which the ghost of the composer Gluck returns to inform Hoffmann of the speciousness of modern audiences and performers: "Do you think that the composer scribbled in the overture so that it could be played just as one pleases, like a little piece for the trumpet?" Hardly: every indication of the artist's purpose is hallowed.

E. T. A. Hoffmann, by naming himself, hallowed his purpose and his path. When, on his forty-sixth birthday, in 1822, friends arrived at his home, they found him asserting, "Let me only live, no matter in what condition!" For five months, his wish was granted: inch by inch, the paralysis that would kill him proceeded at a snail's pace through his body—from his outer limbs toward his head. Throughout the ordeal, Hoffmann continued to write, or dictate, or cry out. Much as Offenbach struggled to create art through the agony and pain of his mortal existence, so Hoffmann before him concentrated every aspect of his mortal being into the creation of his art. And in this he was emulating the final hours of his beloved Wolfgang Amadeus Mozart, who died in the ethereal passion of composing his Requiem mass.

Throughout the quack cures, throughout the pain of his purported remedies, Hoffmann devoted himself to art. He, who would never know the oceanic ecstasy of applause that was barely within Offenbach's gaze and just outside his grasp, was nonetheless striving for that word of all words, for that impression that would transport his reader (and himself) outside and beyond his own life. It was on June 24 that Hoffmann lost all feeling in his body below his neck. It is clear that Hoffmann (who wrote himself into so many of his fictions) had become the embodiment of the creative process itself: he had assumed the posture of creative cerebration—nothing else mattered. He commented to his physician, "I shall soon be rid of this illness, now." Was he referring to the paralysis whose abatement he hoped would be imminent? Or was he describing the story he was dictating as a malady of which he yearned to be free? Or else, was he alluding to his life as an illness, a disease that separated him from the state of pure art?

The next morning, on June 25, he resumed the dictation of his story "The Enemy." Did he believe that as long as he called out the words, as long as he created, as long as he wrote and formulated art—that he would remain alive? I think that death was the enemy Hoffmann strove to defeat word by word, page by page, moment by moment . . . until he fell voiceless: he could no longer continue. He could no longer create art: he would not master "the enemy." He requested that he be turned to face the wall. His wish was granted, and he died.

"And at that moment, Theodor, at that very moment there was a knock at the door. I opened it and there stood Hoffmann!" So would E. T. A. Hoffmann follow (in his art) the amazing revelation of his purported death. What does it mean that I think I perceive his Hoffmannesque qualities to the extent that I deign to fabricate such a sentence? I believe I know how he would create the illusion of his own demise. In writing about his death, I affirm his life. The more he changes, the more elusive he and his art become, the more inspirational he remains. Offenbach changed him—put him to music—and in that state of sublime creation succeeded in expressing the essence of Hoffmann and of himself.

And that essence was change itself—volatility, evanescence, the ephemeral. Hoffmann, as a writer, as a critic, as an artist, praised that moment of creative fire when something new and unexpected appears abruptly from out of the complacencies of life and its established forms. He yearned to depict what was not and in so doing represented for us all an enduring element of ourselves; it is best understood by its presence under a myriad of shapes and manifestations—the human willingness, the human determination, to change, to grow, to become more than who we are. Hoffmann's life—a collage of redefinitions, relocations, career changes, personal and professional disasters, creative disappointments—was nonetheless redeemed by the affirmation of his most romantic creation: himself. Throughout everything that happened to him (or perhaps because of it) he was—ineluctably—E. T. A. Hoffmann; and as Hoffmann he remains, a Renaissance man centuries after the Renaissance, a prophet of the artistic mixing of forms; the exemplar for Offenbach of the tormented artist.

Offenbach, too, was in the midst of change. Notoriously popular for his operettas, he was, as a result, notoriously underrated by the critics at large: he wished to demonstrate that his talent was serious, that he could create a work of depth and texture that would nevertheless entertain and fulfill his audiences—he desired, in short, to be someone other than Offenbach; imbued, however, with all of Offenbach's genius. In order to achieve his purpose, he seized on the artistic correlative of the life and works of E. T. A. Hoffmann: he sought to represent Hoffmann on the operatic stage in order to most deeply and profoundly express himself. What was it in Hoffmann that so touched and moved Jacques Offenbach?

From Mozart to Hoffmann, draw a line—a line that was devised by Hoffmann, by his appropriation of Mozart's name. In each case, an artist created art and became himself an aesthetic object. What kind of art is created by an artist who is a work of art? Invariably, this art represents some ideal, mythical, tormented quality with which we associate the works of art to the artist's tragic death. But the artist's actual work is always more striking and more outrageous than that familiar idealized art. It will always and forever be necessary to hear Mozart again, to read Hoffmann one more time—because they are never where we expected them to be when last we left them. They have changed: or have we?

Offenbach's last testament was to extend the line to himself. If Hoffmann's story may be told within the duration of Mozart's *Don Giovanni* (after all, it takes place during a performance of that opera), then Offenbach's story is itself the narrative of how he has chosen to work with Hoffmann and Mozart as a supreme personal artistic statement. Was it not inevitable that he would die before it was completed? What did he leave behind for us? He is somewhere on the line—a mere point; but he is also everywhere on the line—every point, every possible variation of meaning and life.

"And while Green babbled, Dennis, while he told us about his interminable journeys to Munich, Paris, Venice, Florence, Nuremberg, and the like, and all about the bizarre and dubious 'archvillains' who were ceaselessly harassing him and sabotaging his love affairs in these distant lands, the opera concluded and Lotfi entered . . ."

What's that, Lotfi? *Don Giovanni* is over? Ah, beloved Mozart? And what of La Stella? A triumph! But of course! Did I not predict it? Did I not announce to you all the magnificence of that splendid diva? I am compelled to say that I am not only a supreme artist of the page, a writer par excellence, but I am an artist of critical suavity: I am able to sense the divine presence of a fellow artist and intensify that artistry by placing it in an appropriate context. I hope you all will not take this as the ravings of some braggadocio if I confide to you that I have arranged for an assignation with La Stella after this performance. She is the epitome, the consummation of every woman I have ever loved, of every work of art I have ever created! When she sings, her voice fills me like the music of a heavenly choir! My whole being is consumed with a tender, burning fire and her eyes pour forth their flame into mine like glorious stars. La Stella, I am yours!

In the meantime, my friends, let us drink! Here, Nicklausse, why are you glaring at me? Have some more, Ricard: there, that's a good fellow! Another brew for me, Lotfi: thank you kindly! And now, let's sing:

> "Lotfi's a fine fellow, *tire lan laire, tire lan la!*
> We'll mooch him 'til he's yellow, *tire lan laire, tire lan la!*
> We'll make this day a fun day, *tire lan laire, tire lan la!*
> 'Cause the opera's dark on Monday, *tire lan laire, tire lan la!*"

That's it, faster, faster! Lotfi, keep the beers coming as chasers, but let me have some whiskey. Thank you, sir! To your health! And again? Cheers.

And now, just as I thought, I am once again inspired! But wait: who the hell is that? That schmuck over there waving and pretending to be my friend: who the hell is that? He has that same slimy, deceitful face I have been seeing my whole life. You, bedbug, state your business with me! Do you seriously believe that *you* have an appointment with La Stella? What's the matter, cat got your tongue? Or are you waiting around to see if talking will help? Still nameless? Well, well: behold, my friends, the *last* verse of "The Song of Mandelbaum"! (Nicklausse, why are you looking at me that way?) I dedicate it to this schmuck in the corner, this *putz*:

> In life it all comes down to playing a part;
> (It comes down to playing a part)
> And we make our choice to live for money or art;
> (A choice of money or art)
> But when you're a *shtunk* and your mind's full of trash
> Then you find yourself whoring around for the cash! For the
> cash!
> Voilà, voilà, Mandelbaum!

As for that face, that face, I followed it, the music, along a line, a point on the line, all the points, where was I? My mind was wandering, I resume: Voilà! There you have the story of my life and my loves. No, that's not it! What have I done—this fiasco of words and points and lines—naming names, telling stories, what have I done? I have killed Offenbach! I have killed Hoffmann! Who am I? My reflection! I have lost my reflection! I cannot see myself in the mirror! I see nothing, nothing!

Have patience, friends! I will provide you with yet another verse of "The Song of Mandelbaum": let's see, what rhymes with "baum"? *Traum* (*dream*)? But that's German—too contrived, I admit. To hell with it! To hell with "The Song of Mandelbaum"! Bring on that glorious intoxication that wine, beer, and whiskey provide! Spirits of the bottle: I welcome your madness and oblivion! Let us all drink to forget; let us drink to the end of time and memory. Everyone: "Lotfi lets us drink our fill, *tire lan laire, tire lan la;* but the drink he serves tastes like swill, *tire lan laire, tire lan la . . .*"

Enough! *Basta!* There lies my shattered life . . .

FIRST ENDING

Hello again. M. Muse here. It's redemptive choice time. I've got to make my move before that brazen hussy, that La Stella, sashays into the tavern. Would you look at him? Would you look at that Green? I don't know which irks me more, his self-pity or his self-destructive infatuation with that vocalizing vixen! First, I'll bathe the room in a soft, golden light, and I'll cause everyone to be frozen in time. Next, I will direct a single violin to soulfully accompany my exquisite recital. Then, I will address my great friend directly: "And I? I, the faithful friend whose hand dried your eyes? Thanks to me your pain was numbed, and it rises like wisps of dreams to the sky. Am I nothing? May this storm of passions be stilled in you! The man is no more! Be reborn, O Poet! I love you! *Je t'aime.* Green, be mine."

With a deep sense of wonder and satisfaction, I observe my great friend rouse himself from out of his inebriated stupor, and, as if in a state of epiphany, or the ecstasy of inspiration, cry out, "O God! What is this passion with which you sear my heart? Your voice fills me like the music of a heavenly choir! My whole being is consumed with a tender, burning fire; your eyes pour forth their flame into mine like glorious stars! And, oh my beloved Muse, I feel your fragrant breath on my lips and on my eyes! O God! What is this passion with which you sear my heart? Your eyes seem to pour forth their flame into mine! Beloved Muse, I am yours!" His words touch me most deeply and I yearn to reach out and embrace him, but before I am able to effect this posture, he has again lapsed into the profoundest of trances.

I know that this trance only mimics the appearance of the sleep induced by a degenerate drinking bout. What might appear to be Green collapsed in a drunken stupor I perceive as the productive gestation of creativity within his artistic soul. But wait! Someone is coming! I will again assume the guise of Nicklausse and will cause motion in the tavern to resume. Aha!

It is that doxy, that floozy, that La Stella! Look at her: gussied up as if she expected that my Green would ever stoop to an evening with her! Here she comes: silence!

She is shaking poor Green, whose adorable head lies supine on the table. She speaks: "Green? Asleep!"

That dimwit! Naturally, she is unable to comprehend the expansive degree of compositional séance in which Green is absorbed. He has given himself to me and is devoting himself to singing my praises. I shall get rid of her: "No, dead drunk. Too late, madam. But may I direct your attention to that gentleman in the corner who has been staring at you most assiduously since your conspicuous entrance?" It has been said that the rapidity with which one abandons a pursuit is an indication of how insincerely one initiated it: if that is so, then this ribald harridan had no meaningful feelings for my great friend. In a flash, she has thrown him over for that lecher in the corner! And now they exit together, bodies voluptuating in sequence, the *petite dame* and the Mandelbaum: what a pair—two trulls, out for a stroll! Good riddance to bad rubbish!

In a moment, Green will compose himself, tear off the poster of La Stella from the wall, dip his quill in ink, and begin writing, on its reverse side, the story you are now reading. There is nothing of which I am more certain. But at precisely this moment, he slumbers on, readying himself for that cosmic moment. Ahem! Does he not realize that I am waiting, that I desire that he honor his commitment to me? Excuse me, I'll be right back. "Green? Green? Wake up! Don't sleep your life away!"

Now he stirs, at last. But soft. I, La Muse, must especially remember that even with my divine inspiration, the path of art is steep and awkward: but, ah! what views of grandeur one obtains at the peak! As he sleeps the repose of the creatively endowed, the nap of geniuses, I shall confide to you that, from a certain romanticist viewpoint, there is no difference between the heightened consciousness of divine creative inspiration and the heightened consciousness precipitated by the excesses of spirit ingestion. I, of course, assure you that Green, under my spell, is absorbed in the creative structuring of the tale you are enjoying; it is only my camouflage that disguises his authorial efforts. But now, as the villainous scourges who tormented my great friend recede into the distance, and as his nightmarish past disappointments fly upward to the embrace of the heavens, ere he awakens, stretches, and, in the calm serenity of my divine pleasure and grace, begins to write, I send down my mantle.

CURTAIN

SECOND ENDING

"And at that moment, Dennis, as Green suddenly drained his glass and hurled it to the floor, the old wooden door to the tavern opened and an opera employee entered carrying the mountains of flowers that had been offered in tribute to the great diva, La Stella."

Whoops! Excuse my hasty reintroduction: I am La Muse, and it's showtime! Unbeknownst to Green, I will discreetly reassume my guise as Nicklausse. That creature is about to arrive for her insidious rendezvous. I shall address him thus: "It's decision time!" Look at him, looking at me! I step aside and await his redemption.

All of the students cry out, "La Stella" as the strumpet strolls through the tavern. Who wouldn't applaud wildly for a woman dressed like that? I would applaud her audacity, her natural resistance to the evening chill, her imitation of a burlesque dancer, but applaud her as an artist? Oh, come now. Here she approaches my great friend; she is smiling and expectant, but wait! She sees that something is amiss! Green gathers himself up from his intoxication with great composure, like an elegant Foster Brooks; he speaks to her: "It would appear . . . Have we met . . . ? I don't remember . . . The way time flies . . . I'm sorry, I wish I could remember . . . No! Be quiet! Not a word! Stella should stick to warbling! An inane smile might suit you better!" Yes! He has done it: she turns from him in amazement and faces that strange man in the corner; he offers his arm, she takes it! Yes! Yes! I still have it! Green now addresses the group: "There's the great schnorrer who may suit her and be able to fulfill her shameless desires! That's right: get into your asinine limo!" Then, just as suddenly, Green falls onto a stool and sprawls over a table! I approach him as Nicklausse, but I am allowing myself to transform into my true countenance of La Muse: "Poor Green, dead drunk. But cured?"

In my full radiance, I speak to him with love: "Forget your dream of love and happiness, but don't forget me, your friend, your mentor whose hand dried your eyes and through whom your slumbering sorrows rise heavenward in dreams. Is that not something? May all the storms and false emotions of your passions be soothed away! So the man is no more? Then live again the poet! I love you, Green: Put your trust in me! Put your faith in me!" Now to the kegs and bottles, my servants: Come to me! Rise up! Finish your work! Then vanish along with me. I can't hear you: get glugging! "Green, your Muse will put away this strange guise; never again will the past loom before you."

I confess that I am overcome with emotion: this is a supreme moment indeed! "From the embers of your heart your genius is rekindled! Smile serenely on your sorrows: your Muse will comfort you in your blessed suffering." All right now, magic kegs and bottles, let me hear you! Can you sing, "Love makes a man great; tears make him greater"? Good, that's it! Now I want all of you to sing with me as the music swells for a grand finale: "From the embers of your heart, your genius is rekindled! Smile serenely on your sorrows, whatever they may be. Your Muse will comfort you in your blessed suffering."

"Right then, Dennis, as the music flourished to a climax, and the unseen, invisible spirits and voices joined in the refrain, Green arose from his stupor, calm, composed, sober, almost as if in a trance. He addressed the group, but there was no one remaining. There was a swirl of light and motion, but not a body remained in the room. The music became louder still, but I could barely hear him call out: 'I've got it! The *final* verse to my song:

> Whether inspiration for Art descends from above,
>   (Inspiration may descend from above)
> There is no higher art one makes than living for Love,
>   (No higher art than Love)
> There is, be assured, no conceivable ruse
> To finding on earth your living muse!
> La Muse: you have found here on earth your muse!
> Voilà, voilà, Geoffrey Green!'

His face was serene and placid: I saw him, Dennis, grasp a pencil in his hand, and begin to write."

CURTAIN

Ah, Hoffmann, Hoffmann! Why do you obsess me so? Why am I so absorbed in what you represent that I am haunted by the endless varieties and distortions of the opera that dramatizes your immortality as the mythic embodiment of a romantic author? Why is it that I am unable to put your story—Offenbach's story, my story—to rest? Over two hundred years ago, you wrote in your journal: "Black day. Worked till midnight." And ten days later: "Ditto. Black day." A week beyond that: "The Muse is in flight. . . . This journal . . . is the evidence of the pathetic mediocrity that engulfs me." I cannot deny that I respond to these words, that I feel most intensely your struggle both to survive and to create art. But you sought not merely to be an artistic machine; you wished to live life to its limits—and from that intensity, from that profundity, from that excess, produce your art. A few months later you inscribed in your journal: "Drinking l'Évêque. . . . State of dreadful tension in the evening. All my nerves excited by the spiced wine. Obsessed by premonitions of death, by doubles." As am I, Theodor, as am I! We work persistently, we wrestle with the torments of form, with the demons of structure and words, the ghosts of memories, images, ideas. For whom do we work? Imaginary visions of appreciative masses? A fantasy of devoted readers who hang on our every word? No, Theodor, we yearn for the solace that results from perfect understanding, sublime appreciation, exquisite empathy and identification. We write for that double who is our best side, the embodiment of our finest impulses, and yet who haunts us eternally.

Hoffmann worked like a demon on his art—producing music, fiction, criticism, and essays: almost as if his art was the double of his life, necessitating that it be undisciplined, wild, obsessive, tormented, and touched by a genius for intensity of sensation and impression. His stories influenced everyone: he is among us still. And yet, who reads him today? For whom does he exist? His opera *Undine,* for example, anticipated Weber's

Der Freischütz and was admired greatly by both Weber and Beethoven. When I went to a variety of record shops and music publishers, I was told that Hoffmann's *Undine* "does not exist" in accessible form. Hoffmann, Hoffmann, for whom did you work? For whom did you write so hard? For whom did you live so passionately? When you called out your desire to remain alive, was it so that you might continue to work for posterity? Or were you concerned with the feeling of life that creation provided for you *in life*—as a means of knowing yourself, being yourself, as fully and decisively as possible?

I am on my way to a new production of Offenbach's *Les Contes d'Hoffmann* at the Met. In recent years, new discoveries were made that inspired researchers to believe that they had uncovered the essential, the true, the real Offenbach opera. New material was found in a closet of a villa that was owned by a descendant of one of Offenbach's heirs. The opera was again reformed, reshaped, molded to what we might conceptualize as Offenbach's pure and untarnished conception. Fritz Oeser, who made some dramatic discoveries and assembled an edition that had as its goal the re-creation of Offenbach, presented some striking and deeply felt music: some of it, however, was criticized as being of his own composition rather than Offenbach's. What he presented was criticized for being far longer than what we presume Offenbach eventually would have shaped had he lived through the process of revision-through-performances. But Offenbach did not survive. And now Oeser is gone. But there is a new attempt at assembling Offenbach's opera in "complete" form. It is not yet released and is only a specter; but its mastermind has written publicly that his version has uncovered Offenbach's original conception for the Giulietta act! Nevertheless, this reconstruction will *not* be a part of the recording that is being made of this new critical edition—because we are never able to cease our interactions, our manipulations, our doubling, of Offenbach and Hoffmann. Whose opera will I see at the Metropolitan? Will it be a portrait of Hoffmann that justifies him somehow? Will it shape Offenbach's self-designated masterpiece in a manner that does him credit? Or will it represent the inclinations of shadowy doubles that obsess the minds and spirits of these creators? I fancy that Hoffmann will be sitting near me at the opera, gazing upon the representation of himself that has been devised for posterity. I imagine that Offenbach is in his place in the wings, frantically tampering with his score to match the changes that are being inflicted on his opera: both of them smiling at the acclaim.

Offenbach saw himself in his creations, imagined himself as the creatures of his mind. He identified not only with Hoffmann as a fellow artist but with the Hoffmann characters that interacted with their creator in Offenbach's opera. He pictured himself as an Antonia, Hoffmann's true love, a singer, who was somehow constitutionally prohibited from singing her true song, with her real voice. If Antonia were allowed to sing fully and passionately, she would die. Offenbach felt that, like Antonia, he had spent his life "singing" operettas; his true, authentic voice, however, was opera: to "sing" in his pure voice, to complete *Les Contes d'Hoffmann,* would kill him, and it did. Yet soon I shall again see Offenbach's opera; and I feel it is safe to propose that it will not fully capture the desires and sensations of its composer. Nor, I feel certain, will it represent—in any acceptable degree of historical accuracy or even poetic justice—the essence of E. T. A. Hoffmann. But I will be moved and enthralled and afire. In that space between the mystery of what Hoffmann was and how we shape him today, Hoffmann lives—eternally; in that space between the enigma of what Offenbach conceived of as his opera and the strange and continually expressive versions and varieties that are performed in its stead, Offenbach survives—for as long as there is music and as long as there is opera.

And here I am, addressing this dilemma, addressing my audience, addressing my readership (wherever you are), addressing posterity. Here I am, attempting to infuse life into two creators who live for me but who may not even be known. Here I am, attempting to play in, around, and with forms whose structure is largely unknown to the majority of individuals— the majority of whom no longer find reading an interesting or essential or even pleasant pastime. Who will read this story? Who will understand it in the intricate and spirited manner in which I designed it to be read and understood? For whom do I write? For whom do I write?

Do I write so that someday I will end up immortalized as Hoffmann is on the stage—a veritable automaton whose essential self is unavailable, an Olympia whose resemblance to a real woman must be effected through rose-tinted glasses? Or do I write so that my work will be universally admired—and bastardized: repugnant to my own sensibility—an Antonia whose voice, if allowed to sing unfettered, is a double, a harbinger of death? You out there, you have read my words to this point, through all these lines, through and beyond these two or more endings: Which ending do you desire? How do you think you ought to recombine these elements so as to fashion the story that best expresses the vision of its author?

Do you care after all why I write? Or for whom? Which ending do *you* desire? To hell with what I wanted or intended! What do you want? You don't care especially for the name "Green"? Well, then, what about "Verdi"? Or how about "Hoffmann"? Call me Hoffmann, then. Perhaps all of my words are dictated by the example of shadowy artistic figures long gone. What, confound it, do you want?

Despite my work on these words, despite my efforts to say this and not that, regardless of my decisions to place points here and not there, you will change what I wrote anyway—or else, misunderstand it: as I and you and everyone before us have changed and misunderstood Hoffmann and Offenbach and all artists of significance and not passing fancy. Shall I merely sit at the opera and listen to the ghosts of ghosts enact a phantom travesty of what a writer like me once struggled to shape and create? Or shall I expose this outrage, create writing that is about the misunderstanding and transformation of meaning, demonstrate that I, at least, am writing with an awareness of its absurdity, and I do so willingly—*and by choice, by design*. Ah, Muse! Where are you? I am abandoned and desolate.

But what do I hear? A lone violin: an inescapable urge to write possesses me. I know that there are no readers, no audiences, no crowds of admirers.

I write for you—and, therefore, for me.

I write for us.

I hear your words of love, and encouragement, and they melt together with my dream that there would someday be a you for whom I would write. And so I wrote *then* so that there *would* be a you. And now I write so that I may continue to live with you, to be with you, to speak with you. Because I love you, my Muse, M. Muse, my double, my other, with everything that I call my soul, for the eternity of my days.

I don't believe in some vision of romanticized decadence, of art forged out of anguish and self-destructiveness. I don't believe in some self-designated masterpiece at which one labors while the sand slips steadily out of the hourglass. I believe in you. I believe in joy. I believe in us. I believe in life.

And so I write. And live on.

You: my Muse, my reader: take these words to heart.

Here is what I write for you: carry it on, write it yourself.

Make my words fly, I implore you!

Make these words sing paeans of beauty to the skies!

I'll be watching in the wings, in the shadows, in between the lines.

My fate, my life is in your hands.

For as long as time itself, I will spin tales with you, incessantly, always and forever.

And if (or when) I am ever no longer here, if I am changed so severely as to be unrecognizable; if the page on which I reside should fade and crack and disintegrate into dust so that I am no longer a presence for you—*you* will create me anew! You will imagine me all over again! I will be your Muse as you have been mine.

You are my reflection.

I will always and forever be here, right here, with you: unceasingly—with a song of change, and hope, and love.

PROGRAM NOTES

VOICES IN A MASK BY GEOFFREY GREEN

Based on images of disguise in literature, theater, and opera, *Voices in a Mask* turns on the question of identity. The voice, the writer's instrument of identity, is also the vehicle for disguise. In opera, the moment when the voice is most true and naturally placed is when it is "in the mask"—in the region of the face around the nose and eyes that best projects it, but visually, this conceals our features. Voice, in other words, is a vehicle of personal expression for both singers and writers, yet mask is a dramatic and psychological figure for disguise. This short-story cycle explores the themes of identity and subterfuge in a series of fictions that range from the comic to the poignant and the uncanny, but always exploiting "operatic"— and sometimes over-the-top—flourishes.

Overture. This is the opening frame that provides the thematic entry for the book: the writer-director addresses the audience directly.

≈≈

Voices in a Mask. The title story develops themes of disguise and identity, riffing on *The Makropulos Case* (Karel Čapek's play and Leoš Janáček's opera), Gioachino Rossini's opera *Otello,* and the life of early diva Maria Malibran in historical New York and Venice, among other things. The story is set on January 5, 1996, when a real singer at the Metropolitan Opera House in New York City died during a performance of the opera.

≈≈

The Keeper of the List. Wolfgang Amadeus Mozart's and Lorenzo Da Ponte's Don Giovanni character is depicted here in disguise as his servant Leporello, with accompanying theme and variations on E. T. A. Hoffmann's story "Don Juan." The literary character is represented as an author and vice versa.

≈≈

A Flood of Memories. Giacomo Puccini's opera *Tosca* is reconceived in New York City combined with the actual story of the arrest of the Italian tenor Enrico Caruso at the Monkey House of the Central Park Zoo. The writer-singer-actor directly addresses the audience.

"This Very Vivid Morn." The story is derived from another actual death at the Metropolitan Opera House, the accidental killing of an extra by the American baritone Lawrence Tibbett during the rehearsal of an opera based on Robert Browning's dramatic monologue *The Ring and the Book.* Along with real events, the story moves in and out of Tibbett's life, Giacomo Puccini's opera *Girl of the Golden West,* and Giuseppe Verdi's opera *La Traviata*—and into the author's life.

"Your Sister and Some Wine!" Giuseppe Verdi's opera *Rigoletto* and Victor Hugo's play *The King Amuses Himself* are recast as an over-the-top opera production set in 1990 Los Angeles during the censorship and culture wars of the first Bush administration. The TV detective series *Columbo* goes to the opera. The author-composer frames the story.

"Such Dear Ecstasy." This story represents the death and life of the Italian composer Vincenzo Bellini. Ostensibly set in Paris in 1835, it traverses place (Italy, San Francisco, New York) and time into Bellini's operas and the opera *I Puritani* itself, its performance, its characters, and the author's life as a link in a cultural chain.

Creatures of the Mind. The concluding story works with the life and art of E. T. A. Hoffmann, the opera by Jacques Offenbach (*Tales of Hoffmann*—taking place *within* Mozart's opera *Don Giovanni*) on Hoffmann's mythical life and work, Offenbach's life, the author's life and self-created myth, ending with the writer-director-author returning to directly address the audience-reader-muse.

BACKGROUND AND ACKNOWLEDGMENTS

Voices in a Mask emerged from conversations I had with opera singers, conductors, musicians, actors, and a great many writers. My own musical training and experience as well as my research guided the project. I would like to thank San Francisco State University for a sabbatical leave that supported the writing and for travel assistance that supported my research. *Voices in a Mask* was read in its entirety by John Barth, Robert Scholes, the late Leslie Fiedler, Curtis White, Donald Runnicles, Thomas Hampson, Frederica von Stade, Clifford Cranna, and Michael Krasny—all of whom contributed valuable suggestions and insights. Marjorie Perloff, the late Alfredo Kraus, and the late John Hawkes read selected portions of the manuscript and also assisted me with their responses. My research and preparation benefited from the New York Public Library, the New York Performing Arts Library, the Morgan Library, the San Francisco Performing Arts Library, the University of Bologna, the University of Urbino, the gracious members of the staff of the Gran Teatro La Fenice, the Metropolitan Opera of New York, the San Francisco Opera, the Lyric Opera of Chicago, La Scala, and many others. Whenever provided, the translations are my own.

It is my good fortune to have had inspiring conversations (short and long, spoken and written) on opera, literature, music, theater, and life with the following individuals: Daniel Barenboim, Cecilia Bartoli, Giancarlo Bongiovanni, Richard Bonynge, the late Wayne Booth, Marina Busani, Robert Coover, Irene Dalis, Joyce DiDonato, Plácido Domingo, Umberto Eco, Geoffrey Faust and Doré Ripley, Vita Fortunati, Raúl Giménez, David Gockley, Edita Gruberova, Norman Holland, Hei-Kyung Hong, Marilyn Horne, Vesselina Kasarova, the late Ardis Krainik, the late Alfredo Kraus, Franco La Polla, Father Owen Lee, Andrew Maguire, Lotfi Mansouri, Aprile Millo, Gabriella Morisco, Kent Nagano, Jessye Norman, the late Carroll O'Connor, the late Luciano Pavarotti, Carey Perloff, Marjorie and Joseph Perloff, Pamela Rosenberg, Julius Rudel, Donald Runnicles, the late Edward Said, Nello Santi, Robert Scholes and Jo Ann Putnam-Scholes, Joseph Volpe, Frederica von Stade, Bernd Weikl, and Curtis White. My students, colleagues, and friends have always provided me with pleasures too numerous to mention. Melissa Barclay, herself a writer, typed the manuscript with great goodwill. My father, Marvin Green, infused me with his love for opera. He is a character in this book—and then some! Several dear family members are no longer living, but their lives fuel the energy of these pages: my brother, Arne; my mother, Martha; my father-in-law, Joseph Strzelczyk; and my mother-in-law, Lorraine Strzelczyk. My wife, Marcia, read every page, provided ongoing encouragement and enthusiasm, and never lost faith in what has been a long project. With her, my life is always filled with music.